HOUSE OF A THOUSAND EYES

KATIA LIEF

House of a Thousand Eyes

Katia Lief

Dedication

In memory of my mother
Gail Voelker Barrnett

The Bridge

"An appeaser is one who feeds a crocodile,
hoping it will eat him last."

Winston Churchill

ONE

Dostoyevsky on the East River

NEW YORK CITY, May 21, 2013

"The cleverest of all, in my opinion, is the man
who calls himself a fool at least once a month."

CON MATHIS READ the words as he zipped up his fly. Alexei
Dvorshetskii, his boss, had had all the Dostoyevsky quotes
around the office framed in gold.

"Talking nonsense is the sole privilege mankind
possesses over the other organisms. It's by talking
nonsense that one gets to the truth! I talk nonsense,
therefore I'm human."

in the kitchen, above the sink.

"A real gentleman, even if he loses everything he
owns, must show no emotion. Money must be so

far beneath a gentleman that it is hardly worth
troubling about."

on the wall, behind Olga the receptionist. That one
was Con's favorite because the irony was perfect. Dvorshetskii sounded like Dostoyevsky. Obviously. But it didn't
make him literary or even smart beyond the walls of his
hedge fund. A rumor had circulated around the office that
Dvorshetskii had never gone to college, and Con was
willing to believe it.

"Morning!" The bathroom door was swinging shut
before he realized that Pavel Gavrikov had walked in.
Gavrikov was the most senior partner at Worth & Kimble,
one notch below Dvorshetskii.

"Morning to you, too."

Gavrikov could have taken the far urinal but chose to
stand directly beside Con. "What if I told you I fucked a
girl younger than my daughter last night?"

Con buried a shiver in an exaggerated shrug. He had
absolutely nothing to say that wouldn't have gotten him
fired on the spot. Everyone knew that Gavrikov's daughter
was nineteen because he kept a picture of her on his desk,
dolled up for her senior prom.

The Russian's thick bronchial laugh followed Con out
of the bathroom. He returned to the quiet oasis of
analysts' cubicles and slotted himself in at his desk, where
both screens were awash in a digital waterfall of flickering
numbers. He was so close to his goal and then he'd be out
of here.

For lunch, he ordered a sandwich that Olga brought to
his desk.

Gradually, daylight from the far windows shifted over
the cubicles, promising the demise of another day.

Just past four, Alexei Dvorshetskii's secretary called

Con to the throne room. The first time he was summoned, eight months ago, an icy vodka had eased the realization that he was merely being welcomed to the firm, not discovered as a fraud who didn't deserve the job (six figures, easy hours most days). The second time, about four weeks later, the true nature of the work was finally revealed.

Dvorshetskii's corner office had a plate-glass view of the Statue of Liberty to the south and the Manhattan and Brooklyn bridges to the north. From up here, the river was green and smooth as a mirror.

"Come in." Dvorshetskii gestured toward one of the chairs opposite his desk. "Please." He leaned back in his chair and smiled. He had a silver tooth, front and center, which he seemed to cherish as a reminder of his roots in the former Soviet Union. He had more than enough money now to have the tooth replaced, but he didn't. Behind him was a bookcase filled with leather-bound Russian classics Con guessed had never been opened. On his desk, a digital display faced out to rotate pictures of his young bleached wife and their three children in various luxurious hotels and on various tropical vacations. Beside it sat her last Christmas gift to him, a bottle of Clive Christian No. 1. The top of the bottle was a gold crown, and the label proclaimed, "The World's Most Expensive Perfume Spray for Men." Sandalwood hung like fog around Dvorshetskii, whose neck bunched around the knot of his silk tie.

"How are things going?" Dvorshetskii asked.

"Very well." Sweat percolated under Con's collar. He ignored it, hoping it wasn't noticeable. "Accounts are stable. Investments are growing. In fact, I'm in the middle of working on a report for you."

"Good." Dvorshetskii opened a desk drawer, pulled out a fat padded envelope, and slid it across the desktop to

Con. "We're doing a new export outfit in the Caymans, Matryoshka Ltd. My wife came up with the name. What do you think?"

"Those nesting dolls?"

Dvorshetskii nodded.

"Very nice." Holding the envelope on his lap, Con guessed there was at least a couple hundred grand in there. He summoned all his skills to calm his pulse: mental focus, even breaths. "I'll take care of it. Anything else?"

Dvorshetskii leaned over his desk and shook Con's hand, squeezing it a moment too long. "This won't be forgotten."

"Thank you."

Con locked the envelope into his desk drawer and set to work opening a new bank account overseas. The cash itself would be carried to the Cayman Islands by a courier known for his discretion.

At ten to five, a door slammed open into the analysts' nest of cubbyholes. Olga came running in, shouting, "I told you, he not here!" The panic in her voice ignited a riptide of anxiety in Con. He swiveled to see her straightened blonde hair floating behind her like an unhinged sail, her forehead pleated with distress.

A herd of federal agents in blue windbreakers swept past her in the direction of the executive offices—they were early, damn it. Why were they early? They were supposed to arrive at five-thirty after he was gone. He huddled unnoticed in his cubicle while the office exploded into chaos.

Within half an hour, the entire staff was being herded into a large police bus parked outside the building, like they were going on a field trip. Con stood in line, stoically ignoring the nervous chatter of his colleagues.

"Where are they taking us?"

"I saw Dvorshetskii and Gavrikov in handcuffs."

"What's going on?"

"Money laundering, I heard."

On the bus, he sat pressed into a window seat beside a heavily scented young secretary whose name he didn't know. He looked out at the streets of lower Manhattan as the bus ferried them downtown. It was the start of rush hour and office workers were pouring out of the buildings onto the sidewalks, filling taxis, streaming to subways, lighting cigarettes, and trailing plumes of smoke as they transitioned into the temporary freedom of evening. Another day, over. Tomorrow it would all start again. He closed his eyes until the bus pulled to a stop in a tunnel-like driveway beneath the belly of the monumental building at 100 Centre Street.

One of the cops riding with them stood in the aisle, by the driver, and announced, "Welcome to Central Booking. The process will only take a few hours, most likely. Keep calm and follow directions and you'll be outta here before you know it."

A woman with a fluffy crown of gray hair, who Con recognized from bookkeeping, raised her hand. "Are we all arrested, officer?" Olga, seated beside her, let out a wail and buried her face in perfectly manicured hands.

"Everyone's gotta get booked. The lawyers will sort it out after that."

Con figured that nearly everyone on the bus would walk, sooner or later. This was mostly to scare them into talking. The racket hadn't involved very many people, just a few anointed as trustworthy enough or greedy enough— or dumb enough—depending on your point of view.

He followed the perfumed secretary down the aisle and off the bus. They trooped single-file through a dank entry and up the stairs to Booking, escorted by more armed cops and federal agents than seemed necessary to keep the orderly group of finance workers in check.

When the door to Central Booking clanked open, a cloud of something fried wafted out. Behind the desk, the sergeant's chin shone with grease, a balled-up napkin beside a stack of blank intake forms. One by one Worth & Kimball employees were booked into the system, as the line grew more agitated.

"Why am I being arrested?"

"I don't know anything about this!"

"My kids are going to wonder where I am."

Some, like Con, kept their heads down and said nothing. Perfume had bonded with the young woman in front of her on line, and leaned in, away from Con, in a fervent tete a tete. The man behind him, clutching his phone, was busy with a relay of texts. Con buried himself in the safe confines of his solitude.

Dvorshetskii and Gavrikov must have been brought in separately because there was no sign of them. Con wondered if they'd been kept apart for their own protection.

Once Con was booked and relieved of his phone, wallet, and keys, the sergeant handed him a slip of paper with a number on it. "Straight through, door on your right for mug shots. Follow everyone else."

"Fried chicken?" Con touched his own chin.

The sergeant used the back of his hand to wipe away the grease. "Ham and cheese panini."

"Are we allowed to use the bathroom?"

Sergeant's eyes were hazel when they flashed at Con, a tender balance of green and brown that turned the cop, suddenly, into a person. "Talk to that guy standing over there, in the hall."

Con saw him: short, muscle-bound, clean-cut, wearing jeans and a navy blue Yankees T-shirt. "Will do."

Yankees nodded when Con requested his pee detour. "Follow me."

As they passed the open door of processing, Con glimpsed Perfume readying herself to be photographed. He hadn't noticed how pretty she was until she brandished a mystified smile for the camera. He ached a little because he knew he'd never see her again.

He followed Yankees to the top of a stairwell. When the door heaved shut behind them, sealing off the noise from the hall, the cop said, "Meet you downstairs. Just be a minute."

Con trotted quickly down to the ground floor where he was able to let himself out onto the sidewalk. He had to shade his eyes against the bright sun. The air, laced with traffic fumes, somehow smelled sweeter than the girl's perfume. He watched as the empty bus that had brought them here slid into traffic. Into its yawning curbside opening pulled a black SUV with tinted windows.

A fed Con recognized from the raid emerged from the driver's side. Another fed hopped out of the passenger side and opened the back door. When a shiny dress shoe slid into view, followed by a shackled pair of beefy hands that were unmistakably Dvorshetskii's, Con retreated into the building so he wouldn't be seen.

"Here you go." Yankees was just coming down the stairs. He handed Con his belongings. "Something wrong?"

"Big catch getting reeled in outside." Con returned his things to their assigned pockets. "Stick your head out and see if the coast is clear, okay? Big balding Russian and his skinny sidekick."

Yankees slipped out of the building and in less than a

minute was back. "You're good to go. This the case they're calling Dostoyevsky?"

"Eight months of my life."

"How you like it over at Hogan?"

"DA treats us well."

"I think about transferring sometimes. Booking can be a grind."

"Con Mathis, Rackets Investigations." Con offered a hand, and the men shook. "Feel free to get in touch."

Back outside, Con found his sunglasses in his jacket pocket and put them on. The city now tinted a forgiving shade of russet, he heaved a sigh.

Finally, his role in the long case was over. Playing Kurt Lettieri, one of a dozen analysts at Worth & Kimball, had quickly grown routine, but Con had had to remind himself not to get bored; it was when you lost your focus that you could make a mistake. Dvorshetskii and Gavrikov (allegedly) worked for a Russian kingpin hot on the DEA's radar. Con knew he'd be safe as long as they didn't connect him to the leaked information. Why would they? He'd been very careful, every step of the way.

Waiting for the walk light, he became aware of the neon bar sign across the street, glowing red in the twilight. He deserved a drink. Maybe two. Then he'd call it a night, walk home over the Brooklyn Bridge, and reclaim himself. Already, he could feel the hard shell of fakery melting off.

Two hours and three drinks later, tendrils of cold reached through Con's suit. He felt good, relieved, the job finally over. The chatter of a pair of teenage boys, loitering on the bridge and sharing a joint, caught his attention. They shivered in denim jackets that hung open over their illustrated T-shirts. A guitar. A tilted bowling pin with an illegible word stenciled above it. Guitar turned to the railing and flicked the orange ember of a roach into the East River. Con kept walking. In the near distance, traffic blurred beneath the Promenade, which was relatively quiet at this hour. Manhattan loomed behind him.

The boys leaned back over the railing, arms spread for balance, and faced the sky. They laughed as the wind whipped their long hair into a frenzy.

Guitar pointed up. Stopped laughing. "What the fuck?"

"Oh, shit." Bowling Pin wasn't laughing now, either.

Con arched his back and shielded his eyes and saw it too. A man stood on top of the bridge's east tower. Con tried to tell himself the man was doing repairs but it was late for that, and he was alone. Moving slowly, the man took something out of his front pocket and stooped to lay it down. Then he straightened up and walked forward.

"Fucking dude's gonna jump," Guitar said.

"That water's gotta be cold."

"You ever wonder how it feels to fly?"

"You got another blunt?"

"No man. But yeah. I wish."

"No!" Con shouted. "Don't do it! Wait!"

The man hesitated and looked down, his face a distant tangle of suffering.

Running to get closer to the tower, Con ordered the boys, "Call 911!"

"Yeah, right," Bowling Pin snickered.

"Like we're gonna call the fucking cops."

"I said call them!" The ferocity of Con's tone inspired Bowling Pin to pull out his phone and dial.

The jumper stood on the northern edge of the tower. Con was close enough now to see that the man's whole body was shaking. He was scared. Uncertain. Just as Con always imagined his own father had been in the crucial moments before he had leaped to his death from this bridge nine years ago. Except his father had jumped off the west tower, and instead of May, it had been November. Moonlight shimmered over the man and transformed him into Conrad Sr., and suddenly, for Con, it wasn't too late.

Cupping his hands around his mouth, he screamed, "Stop! don't jump!"

But the man either ignored him or didn't hear. He leaped into a gust of northward wind that seemed to grab on and play with him a moment before submitting to gravity. The splash from below was almost insignificant, but it echoed through Con as he ran, sweating, the rest of the way home.

TWO

Girls Aren't Jumpers

NEW YORK CITY, May 21, 2013

Larissa Berger loosened the knot behind her neck; she'd tied her halter-top too tight again. None of her clothes really fit. The stiff band edging her red hot-pants bit into her skin when she walked, but she dug the way the sequins threw off rays of headlight whenever a car slowed down to talk to her. Made her feel like her idea of a Rockette. And the four-inch stilettos made her tall. She liked that, too.

Guy pulled up now in a black sedan fresh from the carwash, water beading on his fenders. Dyed comb-over. Face a lunar landing of bygone acne. Wedding ring, of course.

She trotted into the empty Costco parking lot and he followed, rolling down the passenger window with the button on the driver's side.

"How much?"

She leaned in, giving him a close-up of her cleavage. "Depends."

"I don't have much time." He glanced at his crotch.

"Twenty. Thirty if you want a bump with it." The profit was in the drugs.

"Get in."

"You gotta pay first, honey."

While he was digging for his wallet, one of her phones buzzed inside her purse. She stood up out of the window and saw who it was.

"Listen, baby, I'm working. Can't talk now."

"I just saw someone jump off the Brooklyn Bridge."

"He live?"

"I never said it was a he."

"Girls aren't jumpers, they're pill poppers."

"There's no way he lived."

"Where you at?"

"Home. I'm freaking out."

Wedding Ring kept glancing at her, drumming his hands on the steering wheel. She took a step away from the car and lowered her voice. "I can't talk now, Con. I'm working."

"I just thought if I could see you."

"I'll call you later, okay? You hang in there for me."

"Larry, I just want to talk. I need to talk."

"I know you do, honey. I know you do."

The car window spooled up, dragging stripes of water. The way the john put his car into gear, he was pissed. Probably used up his ten-minute grace period before his wife started calling to find out why he wasn't home from the car wash. Big deal. He'd be back. Larry adjusted her halter-top and strolled onto the avenue, the sparkle off her hot pants all the advertisement she needed.

THREE

The Glittering Palace of a Kept Promise

NEW YORK CITY, May 21, 2013

So this was it.

And it was spectacular.

Polished steel and glass exchanged rays of self-generated light. The whole place resonated with it. Emmy Schumann's heart sang to realize that at last, she was inside the guts of such a resplendent creature as the Time Warner Center. She'd studied online images of the shopping mecca during her preparations for her first visit to the United States, to New York City, but none had done the reality justice.

Shoppers flowing in behind her sizzled with energy as they checked their phones and glanced around, as if taking orders from some higher power, before veering toward one store or another. The exhausted satisfaction of those who flowed out, arms anchored with bouquets of vibrant bags, was no less thrilling. Jet lag evaporated as Emmy moved forward into the enormous atrium—the glittering palace of a kept promise. She was here. This was it. She felt both welcomed and terrified. She had no idea where to begin, but she could hardly wait.

As a girl in the former German Democratic Republic, there was a time when she'd wanted nothing more than to be a glitter punk, to deck herself out from head to toe in luster and dazzle, joining a verboten breed of teenage rebel unwilling to succumb to the moral righteousness of unabated want. But even in the privacy of their home, her mother, a staunch comrade, wouldn't allow that kind of cultural cross-dressing like some kids' parents did. Emmy was bored by the boyish utilitarian clothes they all wore by default, their Zeha sneakers, the colorful fabric bags slung from their shoulders like flags of unity, the parade of boxy Trabants on every road—everything to celebrate their sameness. Walking to school past the raked sand edging the Wall, her eyes would search hopefully for telltale footprints, wondering if it would be possible to hide her own within them and escape to the other side, to the seedpod of West Berlin, where it was said that the streets were lined with gold. But then she'd think of her mother and her heart would sink. It was just the two of them; she could never leave her mother behind. Those days, if you managed to get out without being shot, there was no going back.

When she was fourteen and the Wall came down, Emmy was one of the first ones through. Seeing the west for the first time was a sharp disappointment. Physically it was the same city but in better condition. There was more and better stuff, but nothing as grand as she'd expected. She returned home that chilly November night thankful for the sulfur reek of their coal oven, their paltry kitchen that was just like everyone else's, and a mother whose love felt relentlessly distant waiting for her with questions about the other side.

Now, dazzled by the abundance evident from every angle in the shopping center's vast lobby, she paused for a breath, stopping at the foot of Botero's Adam—a humongous bronze heavy-chested sculpture with genitals blanched by the curious hands of distracted shoppers. She rubbed the tips of her fingers along his cylindrical penis. Judging from the dark patina of Adam's corpulent bronze partner, Eve, no one had bothered to caress her. It wasn't fair. But Emmy didn't pause to right the situation, because why should she?

She had been sent here to kill someone. To retrieve a key, and leave the man who possessed it dead. In the meantime, she had some serious shopping to do. The delivery of abstract kindnesses was not in her purview.

She had several free hours until she was to meet with the gun dealer. Time to put the call from her grandmother out of her mind; the old woman had phoned out of the blue, right before Emmy got on the plane, and delivered some demented news. Something about long-lost family in America. But Grandma's mind had been skidding off the tracks lately and Emmy didn't know what to do with the dubious newsflash. She wanted to forget about it, to be here now, and decided to right herself with the shopping spree she'd long fantasized about.

It was only because Mutti—the grand wizard and woman who pulled her strings—had snapped her Achilles tendon running for a bus at Alexanderplatz and couldn't do the job herself, that Emmy was here. The thought of the woman collapsing on the street, buckling like a rag doll, had at first struck Emmy as perversely amusing. Then of course she'd rallied and helped, before and after the surgery, becoming a nurse to the temporarily bed-bound control freak who had ruled Emmy's life for longer than she cared to admit. The prospect of what she was tasked to do, followed by a payday the likes of which Emmy had never dared dream, well, it had bubbled giddily in her imagination from the moment the ticket was in her hand, turning a wild idea into vivid reality.

Everything she bought today would go on the credit card Mutti had given her for the trip. Emmy did not intend to hold back.

THE CORNER of East Houston and Allen Streets was crowded with a panoply of the world's cultures: two dark Africans packing up their folding table and plastic-wrapped packs of socks; a hairy-legged man in a kilt, shouting into his cell phone that it was over, that was it; a half dozen teenagers of various ethnicities in clothes that were either too snug or too loose but nothing in between, their tight-packed group moving like a single body. Heavy traffic at the busy intersection periodically exploded into a hideous shriek of honking horns.

Emmy located the sliver of a store called Mini Cart and carried her shopping bags to the refrigerated deli case. The place smelled of tobacco and stale candy. She waited for a man in a white apron and paper hat to acknowledge the presence of his new customer. His pupils were large and black, like the eyes of someone who has just died. He didn't speak.

"A sandwich, please." She recited her precise order from memory: "Black Forest ham. Stilton cheese. Dijon mustard. Roasted red peppers. Cut on the diagonal."

He stared at her with those eyes. She hadn't quite finished.

"On rye toast."

He made the sandwich, wrapped it in wax paper, and put it into a white plastic bag with a yellow smiley face.

Then he slipped something else into the bag and carried it to the register. The cash drawer dinged open to the price of the sandwich: $9.50.

A young couple walked to the back of the store and perused the cold beverages.

"That's expensive for a sandwich," Emmy said.

"Yeah, well." She was surprised by the deep bass of his voice.

She reached into the pocket of her jacket for the tissue into which she had wrapped two one-hundred-dollar bills, as instructed, and handed over the little packet to the deli man. With his thumb, he flicked open the tissue to finger the edges of the money, surreptitiously counting. Then he handed her the bag and returned to his post behind the cold cuts.

"I hope you didn't add too much mustard," she called after him, with a laugh, but he ignored her.

She twisted the loose skin of the plastic bag around the sandwich and the hard little handgun—a .40 with an integral silencer—compacting the package so she could wedge it between the jeans and cashmere sweater that formed the top tier of her A/X purchases. It wasn't that far to her sublet but, weighed down by all the bags, she decided to hail a cab. She would eat the sandwich for her dinner. There was still some research to finish on her laptop, to get ready. And then, later, there was someone she needed to find.

FOUR

asap

———

NEW YORK CITY, May 21, 2013

CON LEANED back in the worn leather Eames chair that used to be his father's, a freshly poured bourbon settled in his lap. The contents of his pockets lay scattered on a side table: wallet, two phones, loose change, top of a pen from the office. With the lights off, the first hints of darkness dribbled across the high white ceiling. Evening gathered in the room's corners where the elaborate molding bent off in a new direction.

His personal phone started to ring and ring and flash and flash Larry Larry Larry. Larissa Berger, his best friend in the world, was finally calling him back. Feeling paralyzed, he waited until the hooting phone fell silent.

He should have been celebrating the Dostoyevsky bust, a job well done, but instead, he'd tripped and fallen into the past.

He couldn't stop thinking about his father.

"His neck was broken on impact," the coroner had

written in his report, all those years ago. "Conrad Mathis, Sr. died instantly at 2:31 am on November 5, 2004." Along with his heart and brain, his wristwatch had also stopped the moment it hit the water. It was a Junghans, a German brand Con may never have heard of if not for his father. He could still hear the melodious voice explaining the provenance of one of the only physical reminders he possessed from the country of his birth. "There are some mementos I'm happy to consider, such as this watch. It was a gift from someone I hated. Embrace your enemies, son, never forget that." After the suicide, once it was released by the coroner, Con had had the watch refurbished and worn it ever since. That, and an old skeleton key to nowhere that his father had brought back with him from Germany when he was a young man, were the only souvenirs he'd carried out of his past.

In the years since the suicide, Con had often walked home across the bridge to inoculate himself against the brutal fact that this was where his father had ended his life, to make the bridge just a bridge. But now it was more than that: It was the vivid backdrop for the event itself. Now that he had seen a man leap to his death, a man who mid-flight transformed into his father, the image had come alive. The desolation of that face had shattered Con's hard-won armor. The irrevocable sound of that splash.

"I'm going to do it," he slurred aloud to no one. "I'm writing to Grandma. Right now. No more waiting."

He opened his laptop and (with drunken imprecision) fished out the email address for the nursing service he'd found connected with his German grandmother's name, last time he'd almost contacted her. He'd searched for her several times but, other than locating her name on an obscure PDF some administrator should have made private, all he knew about her was that she'd moved onto a locked Alzheimer's ward someplace outside Berlin. And he knew her name: Bettina Faber. Frau Faber, mother of Conrad Mathis, Sr., mother-in-law of Ruth Ginsburg Mathis, grandmother of Conrad Jr. and Sophie Mathis, none of whom had ever laid eyes on Bettina or even heard her voice.

Twice he'd written emails to his far-flung grandmother. Twice he'd deleted them without sending. What was the point? How much could she possibly remember with accuracy?

But this time—he clicked open a new message—this time—he started typing.

Dear Grandmother. Dear Bettina. Dear Mrs. Faber. Dear Frau Faber. He had to choose some way to begin.

Dear Mrs. Faber,
I am your grandson, Conrad, named for my father,
your son.

Dear Grandmother,
I am your grandson, Conrad Jr., and although
we've never met I have some questions I hope you'll
be able, and willing, to answer. Please forgive this
intrusion, but I've always

Dear Bettina,
I am your grandson, Conrad Jr., and although
we've never met I have some questions I hope you'll
be able to answer. My father had a complicated
past that he never discussed. I know nothing about
his life in Germany during and after the war. He
was happy with my mother. Our family was stable;
we had no real problems. We were all shocked

when he took his own life. There are so many
things I never asked him, such as:
1. He said he lived in Berlin. East or west?
2. What was his position during the Cold War?
3. What role (if any) did your family play during
World War 2?
4. In your opinion, why would a happily married
man with a good family, a man who was a
successful journalist, take his own life without
warning or explanation? What did he leave behind
in Germany? For example, was anyone in your
family a Nazi? Is that why he killed himself? Guilt?
What about the Cold War? What side was he on?
What did he do for a living before he was a journalist? How did my father fit in during and after the
war and all those years before he came here?

Con stopped himself from revising out that last frantic
bit because it was at the heart of what he needed to know.
He'd ripped the problem of his father's suicide to shreds,
chewed every strand of it, choked it down, thrown it back
up, inhaled the vapors of what was left, poisoned himself
with a chaotic reduction of formless elements he couldn't
digest. No one killed himself without reason. But in all this
time, he had failed to understand. Eventually, he'd looked
away from the waste of his questions, but sometimes,
tonight, the yearning reclaimed him.

There were facts:

Conrad Sr. was born in 1941, in Berlin, the only child
of a schoolteacher and a housewife.

He left Germany in 1979, the same year he married
Ruth Ginsburg in New York and Con was born. A
daughter followed eight years later.

But the facts were minimal, and in the darkness between them shimmered the problem.

As Con reread his email, shame crept into his determination. Why send such a desperate missive into the past? To a virtual stranger? His father was gone, he was dead, and nothing Con could do would ever bring him back.

Today was supposed to be a good day; a day to celebrate, not wallow.

With a quick tap of his fingertip, he deleted the email. Picked up his phone and listened to Larry's message asking him to come out and play.

"Hey, Con. Getting on the train now, bitch of a night. Still want to talk? Text asap if you feel like meeting for a drink at the Mercury Lounge."

Without hesitation, he texted her: asap

He finished his drink, filled his pockets with the regulation items he carried everywhere—wallet, keys, phones—and without bothering to change out of his suit, locked up and headed for the subway.

FIVE

House of a Thousand Eyes

EAST BERLIN, August 13, 1961

CONRAD SCHUMANN SLIPPED his rifle off his shoulder and took aim the moment he heard the thud. Across the road from where he guarded the border, a woman had stumbled rather dramatically. He blinked away perspiration dripping into his eyes from beneath his helmet and saw that the woman appeared to be in her thirties. She was loaded down with shopping bags, and something seemed to have fallen from one of them. A knot of garlic shed its papery skin as it bounced along the cracked pavement, settling just short of the snake of barbed wire separating east from west.

The slope of the woman's cheekbones stirred something in Conrad, and for a moment he imagined touching her skin, its softness, even its taste. He thought fleetingly of Emilie. How long since he'd seen her? Swallowing the aching regret of her loss, he consulted his watch. It was nearly quitting time, and he was getting hungry. He reshouldered his rifle. He was about to fetch the garlic and toss it back to her when Hans, a fellow guard, beat him to it.

The woman was just out of sight when the explosion ripped Hans from the ground. Conrad rushed to his side along with Axel, his oldest friend and also a guard. As the smoke cleared, it was obvious that Hans was dead. The back of his head was crushed, threads of blood spinning lacework on the arid ground. His blue eyes, frozen, stared at nothing.

A siren wailed into the cacophony of panicked voices. Fellow East Berliners watched the scene through the dusty windows of apartments whose view had been radically transformed from open street to barbed wire. Conrad scanned the length of the street for any trace of the woman. Somehow, she had vanished into the havoc.

THE NEXT DAY, vultures appeared. The first three reporters came on foot, with notebooks, and the fourth on a rusty blue bicycle with a camera strapped across his back. Conrad refused an inner pull of jealousy; he'd had a bicycle as a child but it was stolen by the son of a neighbor who had been a Nazi. Conrad's parents hadn't dared complain. Axel would have remembered the bike, as he himself had borrowed it on occasion when they were boys. The friends glanced at each other now and in silent agreement refused to show any sort of response to the predators on the other side of the border. Hans had died a martyr for socialism, and if they couldn't figure that out themselves, it was their loss.

"Officer!" The reporter slid off the bike and uncapped his camera. "Give us a wave."

Conrad walked the border without changing his gait or

even looking at the young man, who appeared to be twenty-one or two, not much older than himself. He had to realize there was no way Conrad could reply. If he did, his commander would give him a severe talking-to; but worse, his own conscience would destroy him.

They hurled their questions like stones.

"How did it feel seeing your comrade die?"

"Has the bomber been identified?"

"Why did she do it? In your opinion. Why?"

"What will happen to her now?"

And then a ripple of laughter passed among the Westies. Journalists loved interpreting the German Democratic Republic for the benefit of the rest of the world, though what they came up with was predictable, generally something about Soviet imperialism, hypocrisy, tyranny.

Conrad ignored them. He had been raised well and was proud of his work guarding the border. The two halves of Germany were too philosophically opposed to coexist. For the GDR to thrive, the capitalists needed to be kept out. As for the question of East Berliners being kept in, his father, a schoolteacher of some local renown, had explained that the resources of a new nation were vulnerable, and it was intolerable to continue allowing people to live in the east and work in the west, reaping the benefits of socialism while enriching themselves on filthy capitalism. "The soullessness of greed," his father had called this kind of dual citizenship in a broken Germany. Still, Conrad was as surprised as any when the coils of wire appeared overnight, the root of wall that enforced new rules of non-emigration. Within days, though, he was used to the idea and signed on as a guard while a permanent wall was gradually constructed.

"Give us something," a reporter shouted. "Anything. A smile."

Conrad marched steadily along his route. It wasn't his problem if they'd missed the garlic bomb yesterday, if today their cameras were hungry for some sustenance. It wouldn't come from him.

When finally his relief appeared, he handed over his rifle and saluted. He noted with some disappointment that Axel, with whom he often shared an after-work beer, was still on duty. Conrad started for home.

"I saw you admiring the reporter's bike." Herr Muller, an older man his sister, Gabi, had briefly dated, pulled to a stop on his own gleaming black bicycle. He patted the handlebars. "Want to take her for a spin?"

"It's a beauty. Where did you get it?"

"Bought it from a colleague last year." Conrad tried and failed to recall what it was that Herr Muller did for a living. "I'm thinking of getting rid of it. It takes up too much room in my apartment, and I never ride it."

"You're riding it now."

"Thought if I took her out, it would help me decide."

"And has it?"

Herr Muller shrugged, and suddenly Conrad remembered why his sister had broken up with him. It wasn't his relative age, but his inability to settle on anything, anything at all.

"Go on, try her out, I don't mind."

Conrad took her around the block, twice, waving to Herr Muller each time he passed. He enjoyed the sensation of gliding. It was exhilarating. He decided he wanted the bike.

"I'll buy it from you," he told Muller, thinking he could free the man from his indecisiveness by putting it bluntly. "Name your price."

When Muller smiled, a web of deep lines radiated across his temples. He was even older than Conrad had thought. His parents felt his sister had made a good choice marrying a man closer to her own age. They had two children now and Lutz worked faithfully at the butcher shop where his own father had spent his life. He was your typical good man, or as his sister had put it, "a decent catch." But Conrad had his suspicions after hearing from a friend who spotted his brother-in-law in Normanstrasse, in Lichtenberg, walking in the direction of Stasi headquarters. It was one thing to work openly for the GDR like Conrad, in uniform, so everyone knew who you were and what you stood for. It was quite another to work secretly as an Inoffizielle Mitarbeiter, informing on your friends and family. It was impossible to know who was an IM and who wasn't.

You had to watch your ground at all times, not that Conrad had anything to worry about. Even so, it was well known that when a Berliner was seen in Lichtenberg, chances were he was paying a visit to the House of a Thousand Eyes.

"Name your price." Muller laughed. "You talk like a true Westy."

"I only meant that—"

"Relax, son. Can't you take a joke? I'll tell you what: keep her until tomorrow and we'll decide on a price. Same time and place. Who knows? Maybe I'll even give her to you for nothing."

Conrad rode off under the chalk-blue sky, eventually arriving home in Friedrichshain, circuitously, over an hour later than usual. His father was standing outside their building, banned from the apartment to smoke his cigar on the sidewalk. He was chatting with the grocer, who also smoked, when Conrad appeared, in his uniform, riding Herr Muller's bicycle.

The rage that spread across his father's face so startled Conrad that he almost fell off the bike. "Are you out of your mind?" his father hissed in a tone new to Conrad, who had always admired his father's even temper. "Get off that bike. Get off it now."

"Take it easy, Erich," the grocer advised in a low voice, practically a whisper. "You don't want to attract attention to the situation."

"What situation?" Conrad asked. "It belongs to Herr Muller. You remember him, Father—the one Gabi threw over for Lutz. He loaned it to me until tomorrow." For reasons Conrad couldn't decipher, it seemed like a bad idea to mention that he was in fact considering buying the bicycle.

The offending bike now stashed in the front hallway of the apartment he shared with his parents, he overheard them whispering frantically in the kitchen though couldn't make out what they were saying. His mother was baking Pfeffernusse; the aroma of the spice cookies drew him forward. When he appeared in the kitchen doorway, she waved him away. Eventually, his father appeared with a bottle of schnapps and two glasses and sat his son down in the living room for a man-to-man talk.

"The Schumanns don't ride bicycles," his father began. Conrad noticed that, when his father ran his fingers through his thinning grey hair, a tremor shook his hand.

"What's wrong?" Conrad asked. "Is it your health?"

His father drained his schnapps and poured another. Conrad hadn't touched his. "My health is fine, and so is your mother's. But please, listen to me. The bike has to go."

Conrad was nineteen. In two months, he would be twenty. He crossed his arms over his chest and waited for the explanation he believed he was due.

"It's like this," his father finally began. "These days, a bike is not a bike."

"Which means?"

"The woman who threw the garlic yesterday, has she been found? Have you thought about what will happen to her?"

"She's a traitor. She killed Hans. Why do you care what happens to her?"

"Let me explain something to you." His father spoke in the tone he used with his students, the same tone with which he had often enlightened Conrad and Gabi throughout their childhoods. His voice fell to a whisper and he leaned in, as if fearful of being overheard. "The bicycle is to get around more easily."

"Exactly."

"Don't interrupt. Let me finish." Agitated, he poured himself a third schnapps.

Conrad's throat tightened. There was something his father needed to say but didn't know how. Never before had he seen the man speechless. He laid his hand on his father's knee. "Don't worry. I'll return the bike to Herr Muller tonight. Gabi might still know where he lives."

"You don't know what a bike means these days. You don't understand." When his father's hand landed on top of his, the sticky heat was overwhelming, but he left his own hand where it was. "IMs ride bikes to get around quickly, and they're given clearance to pass through the checkpoints."

"But it isn't possible," Conrad argued, "that everyone with a bike is an IM."

"Who else can afford a bicycle these days?"

"You once said that, before the war, a lot of people had bikes."

"Conrad, do I have to remind you how little survived the war?"

Of course, he didn't; it was a ridiculous suggestion. Almost nothing survived. Every building in Berlin was scarred with bullet holes. The Jews were all gone. Nearly everyone in the east was scraping by with what little was left after the Soviets cleaned them out, while the west rebuilt itself and snickered at them across the border.

"I've often wondered," Conrad ventured, curious what his father thought about the tender issue of informers, and questioning now the depth of his concern, "if IMs provide a necessary service, even if it makes us uncomfortable when we don't know who is...." How exactly to put it?

"Betraying you," his father spat.

"But is it a betrayal when it's for the good of the country? I don't like IMs any more than you do, but I've wondered about this. Mielke must have a good reason for needing them. It's no secret that splitting the country has been a tricky business."

His father's mouth tightened. A frightening clarity overtook his eyes. "IMs are scum. Mielke doesn't need them, he wants them. He's terrified of losing his grip around our throats."

It was the first time Conrad had heard his father speak so bitterly about the leader of the GDR. He was taken aback and waited for the rest to pour out.

"You remember when you were seven, and I went away for five months?"

"Of course I remember." Their mother had explained that their father was on a teacher-training expedition, which had seemed plausible at the time, but suddenly didn't.

"I was in prison, first tortured, then put in solitary. And what was my transgression?"

Transgression? His father? Never had Conrad known a more loyal citizen than his father, which is why he'd been trusted with the honor of educating the new country's youngest minds.

"I sat down for a cup of coffee one afternoon. At the table next to mine was a man. I'd never seen him before. I didn't know his name or anything about him, only that he was drinking a beer at the next table. I asked him the time. That was my transgression. I was picked up the next day, accused of subversion. Apparently, the man with the beer was a spy for the Americans. They wanted to know what we talked about. They wanted to know if he "recruited" me. They kept me awake for four straight nights. No sleep, Conrad, you have no idea how insane that makes you. No sleep at all, and very little food or water. I thought I would never see you children or your mother again. I was out of my mind."

"So you confessed?"

"They never broke me. Not like that, anyway."

"How, then?" Conrad knew as well as anyone that traitors, even perceived traitors, weren't released back into society without paying a price.

"A promise was extracted from me. I vowed to teach my students, all of them, year after year, the purest values of the GDR. If I wanted to see my family again, that was what I had to do. And I've done it, haven't I?"

"What were you teaching them before?"

"Mathematics. Science. History. Literature. To ask questions and to think critically. After, I kept my lessons to the benefits of socialism, and still do."

His father watched him, waiting for it to sink in: the new understanding that, for much of Conrad's lifetime, his father was not exactly who he'd seemed to be. "I see now why you don't want me to appear to be an IM."

"Don't let them turn you into a monster," his father whispered, hands gripping his knees, eyes sharp as crystal, "like they did me. I can't live with that. Do you understand?"

"I'll go right now and find Gabi. I'll walk to her apartment, leave the bike here, and when I have Muller's address I'll wait until dark and return it."

CONRAD RODE SHAKILY to Muller's, and in the twenty minutes it took to get there, he tried but couldn't digest his father's confession. All these years, his father, the man he loved and respected above all other men, the man he emulated, the man he'd hoped to make proud by wearing the uniform of the GDR, had sustained his loyalist persona under duress. Conrad felt trapped in a quicksand of bewildered disappointment.

Muller's elderly sister answered the bell by peeking through the curtains onto the street. In moments, Muller himself appeared at the door.

"What's this? I thought we agreed on tomorrow."

"I've already decided. Thank you, but I don't want it." Conrad leaned the bicycle against the bullet-scarred wall of the Mullers' building. In the moonlight, he was able to see that someone had left a thimble in one of the holes. It made no sense to Conrad. Nothing made sense tonight. He turned to leave.

Muller stepped forward and grabbed Conrad's arm. "I won't take no for an answer." In the strange shadows of night, Conrad noticed jowls on the man, who seemed to age rapidly with every conversation.

"I've made up my mind."

"I don't care about money. I'll tell you the truth." And here Muller leaned in to whisper in Conrad's ear. "It's my sister. She told me if I don't get rid of the bike, she'll toss me out. You'll be doing me a favor by taking it off my hands."

"I wish I could help you, Herr Muller. My father asked me to return it. Good night."

"When Emilie ran to the west, she was pregnant."

Conrad turned back to look at Muller, who stood now in a pocket of darkness, his face blackened. Behind him, the thimble glimmered.

"Who ended it?" Muller continued. "You, or her? Or did she leave you high and dry without mentioning she was going to the other side?"

Conrad stared at Muller, but the inscrutable thimble kept intruding on his attention. Why was it there? How did this man know anything of Emilie? He struggled to recall exactly when he had last been with her. How long now since she'd fled to the west? Fifteen months, he guessed, was the answer to both questions.

"I don't understand why you've mentioned Emilie," Conrad said, "when our business only concerns this bicycle."

"Your girlfriend's defection might look bad for you, don't you think so? Especially now that she's given birth to your child."

Given birth. Child. Was it really possible that he, at nineteen, was already a father? His gaze melted against the hard thimble in the bullet hole.

"It seems to me, Herr Schumann, that someone could think you'd have good cause to follow her over. Who wouldn't want to see his own child?"

"I'm not sure why I should believe you, Herr Muller."

"But are you sure why you shouldn't?" He stepped out of the darkness now, his old face pallid in the weak moonlight. "I can fix this problem for you if you let me."

"I'm not yet convinced it's a problem, with all due respect."

"All due respect." Muller laughed. "I'm not your father, boy. Trust me. Take the bike."

"No, thank you."

"I insist. You'll take the bike, and I'll protect you from the powers that be. One hand washes the other. You understand?"

Finally, Conrad did understand.

"And if I refuse?"

"I'll have no choice but to report that fact. How will it look? Someone could think that your uniform is just a costume to keep you near the border, giving you an opportunity to get to the other side before the Wall is fully built. It could look very bad for you, Herr Schumann. Refusal to cooperate. Baby on the other side of the Wall. If that isn't begging to be put under suspicion, I don't know what is."

None of that had ever occurred to Conrad. He guarded the border out of pride as the Wall was constructed, to please his father, and himself. Never once had he considered his daily proximity to the west as a temptation of any kind. His father's words rang in his ears, "Don't let them turn you into a monster like they did me." But his father was not a monster. Who was a good man, if not his father?

"You'll be better off if you accept the bicycle," Muller pressed, "as will your entire family. Your sister also has children now, I understand?"

The barely veiled threat against Gabi's children startled Conrad. Apparently, he was to become an informer, or else. Without considering it another moment, he took the bike from the wall, got on, and rode home. He did not, however, bring it into the apartment. Instead, he leaned it against a tree around the corner, hoping that when he returned for it, it would be gone. But to his dismay, the next morning, the bicycle was waiting exactly where he'd left it. He decided he was better off riding it to work than chancing his father seeing it abandoned against the tree, or Muller intercepting him on his way home without it.

"Did you hear the news?" Axel greeted Conrad as they prepared to assume their posts.

"What news?"

"The woman bomber. She's been caught."

"And?"

"She's a baker's wife with three children at home. She'll be hanged."

Conrad wondered briefly what the woman's name was. He could still see the curve of her cheek. If he knew her name, he would mourn her, so he decided not to find out. Instead, impulsively, he asked, "Since you know everything, Axel, what can you tell me about Emilie?"

"Emilie?"

"Never mind. I don't know why I asked." Would anything Axel said to him now be fodder for the Stasi, that great iron ear that hovered above them and forgot nothing? Conrad tried not to listen to the answer but found he couldn't resist.

"I heard she had a child. Didn't you know?" Axel stepped so near, Conrad was sure he caught a whiff of the currant and raspberry pudding Frau Bauer used to make them sometimes after school. The familiar yet distant fragrance sent a cascade of regret through him. He was to lose his friends, all of them, he was sure of it. He needed to keep quiet, say nothing, hear nothing, but there was one more thing he felt compelled to ask.

"Boy or girl?"

"I've heard both, so I can't tell you."

"Why didn't you mention this to me before?"

"Only to hurt you?"

The morning progressed, and for the first time, he wondered what he was doing and whom he could trust. How was it, for instance, that Axel had heard about Emilie and the baby but Conrad hadn't? Was Herr Muller already an IM when he and Gabi were together, and if so, had he spied on his sister and perhaps the entire Schumann family? What, if anything, did Gabi know about it? Now, as the day passed, minutes mounting to hours, each one compounded his distress. It didn't help that the same band of reporters had taken up their usual spots, waiting for something new to happen.

"A baker's wife!" One of them tried to capture Conrad's attention. "What do you think of that?"

"Do you, in your opinion, think she could have done more damage by loading explosives into a loaf of bread? Why garlic?"

"In your opinion, was the baker's wife a traitor to the people?"

"What was her statement in throwing her little garlic bomb, in your opinion?"

Conrad's job was not to hold opinions. His job was to guard the border. But at the end of that day, when Herr Muller intercepted him, it fully sank in that he now had another job as well. Today Muller rode a red bicycle and traveled beside Conrad along the avenues of the Mitte.

"So tell me," Muller began. "What were you and your friend discussing this morning, by the border?"

"You were there?" Conrad sped up, but Muller only followed.

"I'm asking the questions. So tell me. What's on Axel Bauer's mind these days?"

"Nothing. The weather."

"You mean to say that he didn't tell you about Emilie?"

"How would you know what we talked about?"

At that, Muller laughed and rode off in another direction. As he continued home, Conrad could hear the man's cackle far into the distance. Once again he propped the bicycle against the tree and was disappointed the next morning when it was still there.

He no longer spoke to Axel; it felt too dangerous. And now, he found that when the reporters called out to him, provoking him with their questions, he sometimes listened ponderously. He wished he could take his new concerns home to his father but could see his parents had made a heavy peace with their past choices and only hoped that their children would follow the path of least resistance. A path Conrad believed no longer existed for him.

As he walked the border one afternoon, his attention kept landing on the black bicycle propped against a lamp-post, his bicycle, with its menacing gleam. He hated it. Muller waited for him every evening, asking what the guards had discussed on their breaks. As if he spoke to anyone these days. There, in the distance, was Axel. He remembered bunkering under a homemade tent with his friend when they were children, late at night, bending their fingers to make shadow puppets dance on the glowing white sheet they had pilfered from the hall closet. He blinked away the reminiscence. Axel was lost to him. Any sort of intimacy would be impossible now; no one could be trusted, including him. And Emilie. Someday, when he looked back, would she glimmer in his memory as his one and only love? When he thought of the rumor of their child, blood pumped wildly at his temples, deafening him against the usual discipline of his thoughts. Hans was dead. Axel was a stranger. His father was heartbroken.

Emilie had vanished into a world he staunchly refused to imagine.

Without thinking, Conrad turned to face the lens of a photographer...and heard a click.

"Come on," the man shouted. "Give us something to look at."

Before he knew what was happening, Conrad was flying over the barbed coil, dropping his rifle on the eastern side and landing, suddenly, in the west.

The chaos that followed was instantaneous. Axel and another guard ran to intercept him but were too late. The photographer's camera clicked mercilessly, capturing Conrad's every move. Others joined in. The mechanical clacks and whirs sounded more voracious than any of the excited voices. People were shouting but he heard nothing of substance. It happened fast: in an instant, without thought, he was over. For a moment his body felt light as a feather, though when he landed he experienced the full force of his weight. He thought of his father's disappointments, the open sore of his own uncertainty, and ran.

SIX

Blue Eyes to Die For

NEW YORK CITY, May 21, 2013

Larry Berger stood at the bar of the Mercury Lounge, nursing her bottle of beer. She ignored the pings of bemused male attention that kept landing on her: sparkly hot pants, halter top, sneakers. Not her problem what they thought or wanted. She was here to meet Con. Each time the door let in a new customer, a fresh blast of the spring night snuck in, but it was never him.

She stared at the TV angled over the bar. Hardly anyone was watching the news, but she was. She liked politics the way some people liked sports, with a hunger, and anyway she had nothing better to do while she waited.

The local news was replaying its evening report about the case Con had been working: A coterie of officials that included Senator Kenneth Rapp (R-New York) and New York District Attorney John Newcombe (Con's boss's boss's boss) spoke about today's big event in the world of law enforcement. They'd arrested two "individuals" who were "alleged" money-laundering "masterminds" behind the notorious Russian kingpin Vlad Popov, who was still at large.

"This is a significant coup for the city, the state, the country, and, yes, the world," Newcombe pronounced in a tone of grave enthusiasm that suggested a political campaign—lately a hot topic of cable punditry. The mayor's job was opening up at the end of the year, for instance, but Newcombe refused to publicly address his intentions.

Senator Rapp, who was neck-deep into an unofficial pre-campaign for the Republican presidential nomination, spoke next. "The importance of this arrest cannot be overstated: America's war on drugs is alive and well, and we plan on winning it!" As the crowd roared, he turned to Newcombe to whom he directed his own hearty clapping and then paused to rotate his right hand. It was a gesture that had lately been picked up by late-night comics: that quick pivot of his wrist along with his notably crooked nose had laid the foundations for a celebrity caricature that had already started to irritate Larry.

The way they were both glomming onto the victory of today's bust, which was really an accomplishment of the people who ran the operation, was…what? Larry let a sip of bitter fizz evaporate on her tongue. Obvious. Self-serving. Premature.

"Ooh, you dress up nice," Con snuck up on her with one of his easy-sleazy I'm-fucking-with-you smiles, kissing her cheek. "You go to all that trouble for me?"

"Just for you." She leaned forward and jiggled her breasts, feeling the padding in her bra slip a little.

His gaze rose to the TV with a smirk. "So, what do you think?"

"I'd put my money on Newcombe coming out for mayor any day now. You?"

"He's definitely campaigning for something."

"Why doesn't Rapp just get it over with and announce for president?"

"Huh." The corners of Con's mouth turned down in thought. He didn't think about politics as much as she did. "That for me?" He reached for the bourbon she'd already ordered him, on her tab, because this was his night to celebrate.

"Good work." She jabbed his shoulder the way a guy would, and then succumbed to an urge to open her hand and run her palm along the smooth fabric of his jacket. She knew, because he'd told her once, that all his suits and sports coats used to belong to his father. Con had had them all tailored to fit his slender frame. He looked good in a suit, like a real banker. Rackets didn't have much of a budget to spend on wardrobe, and that Con already had a good one tended to direct him toward the tonier jobs. He also had a degree from Columbia University, bought with student loans he'd probably never pay off. He was smart, and handsome as a movie star, but he didn't seem to realize it. Larry never told him how freakish his good looks were; she kept that to herself so that that bridge would not get built between them. The last thing she wanted was to end up on his trash heap of discarded women.

"I nailed a perp on my way home," she told him. "Guy was mugging a monk."

"A monk?" His smile was all irony and pride. "Way. To. Go."

She lifted her hand, awaiting her high five, and their palms slapped with a comforting frisson.

"Hey, Con, what was that about someone jumping off a bridge? Before. When you called me."

He looked at her with those eyes of his, light brown and sweet as the M and Ms that used to be Larry's favorites. Most kids would search out the bright ones, the reds and oranges, but she'd always liked the ones that resembled what they really were. Chocolate. His hair was nearly the same color. He looked at her so long she had to shift on her stool to adjust the rhythm of her breathing.

"You're making me nervous," she said.

"You know how my dad jumped off the Brooklyn Bridge?"

She nodded. There were no words.

"Walking home last night, I saw another guy do the same. That's why I wanted to talk to you. I just needed to blow off some steam. I ended up writing an email to a grandmother I never met."

"Writing, or sending?"

"I deleted it."

Larry stopped herself from throwing her arms around him. He looked so vulnerable, standing there in his nice suit, with his candy eyes, downing his bourbon. She knew he did best when he didn't think about his father, whom he had deeply loved and whose suicide had felt like the worst kind of betrayal to a son who was just starting to find his way.

"What did the email say?"

"The usual bullshit. Blah blah blah." Flagging the bartender, Con asked her, "You want another?"

"No, thanks." In fact, it occurred to her not to finish the beer she already had. She pushed it away. "You know what, Connie?"

When he leaned close to whisper, "Don't be an asshole," his breath was hot and it stank.

"You know what, Conrad?"

"What?"

"Nothing." He drank too much. That was what. But somehow, she didn't have the heart to state the obvious after his long and twisty day. "You look tired."

"I should go back home," he yawned, "and get some sleep."

"Me, too." She slid off her stool, ignoring all the gluey eyes that stuck to her in her work clothes. Slutty though she looked, she still felt cleaner working Vice than Rackets, where Artie Visch, her old boss and Con's current boss, was as dirty as the average john who pulled up for a quickie. She still thought from time to time about bringing a sexual harassment charge down on Artie, but always reached the same conclusion: she wasn't ready to bomb her career.

Pressing through a rank of bodies three-deep, Larry led Con out of the bar. "We'll talk tomorrow, okay? And seriously, congratulations. I'm so proud of you."

Larry strutted off down East Houston, swallowing the usual stoic disappointment whenever they parted ways after-hours. Despite all the time they'd spent together, she felt like she didn't really know him. She couldn't seem to dig past the cool exterior that held him together so well when he was working undercover and sealed him in when he wasn't.

And that, she figured, was why he drank.

And that, she decided (not for the first time), was why she had no right to try and take it away from him. Maybe he needed to get out of himself sometimes, and maybe it was the only way he knew how.

Con stood on East Houston, the dark avenue streaked bright with two-way traffic, listening to horns honking and watching Larry walk away. She put on a good swagger, and the way she looked in her little outfit: thinner, curvier, unponytailed hair a sexy mess. Well. She was his best friend. He'd seen her dressed as a nun one time, back when she worked with him in Rackets, and the truth was she had a knack for becoming other people. "Do I inhabit the habit?" she'd asked him, and laughed at her own wit.

Con reminded himself that he should go back home and take it easy. In the hours after a bust, it was best to lay low—a mandate at which he had already spectacularly failed. Tomorrow, Artie Visch would want to talk. Con knew that he'd be clearer in the morning if he caught some sleep. But then his mind drifted.

This time last night, he was deep in the final take, knowing the bust was set for the next afternoon. After everyone had left, and the cleaning staff had come and gone, he'd gotten to work. He downloaded his hard drive onto a thumb drive so that the DA would know exactly what the fund knew, up to that moment in time, when they went to court. Thoroughly checked his computer, making sure he wouldn't mistakenly leave behind any unintended footprints. Emptied the trash into a bag he took with him. Even disinfected the insides of his desk drawers. He cleaned and organized until he felt confident that he hadn't made a single mistake. Though he'd be back for one more day, acting out the role of Kurt Lettieri, no one would notice the difference. It would take a little time, a few days or a week at most, for Kurt's skin to shed away, but eventually, it would dissolve into a distant and irrelevant legend of a man who didn't exist. Con never knew how long he'd have before stepping into a new skin, a new cover. Already he began to feel the discomfort of trying to fit fully into the private membrane that was supposed to be his real self.

This time last night. Yes. And tonight: the bridge. That tormented face. He could still feel himself running away, worried he'd be seen by the jumper squad when they arrived (too late), by the reporters who might even beat them there and turn him into part of the story.

He could still hear echoes of blood surging to his head. The insane feeling of a thwarted urgency to turn back and see if the man had survived his fall. As he ran, Con had seen himself catapult from the bank into the river, swim to the man who in his mind was flailing, not dead on impact. Con saw himself rescuing the jumper from drowning, convincing himself that, unlike his father, this suicide was redeemable. He'd wanted to go back. But he'd kept running. Because nothing, not even the jumper's life, was more important than protecting his cover.

He stepped back into the Mercury Lounge, into the comfortable darkness of the bar, and fought his way through for another drink. In the back room, the ten o'clock show was about to begin. A cacophony of horns rose and blended. And then a throaty voice sang above the coalescing harmony, and he followed it.

THE BACK ROOM WAS PACKED, the floor sticky from spilled beer. The loud music rattled Con but in the best way, like running out of the heat and into a hungry ocean.

"Who's playing?" he shouted to a guy barely into his twenties, plaid flannel shirt, face half-hidden behind a lumberjack beard. He looked like easily half the other young men in the room. Con, in his good suit, felt old at thirty-five.

"Friendly Fire. Girl band. Not bad."

"Thanks."

"No problem, man."

Con sipped his bourbon, the liquid turning to smoke on his tongue.

A woman in tight jeans and a hand-knitted top came up and gave Plaid Shirt a kiss on the lips. They moved off together and Con was alone in the crowd that swayed and pulsed with the hyperbolic music. Tonight he would have preferred jazz, but still, this was music. It was great. The girls on stage were energetic, heavily made up, a sexy mob with no discernible players. They blurred into the fogginess of his drunken, exhausted brain. His mindless mind. He wanted to feel blank by the time he got home. Blank and empty of Kurt Lettieri and Alexei Dvorshetskii and Pavel Gavrikov. His father. When would he stop seeing him fly off the bridge in another man's body?

At the end of the early show, Con returned to the bar. When the second show started, he found himself in the back room again without knowing exactly how he got there. His jacket was gone. Tie, off. One shoe mysteriously untied.

By the time he realized the show was over, he was dancing in the mottled dark with a woman about his age. Her face, framed by jaw-length straight black hair, had the porcelain tranquility of a doll's. When the lights came up, he was startled by her eyes: they were the bluest he'd ever seen.

"I know you," he said.

"You do?"

"Why do I know you?"

"Are you serious?" She had a vague accent of some kind.

She seemed to think he was pitching her a line, but the thing was he did know her. Somehow he knew her very well. It was like he'd always known her. Never, not once, had he experienced such certainty meeting a woman. He'd lived with two and slept with many, but this feeling was new and tremendous and sorely needed. Especially tonight.

"Maybe I've seen you around. Where do you live?"

"Only way I'm going to tell you that is if you come home and fuck me."

He didn't want her to see how much that had shocked him, so he kept dancing. "Don't be shy."

"Thanks for saving me from myself."

"I'm pretty drunk," he said, trailing a finger along her damp cheek.

"Me, too."

"You're going to marry me someday, you know."

"I don't even want to know your name."

Her bed was unmade when they got there. There were shopping bags and magazines and messes that they kicked aside while they stripped off each other's clothes. Cheap curtains on the open bedroom window let in enough streetlight to see that she was gorgeous but not perfect, which made him want her even more. Standing in front of her, he pulled out of a kiss and gazed into those eyes. Feeling that feeling again: how he knew her: how there was an inevitability to this. How she was the reward at the end of a truly crappy set of hours. How one day they would tell their children about the night they met by accidentally dancing together.

She broke the spell by taking his erection in her hand and leading him to her bed with the insouciance of a dog walker. She pushed him down, climbed on top, and he plunged in as he sensed she wanted him to. Now this was fucking. It was love and it was fucking and it was fucking good. His mind reeled and snapped and finally, blissfully, emptied completely.

After, they lay facing each other in a haze of sweaty exhaustion, desire transfused into a heavy calm. Outside, an ambulance wailed past and then faded into the lush quiet of a sleeping city.

He must have drifted off. When he opened his eyes, she was awake, watching him. He glanced at the red numbers of a digital clock on her bedside table: 6:27 a.m.

"I'd offer you a cigarette," she said, "but this isn't the old movies and I don't smoke."

"Neither do I."

"No one does anymore."

"My old boss smoked like a chimney. He's worth billions but he had to stand on the sidewalk with everyone else." It felt cathartic to refer to Dvorshetskii in the past tense.

"What do you do?"

"I thought you didn't even want to know my name."

She rolled onto her side and propped herself on an elbow, her hair a lovely nest. "I didn't ask your name."

He hesitated, for one wild moment thinking he could tell her the truth. Because she was the one. But the deal with new relationships was that you didn't talk about your undercover work until it was serious, and maybe not even then.

"I'm a hedge fund analyst. At least I was until today."

"You don't sound too sure." The tip of her tongue wandered out to knock something invisible off her bottom lip.

"What about you? What do you do?"

"I'm not that interesting."

"I beg to differ."

Her smile was simple for the first time in the hours they'd known each other. Her teeth were less white and less straight than he'd imagined earlier. "Also unemployed, more or less. And my name is Emmy."

"I'm Kurt." An impulsive, and comfortable, lie.

"Nice to meet you."

"Emmy. Short for?"

"Emilie. Named after my mom."

It occurred to him to ask if she always came on to men so fast and hard at clubs, but didn't dare. Suddenly their encounter didn't seem romantic, but he still liked her, this was still good. This could still be good. After all, she had every right to want to ask him the same question. Maybe the thing to do was to bypass it altogether and start again.

"I wish I could figure out where I know you from."

"Think about it."

"Maybe you're a passerby."

"No, you're a passerby."

He pulled her forward and kissed her. "Not anymore." He kissed her again. "So, what did you do before you were unemployed?"

"Are you for real? How drunk are you?"

"Feeling soberish now, actually."

Hurling herself over the side of the bed, she reached under, searching for something.

EMMY'S HAND sweeps paths in the moonscape of dust that gleams under the bed, digging past stuff she's accumulated during her brief stay along with random items she hadn't realized were missing. A sock, her Chapstick, a rolled-up poster. And some new things she hasn't seen before, evidently dropped during the strip-fest: a pair of sunglasses, three keys on a ring, a BlackBerry with a cracked screen, a man's gold watch resting against the gun she hid for easy access.

She flicks the expensive-looking watch deeper under the bed and runs her hand along the rubber grip of the gun. Just for the hell of it, she inches her finger into the cold metal loop of the trigger guard: a perfect fit, it feels like coming home.

She thinks, suddenly, of her wretched grandmother. Emmy never should have taken that call and listened to those demented stories about the past. There were things you were better off not knowing. She had come away from the call feeling spiteful. She shouldn't have slept with Kurt. Because she knew herself: taking action when she was angry was usually a mistake. Drinking and taking action was always a disaster.

CON WATCHED EMMY UNROLL A POSTER, fished out from under her bed. It was a promotion for last night's show at the Mercury Lounge, featuring a picture of Friendly Fire. There were four girls in heavy makeup, one of whom could have been Emmy.

"You're in the band?"

"Wow."

"I didn't recognize you. All that makeup." He touched her face, gently. "You took it off."

"Observant. But only to a point."

"They loved you."

"After every show, I give myself a treat. Tonight, you were it, but you were supposed to be all jacked up from the music. It's a game I play with myself. You think you can't have me, because I'm so fucking awesome, and then you get me so fast your head spins."

"You should have kept the makeup on. I would have known you in a minute."

"You weren't even watching the show, you were just getting blasted."

"I was watching the show. And I swear, I fell in love the minute the lights came up and I really saw you. Even if I didn't know why I knew you. I loved you."

"What's your punishment's going to be for being such a liar?"

She ran a finger from his chin, down his neck, and along his chest until she reached his groin. And then she stopped. He was on a roller coaster, suddenly heading down into abject disappointment. But then she upped the ante by wiggling down the bed and taking him into her mouth. Pleasure fountained into his brain.

"Not much of a punishment," he groaned.

Her mouth was agile. Luscious. Firm. Velvety swift. And then he felt the razors of her teeth fasten on his skin. It was just a moment, maybe two. His pulse spiked and, as if responding to some primal cue, his erection began to wilt.

She pulled away, wiping her mouth with the back of her hand.

"Why were you biting me?"

She sat back on her heels. "Seriously? Because you're a dick."

"What did I do?" He pushed onto his elbows, away from her.

"Get out."

"What the—"

"I said get the fuck out of my place. If you know what's good for you, you'll leave right now."

Stunned, Con quickly gathered his things in the still-dark morning. The moment he hit the cold air outside, he hailed the first taxi he saw.

SEVEN

Boy/Girl

WEST BERLIN, August 24, 1961

EMILIE PFAFF'S Kreutzberg building would have been visible from Conrad's side of Berlin if he had known where to look. It turned out she hadn't made it very far, but west was west and east was east whether you were an inch or a mile from the border.

Her window was open. From the street below he saw stained white curtains billowing on a lackadaisical summer breeze. A couple of books were piled beside a crusty-looking glass half-full with water. The high wail of a baby crying followed a breeze onto the street, landing painfully in Conrad's ears.

The building's front door was unsecured so he walked right in. He took the steps in pairs until he reached the third floor, breathless, and knocked three times.

Emilie held her chiseled composure when she opened her door and found him. "I saw the papers." She wore the same crimson lipstick she used to, and the way her soap and perfume melded with her skin still produced a musky vanilla fragrance that was uniquely hers. He yearned to embrace her but held back.

"May I come in?"

"What took you so long?"

"I've been busy." He didn't have to explain why it had taken him nearly a week to find her. Defectors were always held and questioned by the Allies until their motivations were fully understood.

She was dressed for the office, in a skirt and blouse, and was barefoot; the red polish on her toenails was badly chipped. Conrad stood at the entrance of her small living room and listened for a baby. The tepid silence unnerved him. He was sure he'd heard it crying.

"Where is it?"

"What a nice greeting." She plopped down on a tattered couch, bundling her knees in front of her. There was little furniture in the place other than the couch and a table with a single chair. There was no sign of a child. On a mantle across the room, a pair of bricks served as bookends, with a single book lapsed sideways between them. This was the Emilie he remembered: haphazard, improvisational, a reader. Often selfish. "Why are you here, Connie?"

She had once whispered that in his ear at the height of passion. Connie. Teasing him, calling him a woman's name, just at his moment of release. She had been his first and only lover. He had assumed they would marry and was devastated when she disappeared across the border without warning.

"Just tell me: Is it true you had our baby?"

Her eyes were black scythes in a white face. A new pageboy haircut made her severe. Finally, she answered, "I gave it up. I had to. I couldn't make it on my own with a child."

"Why didn't you tell me you were expecting?"

"I didn't know until I was already here, and then it didn't matter anymore. I wasn't going back, and you weren't coming over."

"And yet here I am."

"Why?"

It was an excellent question. "The truth is, I'd rather be home."

"But you defected."

"It was an impulse. I wanted to...." Words failed him. It wasn't as simple as finding her and learning the truth. He'd wanted to get away from Muller, and from the black bicycle. "Was it a boy or girl?"

"I don't know."

"How can that be?"

"They were instructed not to tell me at the hospital. I never even saw it."

"So you don't know where it is now?"

"How could I?"

She had walked away from her newborn, just as she'd walked away from him. Her mercilessness was electrifying. He wondered if she was telling the truth; if there really had been a baby. Cold shuddered through him. Why was he here?

"Want something to drink?"

He sat down beside her. "Why not?"

They drank beer until midnight, after which it was agreed that he should spend the night on her couch. By the second night, he was in her bed. It quickly made no sense for him to leave at all.

· · ·

"THE WALL WILL BE FINISHED SOON," Emilie whispered in his ear. They'd been together a month, one day easing into the next without any planning. "They say it's going to seal off West Berlin completely, turn us into a little island unto ourselves."

Conrad thought of his father and mother, trapped on the other side. He'd written to them several times, but doubted any of his letters had gotten through. "I need to see my parents."

The sheet slid off when she propped herself on an elbow, exposing her small breasts. "I know a way we can both go back."

"Do you want to go back?"

"That's not what I mean." Without her lipstick, the wild self-assurance of that slash of vivid red, her smile betrayed a rare vulnerability. He kissed her.

"What do you mean?"

"You'll see." She lay back on her pillow and closed her eyes. A blue shadow from yesterday's makeup lingered in the relaxed folds of her lids. Wetting a finger, he smoothed away the color. He disliked it when she became mysterious.

"Explain," he insisted.

"Do you really want to go back?"

"Yes, but only if you come with me." He kissed her, and she threw her arms around him.

"Someone very special is in town," she whispered in his ear. "He can help us. I'm told he's willing to meet with us today."

A SLENDER MAN in a suit and tie reclined in a chair in the back room of the construction outfit where Emilie worked. His dark hair was brushed neatly off his forehead, and his fingernails were conspicuously clean. There was no denying his elegance. He held a tiny espresso cup on a saucer, balanced on his knee.

"This is Mischa," Emilie told Conrad, the moment they walked in. He wondered why she hadn't introduced him, as well. Did the man already know who he was?

"A pleasure to meet you, Herr—"

"Wolf." His voice was as unimpeachable as his manicure, without tone. The name Mischa Wolf rang a distant bell in Conrad's mind. And then it struck him like a thunderbolt.

Markus "Mischa" Wolf was second in command of the Stasi, the notorious spymaster who ran the Hauptverwaltung Aufklärung. It was rumored that the HVA sent its tentacles worldwide, and well known (if rarely discussed) that the East German secret police recruited far and wide, and greedily. It had to be some kind of absurd dream, finding Wolf in the dusty back room of a minor capitalist enterprise in West Berlin. Unless of course, this business was a front. Conrad glanced at Emilie's pretty face and saw nothing different from before.

Wolf set his cup and saucer on the arm of the chair and stood. He was tall, with a guileless manner that commanded the room. "It took some time to figure out how to get you here."

"I can't imagine why you'd be interested in me, Herr Wolf."

"It was Emilie's idea. I'm told you're trustworthy."

She nodded, earning a small smile from Wolf. That they addressed each other on a first-name basis made Conrad wonder how long they had been acquainted.

"Trustworthy? I myself crossed the border I was guarding."

"You behaved exactly as we anticipated."

"I don't understand," Conrad lied.

In fact, he understood perfectly. Finally, things made sense.

Herr Muller had been just the beginning. The bicycle. Muller's threats against his family. That spin around the block had always led right here. For a frantic moment, Conrad even wondered if the woman with the garlic bomb had also been arranged by the HVA, to attract the press, to bring the bicycle, to spark his reminiscing and make him susceptible to Muller's offer of a bike. The story of a baby. How had they known precisely how to tunnel into his mind?

He felt the urgent need to speak with Emilie privately. How long had she worked for Wolf? When had Conrad been factored into it—before or after her defection to the west? He wondered if she had been in love with him from the start, in her own strange way. Her face revealed nothing. As his mind awoke, he recognized another fact of life: There was never any baby. It was merely a lever to bring him over, as planned because Emilie asked for him. But it was Emilie they really wanted. Emilie, with her looks, her brains, her confidence, her inscrutability, would doubtless make the perfect spy.

Light-headed, Conrad turned to leave. But when Emilie's hand landed in his, with its blast of warmth, he found he couldn't get to the door.

"What exactly do you want from me?"

"Eyes and ears," Wolf answered. "Keep us up to date."

"How long have you been doing this?" Conrad asked Emilie.

"Connie, you've got to understand. The Wall is just the beginning. Once West Berlin is isolated, once they're hungry, the Wall comes down again and the GDR will run the entire city. No more separation."

"They? We're here now, too."

"You don't need to worry. There's a plan for how it's all going to work. All we need to do is pass along information that could be helpful."

"What kind of information?"

"Anything. Anything we might notice. Whatever we might overhear."

"You told me we could get back to the east. Is this what you meant?"

Emilie looked at Conrad with a spark in her eyes. He hated what she had done to him, and yet he loved her. "We'll get back home by staying here and working together. We'll have each other. It's going to be perfect, don't you see?"

Thoughts crashing, Conrad did the political math. If he agreed, they would work for the east against the west, while appearing to have defected to the west, as all the while Wolf and his team surveyed and manipulated them. Double agents, if he'd done the puzzle correctly. And if he didn't agree? He thought of the bicycle, leaning against the tree outside his parents' building every morning without fail, and knew he'd never get away.

"How can you be so sure we won't be caught by the Allies?" Conrad asked them both.

"I'll protect you," Wolf answered.

"How? What makes you think that you of all people can keep us safe in the west? And what about my parents? How can I know nothing will happen to them if I'm caught?"

Wolf smiled, his teeth slightly yellow in the dim light. "You're right, no one can trust anyone these days. But even so, young man, you'll have to make a choice."

EIGHT

Home is Where

NEW YORK CITY, May 22, 2013

THE CAB LEFT Con off on the corner of West End Avenue, and he walked the sloped block down Ninety-ninth Street toward Riverside Drive. Sun gleamed so brightly on the Hudson River that he reached for his sunglasses, only to be reminded that he was traveling light. His wallet was still in his pants when he'd put them back on at Emmy's, but his keys must have fallen out. Bit by bit, he was realizing what was missing. He felt naked, unbalanced, and confused about what had just happened. He'd had a lot of experience with women, seen lots of crazy stuff go down in bed and out, but this was a new one—nearly getting his dick bitten and then unceremoniously tossed out, and for what?

Just then he realized that his wrist was bare. His father's watch was gone, dispatched by lust to Emmy's bedside table or thereabouts. It was the only item of his father's he had left, besides some clothes and that useless key. The watch was the one thing that really mattered to him; he would have to get it back.

And then, as he waited for the old elevator to struggle its way down the shaft, a fourth loss registered: his personal cell phone. The phone was packed with information about his life and work.

Using the case phone he'd been assigned at the start of Dostoyevsky for all his communications with Worth & Kimball, he dialed his personal cell. Voice mail picked up instantly: "You've reached Con Mathis, please leave a message and I'll get back to you as soon as I can." He tried again before the elevator arrived, and again voice mail answered right away. Either he'd turned the phone off or the battery had run down.

His keys, his sunglasses, his watch, and now his phone…he would have to find his way back to Emmy's…if he could only remember her address. He'd stumbled out of there so fast, hung-over and in shock; all he knew for sure was that she lived on a side street in Chinatown.

He hoped his sister had some coffee.

The tenth-floor apartment's front door was still decorated with their mother's glittery No Smoking sign, pre-empting any intention to light up in the house, as if anyone would anymore. Since she'd decamped to Florida five years ago, and Sophie took over the rent-controlled apartment, not much had changed. The sound of her footsteps clomping toward the door gave him heart. This was almost over. He could get some comfort (and his spare set of keys) from his sister, track Emmy down, and then head back to Brooklyn and clean himself up so he'd be ready when Artie contacted him.

"Enter." Sophie swung open the door, looking fragile as a tiny bird. Her skinny jeans were baggy and her collarbones heaved above the scooped neck of her T-shirt. Her head looked too large for her body. Her formerly lustrous long brown hair was turning to mist.

The door slammed behind them with its usual uncontrolled thud.

"Whazzup, sister?" He kissed her cheek and felt bone. "You lost a lot of weight."

"Thanks."

He hadn't meant it as a compliment, exactly, and that she'd taken it as one left him speechless.

"What's going on?" she asked.

"You don't want to know."

"You're right. I don't."

He followed her out of the foyer. The apartment's entryway was as big as some people's bedrooms in this city of astronomical rents. Their parents had moved into this massive apartment over thirty years ago before the urban middle class was relegated to miniature spaces; it had to be one of the last rent-controlled leases remaining in family hands. Sophie paid less for five bedrooms, flowing living spaces, and exquisite citrus sunsets through her many large windows than Con did for his studio in Carroll Gardens. He could have lived here with her when their mother moved out but had never considered it. He cherished his privacy. Sophie, on the other hand, was never alone. She rented out all the bedrooms other than her own and lived off the profit.

He trailed her through the dining room, where their mother's ornate birdcage sat empty in a corner and neat piles of mail lined the edge of the long table. They had always kept spare keys in a cabinet in the breakfast nook off the kitchen. Con removed the molded porcelain hair from a chipped Betty Boop cookie jar—their mother collected "vintage treasures" as she called them, otherwise known as thrift store junk—and fished his spares out of a trove of old keys of various unknown provenance. There were keys from long-gone neighbors, loose keys with no tags or explanations, and a few tiny keys stamped with boxy numbers: 946, 290, 357. There was also his father's old skeleton key from back in the day. When Con was a boy, he'd spirit the foreign-looking key to the apartment's back door and pretend it led to a medieval dungeon where, if he dared venture in, he'd find unspeakable things going on. He'd sit with his back against the door, the key hot in his hand, and make up stories. Then he'd return it to Betty Boop and stir it back in among all the other keys to lost places.

"I could use some fuel to make it home," Con said. "Coffee?"

"In the kitchen. Go ahead. I'll take some, too."

He found a bag of ground coffee in the freezer in a Zabar's bag marked with Sophie's name and started the Mr. Coffee, another relic from his childhood. Sophie drank hers black. She sat on one of the old mismatched chairs with her knees folded under her chin like broken wings. Her bare feet were so bony Con had to look away. Sipping his coffee, he asked her, "Why are you so thin?"

"I don't understand. I mean, look at you. You look pretty shitty yourself."

"I had a long night, Soph. I just closed a case. Don't deflect this back to me—I asked you something. And I never said you look bad." Though she did. "Just really thin."

"I took off some weight."

"Are you sick?"

"No."

"When I saw you a couple of months ago you looked —" He'd been about to say fine, but stopped himself. She must have lost weight on purpose, which upset him, scared him. He didn't know what to say. He finished his coffee. "I should probably get going."

"Seriously, Con, you okay?"

"Generally, yes. Today, not so much. But I'll be fine."

"Did you hear about the guy on the Brooklyn Bridge? There was an article in the Times about him—Martin Boettcher, he was a gym teacher and his wife died of cancer two weeks ago. The way he jumped, it made me think of Dad."

Before Con could respond, Sophie sprang out of her chair and wrapped her arms around him. Her back moved in fragile undulations as he hugged and consoled her. She was eighteen when their father died, and she had persevered bravely in her own quirky way. Only now, holding her, did it occur to him that she may have been slowly shattering ever since. She'd probably want to talk all day if he could spare the time, but he couldn't handle it right now. He had to be ready for Artie when he called. But first, he had to try to get his stuff back from Emmy.

"Sorry, Soph, but I've got to get going." He pulled away with a promise to return soon.

THE PILE of raw fish heaped on an outdoor table on the corner of Mott and Canal Streets reeked in the warm morning air. An elderly Chinese man with a gimpy eye alternated between shooing away flies and heckling potential customers.

"Excuse me," Con said.

"How many?"

"I don't want any fish, I just—"

Gimpy turned his back on Con with the practiced resolve of a vendor who had no use for chitchat. Con opened his wallet and bought one of the limp silver-skinned trout, avoiding its dead eyes as ropy hands slid it into a plastic bag and took the money.

"Thank you, sir," Con said. "I'm wondering if I can ask you something."

The old man's good eye blinked. "Fry in oil, not too long."

"I'm looking for a woman who I'm pretty sure lives on this block. Black hair, blue eyes. White girl, like me." Con's thinking was that not too many non-Chinese lived in the neighborhood, and it couldn't hurt to ask around.

"Every girl round here got black hair. Take a look."

Con obliged, throwing his gaze around the busy Chinatown intersection. "You've got a point there."

"Anyway, no white girl on this block, and I know everyone."

"Thanks."

"Find new girl. Always more fish in the sea."

The fishmonger's heckling laugh followed Con up Mott to Bayard, where he turned and ventured down Mulberry. Expecting nothing, and getting nothing, he used the Kurt phone to call the Con phone again and ran into the wall of his own voice. He was sure Emmy's building was on one of the quieter side streets, not on an avenue. She lived in a shabby walkup somewhere near a Chinese restaurant. That's about all he remembered, and it described pretty much the entire neighborhood. He had no idea what her last name was.

He walked and walked, the smell from his fish intensifying until he offered it to a woman in a stained apron, sitting alone on a stoop. Her arthritic hands gripped her knees as if she was about to get up, but from the look of her, she wasn't going anywhere. She took the fish and set it on her lap, thanking him in Chinese.

Eventually, he'd woven his way through most of the

neighborhood with nothing sparking a clue. This was why he shouldn't drink; he didn't know when to stop. Thirst clawed at his throat. At a market on the corner, he bought himself a bottle of water and this time didn't ask anyone if they had seen a woman who looked like Emmy. He was getting the sense that even if someone did know who he meant, no one would tell him—unshaven, rumpled clothing, smelling of old booze and unbrushed teeth. He thought of Martin Boettcher, the suicidal gym teacher— loses his wife, and suddenly his life turns rotten. He thought of his father, and his aborted email to his grandmother, and the sensation of Emmy's teeth biting him and wished there was some way he could reverse the decision to walk across the bridge last night.

Standing there, drinking his water, a taxi approached with its vacancy light glowing. Smitten with a new idea, Con flagged the taxi.

"Mercury Lounge," he told the driver.

It was a little early for the music scene but a few dozen determined knocks on the door of the club finally brought someone. A chunky hipster in black-rimmed glasses, black vest, and bolo tie looked annoyed to be interrupted during daylight hours.

"Yeah?"

"I was here last night and lost a few things."

Sighing, Bolo led Con through the empty bar to a back office where a laptop was open on a desk. "Lost and found." He pointed to a ratty cardboard box in the corner and got back to work on the laptop.

Con's suit jacket was crumpled near the top. He slipped into it and searched all the pockets for his phone and watch. Nothing but his tie and a Slim Jim wrapper. He hated Slim Jims. Someone must have borrowed his jacket last night.

Con stood in front of Bolo in his wrinkled suit. The more Bolo ignored Con, the more ridiculous he felt. "I can't find my phone or my keys or my watch."

Bolo stopped typing and looked at him with an expertly tuned expression of disdain and disinterest. Apparently, he had heard it all before. "Sorry, man."

"I'm thinking this girl I met last night might know where they are."

"Ask her."

"The thing is—"

Bolo handed him a blue post-it note and a pen. "Name and number. If she turns up, I'll send her your way."

Con handed over his contact information. "She was in the band."

"Which girl?"

"Emmy."

He opened a file on the laptop and paused to read. "Sally, Chandra, Melanie, Jane. You're talking about Friendly Fire, right?"

"She said she was in the band."

"No Emmy in that band. What'd she look like?"

"Black hair to here." Con touched his jaw. "Really blue eyes. In her thirties, I think."

"I don't know her. Sounds like a million girls. Like I said, if she comes looking for you, I'll send her your way."

NINE

White Skies, Broken Doors

WEST BERLIN, December 20-25, 1963

Conrad Schumann huddled in the bitter cold as pearly morning light announced the start of a new day. His hands were fisted into the pockets of his wool coat but still his fingertips felt like blocks of ice. Framed in a doorway, every exhalation produced a foggy cloud that blotted out the scene unfolding in front of him, and hid him as well, though he didn't feel hidden. Here, you were always seen, even if you were the one doing the watching.

He'd be late for work—these days, he and Emilie were junior producers for Radio in the American Sector—but he'd been unable to resist this detour. Emilie had warned him against exposing his curiosity, but this was something he had to see for himself.

It was more than curiosity that had brought Conrad face to face with this unprecedented opening of the Wall— this five-day allowance for West Berliners to cross into the east and visit loved ones for the holidays. His heart throbbed with loneliness for his parents, especially his mother. He hadn't seen them for nearly three years, since he was a foolish nineteen-year-old boy. Now, he was a young man with responsibilities often heavier than he felt he could carry. A hug from his mother would have been enough. Just one embrace. Thinking of her, he could smell the almond butter cookies she always baked for Christmas. Spiced cider warm on the stove, radiating its succor of cinnamon and cloves. If they were lucky that year, a ham in the oven. His mother's light touch on his shoulder when it was time to eat. The soft give of her cheek when he kissed her goodnight.

Two weeks ago, when the agreement was announced to allow these Christmas visits, a line had instantly formed in the cold, stretching long hours through the night for a chance at the one-day permits. For a single, heady moment Conrad had thought that he, too, could apply, until Emilie looked at him and said, "Don't waste your time thinking about it." She was right, of course. Somehow, if he opened himself to scrutiny, they would find out he was Stasi. Wherever he was, he was locked in place.

He watched as thousands upon thousands of eager West Berliners braved the cold on foot, arms loaded with gifts, and passed into the east. A long line of cars nosed their way toward the border like a hungry snake. Guards checked every permit before waving them through. Crowds of easterners waited on the other side, one by one falling out of the group with jubilant shouts, arms thrown open. In their faces, sparks of heartache and loss plagued people on both sides of the Wall.

In his official life, it was Conrad's job to help compile narratives of lives torn apart by the separation of east and west, and turn them into segments for RIAS's program *From the Zone for the Zone*. These stories were among the missives that the radio station traded in, in the name of free speech, and since the Wall went up, airwaves were about the only thing the GDR couldn't successfully block. His own story, however, was one that must never be told.

His real job had nothing to do with radio journalism. As an active measures specialist for Wolf's HVA, he'd grown skilled at weaving disinformation into sanctioned truth. In other words, he was a professional liar, and a sneak, and a rat.

The morning sun rose higher; the sky grew brighter, now veined with blue; and the ache of being left behind grew stronger as Conrad stood in his sheltering doorway and watched the people flood into the east, or as he still thought of it: home.

And yet, in his dual life, he had become conflicted. Confused.

Whenever he thought of home in comparison to here, he pictured white skies and broken doors. It was a bleak memory based on something long gone, but it haunted him. In the memory, which may have been more a feeling than an actual recalled event, it was the day after the Wall was completed and he woke up to the realization of how many broken doors he'd left behind in the east. Each door, filled with the memory of something lost. Someone lost. And the sky: it was always white when he thought of his past, and a shifty blue-green-purple, like a bruise, when he thought of his future, though in fact you saw the same sky from both sides of the Wall.

In the time that he'd lived and worked in the west with Emilie, logic had never depleted the blow at the heart of the feeling of that memory. Here was the new problem faced by turncoats like him: The west was both better and worse than the east, and the east was both better and worse than the west. There was no tenable compromise.

The fantasy of reconciliation would never work. They'd be stuck in this postwar madness forever, wedged between the contradictory political and social philosophies of the Soviets, the Americans, the British, and the French, everyone grabbing their share of a broken country and trying to get everyone else's. What was Germany now? Where was Germany going? Defining it had become a collective and wholly self-destructive obsession.

He watched the east-bound stream of humanity for another hour until he could no longer stand the cold. Then he hopped back on his bicycle and continued on to the office.

In the Schoneberg neighborhood, where RIAS was headquartered, bakeries were just flicking on their lights. Conrad biked swiftly past the staid city hall, anchored by its clock tower, where just five months ago, on a warm summer afternoon, Mayor Willy Brandt hosted John F. Kennedy. Con had watched from the street, spellbound, as the dashing American president announced to the world: "I am a Berliner!" Kennedy had now been dead a solid month. The decision to open the border for Christmas had struck a rare note of accord, some thought in tribute to the slain democratic leader, others in weakness to the wrong ideal.

The mood all along the Kufsteinerstrasse was energetic as men and women emerged for work and children ran for school. Conrad parked his bicycle in front of the curved corner building where RIAS had its offices. From across the street, a shout of high laughter caught his attention.

He paused to watch a pair of coatless girls in skirts and knee socks exploring a mound of ornate rubble until he was confident they weren't in danger of getting hurt. The bombed-out Beaux-Arts building had been reduced to a pile more than twenty years ago and yet here it sat, mostly undisturbed. Every day he noticed it, and every day he wondered if it would ever be rebuilt or at least cleared away. Berliners were used to the urban-archeological leavings of the war: destroyed foundations, empty lots, bullet-riddled facades. Even here in the west, cleanup had been slow and threatened to drag on indefinitely. He could only imagine that the scars on the eastern side of the Wall had deepened since he'd been gone, wizening into a geographic despair.

The girls slipped to the broken sidewalk and buckled to examine their finds. Stones, mostly, masquerading as marbles. Conrad continued inside. The vast building's foyer was barely warmer than the frigid outside air; the station may have been run by the Americans but even they couldn't keep the heat coming on days like this.

As the week passed, every program on RIAS doubled down with news of the holiday crossings. Women brought homemade cookies into the office. Men stood on chairs to hang paper streamers. In the evenings, there was schnapps, though few over-indulged for fear of losing their wits. Conrad didn't know whether to laugh or cry at the prospect of a bunch of drunken spies all thrown in together. For reasons of survival, every side was repre-sented at influential hubs like RIAS.

One morning, he arrived at work to find on his desk a brown paper bag, folded and tied with a green ribbon. There was no note. Inside the bag was a jumble of Kodak slides. He pulled one out at random and held it to the light. It was an image from his childhood: he was eight or nine years old, sitting at the kitchen table doing homework, a plate covered in cookie crumbs beside him. His heart swelled. Somehow, his parents had found a way to get this gift through to him. There were at least a dozen pictures from his childhood, black and white remembrances of the love he'd left behind.

Bit by bit, his mood grew uncharacteristically hopeful, and he thought that maybe in time there would be another opening of the Wall, another chance for a permit, and it wouldn't be beyond the pale to think that he himself could make his way back into the arms of his mother for a brief respite. He would treasure just one more heart-to-heart talk with his father.

On Christmas Day, Conrad and Emilie were at home —having opened their practical gifts and eaten their meager meal and made half-hearted love in the early afternoon—when news broke that shattered any illusion that things had warmed up between east and west.

It was Emilie who turned on the radio to the bass voice of their colleague, Don Fennell, announcing the latest development. A pair of eighteen-year-old East Berliners had scaled the Wall between the Mitte and Kreuzberg, but only one of the boys, Hartmut, managed to land safely in the west. His friend Paul was killed in a hail of bullets courtesy of eastern border guards. As RIAS reported it, the boy was a fallen martyr. Dispatches from the east called him a fugitive. Either way, he would never see his parents again, either. The five-day dream was over. The border had slammed shut, for good.

TEN

Friendly Fire

NEW YORK CITY, May 22, 2013

CON FOLLOWED the smell of roasting beans to D'Amico's on Court Street in Brooklyn, past the butchers and the bakeries and the stroller-mamas with their diamonds and clogs. The coffee smolder that hung over his sunny neighborhood engorged his senses, luring him forward. While he waited for his pound of house blend to be ground and bagged, he considered his plan: call a locksmith; remote-wipe his lost phone; forget his father's watch; call Artie and wrap up Dostoyevsky.

He stopped to buy himself a bright green apple at the fruit and vegetable store on his way home. The sour wet snap of his first bite was intensely delicious. He finished the apple in measured bites, resisting an urge to devour it, and by the time he turned onto First Place he was suffused with the sweet respite of apple, neighborhood, home.

Nearby church bells rang for one o'clock, the final peel of bright sound distorting as a siren bled into it. At the end of the block, a fire truck pulled wrong-way around the corner and ground to a halt beside the hydrant closest to Con's own building. Firefighters jumped off like fleas skirmishing for a host. Another truck followed. Con tossed the apple core into a neighbor's garbage can, pressed the brown-bagged pound of coffee under his arm, and sprinted the rest of the way.

"Whoa, you can't go in there!" A firefighter with the rosy nose of a serious drinker stopped him before he reached the iron fence separating the sidewalk from the front yard. His chest tightened when he realized that smoke was billowing out of his apartment windows. Firefighters were streaming up his front stoop.

"I live here. That's my place."

"Ah, jeez, that's some tough luck," Nose commiserated. "Won't be livable for a while."

"Anyone inside?" Con thought of Marcellina, his landlady who lived alone in the basement apartment, and the other tenants, Sean on his floor, and Jayla and Nolan upstairs.

"The owner."

Con glanced across the street and with relief spotted Marcellina, holding court in her housedress with a gaggle of other matrons from the block. Her head was plastered with blackish dye that dripped from her hairline, threatening her eyes.

"She's the one who called," Nose said. "No one else yet, but we're in there lookin'."

"All the other tenants work regular hours in the city. I doubt anyone's here."

"Lucky thing."

"I'll say."

"You—you don't work regular?" Nose glanced at Con's

rumpled suit, possibly smelled the boozy apple on his breath. But it was none of his business.

Suddenly aggravated, Con asked, "Why are you standing around talking to me? Shouldn't you be fighting the fire?"

"You wanted me to let you go inside and get roasted like a marshmallow? Go ahead, Buddy Boy, be my guest."

A breeze abruptly shifted a blast of heavy smoke. Nose walked away as Con doubled over coughing. When he'd recovered himself, he watched as the fire was tackled and subdued. The thought that he had now probably lost all his possessions eclipsed his disappointment about the phone and watch, and nullified the keys altogether.

"You!" Marcellina's high-pitched voice jerked him out of the stupor of his disbelief that this was really happening.

She came toward him, arm in arm with two women, one of whom was using a wad of tissues to wipe goop off her friend's forehead. The other, in a bright pink cardigan, held the tissue box.

"Marcellina, I'm so glad you're okay," Con said. "What happened?"

"That'sa what I'ma gonna ask you."

"I don't know. I haven't been home since yesterday morning when I left for work."

"Why only your place is aburnin' up? Huh?"

"I was wondering the same thing. Maybe an electrical fire."

"My wires is all agood. This a catastrophe!" She burst into tears.

Pink Sweater said, "Come on, Marcy, and let's clean you up before your hair burns worse than your house."

The trio repaired into the brownstone directly across the street, where Marcellina could both wash the dye out of her hair and suffer the progress of the fire from a distance.

As the blaze was subdued, it became clear that it had confined itself to Con's apartment thanks to the fact that all the doors and windows had been closed until one of the firefighters broke a front window. Word was that everything inside had been incinerated.

A fireman appeared on the stoop carrying Con's bicycle, which he'd stored in the front hall. He felt overwhelmed with gratitude that something of his had survived. His scratched blue helmet was still dangling off the handlebars.

"That's mine," Con said to a beat officer who had come to control the growing crowd of onlookers.

When the officer cleared a path so Con could step forward and claim his bicycle, he glimpsed an ax being swung into the wall upon which his bike had leaned intermittently for the past three and a half years, and he knew it was over for him here. The handlebar was hot so he leaned it against a neighbor's fence and waited for the metal to cool. A few people approached to console him, and he thanked them, but he couldn't concentrate. His gut feeling was that this had something to do with Dostoyevsky. A cold sweat crawled across his face as he wondered if they'd made him. The way he'd snuck out during booking. He could imagine Dvorshetskii's bald rage at being arrested. Pavel Gavrikov's humiliation. Did they send someone to jimmy his door while he was out and start the fire as a warning? Or maybe, knowing first-hand the power of their greed, they would have burned the place down with him inside.

Drops of smoke-murky sweat fell off his face onto his case phone when he tried to call Artie. He dried the phone on his shirt and dialed again. As it rang, he noticed a young man step out of the crowd and aim a camera at him. A young woman nearby jotted notes. Con ended the call before it was answered, pocketed his phone, hustled his bike off the fence, and rode away before the reporters could capture him. He couldn't risk getting his picture in the paper on the off chance that his cover wasn't already blown, that the fire was merely accidental.

Or.

The keys he'd lost at Emmy's.

He thought of last night and a spate of delectable sensations electrified his body, followed by a memory of her teeth sinking into his dick. Dread tremored through him. What exactly was her problem?

Defying the skin-melting heat of the handlebars, he danced his hands up and down in an alternating two-step all the way to the entrance ramp for the Brooklyn Bridge. It was the last place he wanted to be, but Manhattan and the refuge of Sophie's apartment were on the other side. He circumvented foot traffic by pulling up against a barrier and took out his phone.

"Artie, it's Con."

"You're at the top of my list."

"My apartment just burned down."

Artie exhaled heavily. "When?"

"I just got home and the fire department was there. Just my apartment, Artie. The rest of the building's fine."

"Fuck."

"Dostoyevsky?"

"They're getting interrogated right now. I'll see if I can find out if they made you, but there hasn't been any reason to think they did."

"Up until now," Con pointed out, conscious of his misdirection in omitting the fact that he'd lost his keys at the apartment of a woman he barely knew. The last thing his career needed was to be connected personally to Artie's reputation for sexual impropriety. Plus, if Artie knew, word would spread and Larry would find out, and Con didn't want that, either.

"Where are you?"

"Heading to my sister's place. One more thing: I'll need my personal phone remote-wiped. It got lost in the shuffle. I was going to do it when I got home, but now…"

Another whoosh of breath from Artie, this one annoyed. "Why'd you have your personal phone on the job?"

"I screwed up, Artie. I grabbed my stuff and got out. Haven't seen it since."

"I'll call IT."

"Thanks."

"Hang tight, buddy. And don't worry, you did good. I'm proud of my best agent, okay?"

"Thanks."

"You got someplace to go now?"

"My sister's, uptown."

"Good. Stay out of sight the rest of the day. Let me handle things from my end."

Con hopped on his bike and rode, gripping the handlebars and letting them burn his hands. He did not look at the east tower from which Martin Boettcher had jumped last night. Nor did he look at the west tower from which his father had jumped nine years ago. He rode with his eyes fixed ahead. His resolve to overcome this flourishing nightmare was still strong and he welcomed any price he would have to pay at this point, as long as it ended.

"MATHIS," Con answered, seeing that the call was coming from the Fire Marshall. Sophie was at the gym and none of her roommates were around. Con had the living room to himself: his mother's soft couch, her paintings on the walls, the big window with its poignant tangerine sunset draped over the river. He was hungry for dinner and had just been wondering if he should wait for Sophie, if she even ate meals anymore, when his cell rang.

"This is Inspector Joan Bailey, Bureau of Fire Investigation. I'm at your apartment in Brooklyn."

"I hope you talked with my supervising investigator at Rackets. We're worried there's an overlap with an undercover job I just finished."

"Yup, just hung up the phone. Visch is all over it. Says you're his best undercover."

"Artie said that? Aw."

Bailey chuckled, though only slightly. "We're looking at arson, but I figure you know that."

"Yes and no. What did you find?"

"Traces of alcohol, a lot of it, on what's left of the couch. Evidence of a box of matches. Unwinding with a smoke and a couple of drinks after work, maybe?"

"I don't smoke."

"Playing with fire?" A snicker in her voice.

"Just to be clear, Inspector, a) I hadn't been home since the night before, and b) I'm a big boy and I don't play with matches. Ever."

"We'll be canvassing for witnesses, anyone who saw someone coming and going, someone who didn't belong."

"Dostoyevsky's Russians, well, let's just say they don't fly under the radar. If they were there, someone probably noticed."

"Dostoyevsky, the writer?"

"Name of the case."

"One more thing. Your door was locked."

"Locked, as in...."

"Someone turned a key, locked the door, and walked away after the fire was set."

His stomach collapsed; he was no longer hungry. He scrunched into the couch and dropped his forehead in his hand. He thought, again, of Emmy. It was bad enough that he'd had to admit to Artie that he lost his phone, but now the inevitability of confessing that he also lost his keys loomed. He had a choice to make: either add another lie, complicating and deepening his troubles by perjuring himself during an official arson investigation or simply tell the truth about Emmy. Which was? He'd stumbled drunk into a one-night stand with a woman who fucked like a dream, was a biter, oh and maybe was an arsonist? Con wrapped his fingers around his watch-less left wrist, feeling the impending loss of himself like a seed buried inside the loss of his father. The predictability of his implosion. He recalled a distant, heated conversation—over drinks, a couple of years ago—in which Larry had warned him that if he didn't "grow up" his "reckless behavior" would "have consequences." She'd never expressed those concerns again, but every now and then her voice materialized in his consciousness.

"You there?" Inspector Bailey asked.

"That's pretty strange," he said, "about the lock."

"Ever leave your keys out at work?"

Con was sure he hadn't, his keys resided always and solely in his pants pocket. But her question opened the credible possibility that someone at Worth & Kimble might have copied his keys. Ready-made reasonable doubt.

"Yes," he heard himself lying, "I put them on my desk sometimes."

"Why's that?"

"Emptying out my pockets, looking for change for the soda machine." Except he never drank soda. People could testify to that. His breathing got shallow, he felt dizzy, waited for her to respond.

"You must've been pretty thirsty if you ran off to the soda machine without putting your stuff back in your pockets first."

"I biked to work occasionally, and yeah, I'd get parched."

"Well, maybe that's what happened. Maybe someone copied your keys. Maybe they made you and they burned down your place and now they're going to hunt you down and kill you." And then Joan Bailey laughed, a howling belly laugh that she clearly enjoyed. "Sorry, Mathis, long day. That felt good, though."

Women could be such bitches. "Glad to be of assistance, Inspector."

"I wouldn't worry about the lock thing too much. Someone could have gotten in through a back window and closed it after himself. We noticed you don't keep your windows locked, which is strange for someone who works in law enforcement."

"I shut them when I leave," he said. "But you're right, I should lock them. Always."

"Give it a few days and you can go back into your apartment, see what you can salvage."

"Thanks."

"We'll let you know."

ELEVEN

Little Murders

NEW YORK CITY, May 23, 2013

THERE WAS A CLOUD, just one, hovering in the blue sky above a construction pit on the corner of 96th and Broadway. Cotton-white and buoyant without threat of rain, just floating there as if biding its time. Emmy liked this little cloud; if clouds could be pets, she would choose this one. Larger-than-life cranes sprouted from the pit with the majesty of redwoods.

Mutti had been trying to reach her again. Emmy hadn't answered or returned the calls because she still wasn't sure what her next move would be. If she would get going on Mutti's business, or continue her digression as a wrecking ball in the life of her latest fixation: Kurt Lettieri the hedge fund analyst a.k.a. Con Mathis the undercover investigator. That phone of his had revealed a lot. What a liar. Maybe she should have bitten all the way through.

She'd showered after she got back from Brooklyn, but

her clothes still smelled like smoke. She'd have to find her way to a Laundromat at some point. But first.

Using Con's phone (before it went suddenly, mysteriously blank), Facebook, and the online white pages, it had been ridiculously easy to track down his sister.

Sophie was easy to recognize when she came around the corner wearing turquoise sneakers and black spandex hanging off her like a sheath of sorry old skin. She looked like a modern rendition of a Holocaust victim; a kind of skinny that was not supposed to be self-inflicted. Emmy and her generation had grown up haunted by the imagery of wartime Europe, all those harassed and murdered Jews. She hadn't expected to see a living skeleton like that in modern-day New York.

She hung back a good ten paces, followed Con's sister into the gym, and paid for a one-time pass.

Her first crunch was a feeble attempt to raise the ten-pound weight. A pain shot through her neck. She sat back against the cushioned seat and glanced at Sophie, perched on her knees on an exercise contraption apparently aimed at sculpting the middle torso. Sophie twisted mightily, again and again, hauling and releasing eighty-five pounds with every effort. Her spine knuckled its way out of her top's neckline to make a fist at the back of her skull. Emmy believed this was the first time she'd been able to discern the shape of someone's skull bones beneath their hair.

She grunted out another failed crunch and slammed back against the cushion, panting until she got Sophie's attention. And then she smiled, unable to resist sliding in a sharp probe. "You're Ana, right?" Ana Rexic, the Jane Doe of eating disordered women throughout the first world.

Sophie froze a moment before answering, "No."

"My mistake. I thought I knew you for a minute." When Sophie shrugged, her shoulder bones looked like they would burst through her skin. But Emmy didn't look away. "Sorry to bother you."

"Where are you from?" Sophie asked.

"Switzerland." Which could account for her German accent if you were tone-deaf enough.

"Visiting?"

"I'm here on a student visa."

"I don't mean to pry, but I couldn't help noticing that you're having a hard time with that machine."

"It's my first time. I have no idea what I'm doing."

"You warmed up? It's really important to warm up first."

Emmy looked at her as if she didn't understand what that meant, though she did.

"I always warm-up on the elliptical machine."

"Sorry?"

"I already did my half-hour warm-up but I don't mind showing you. Never hurts to burn a few extra calories, right?"

"Absolutely."

"Just give me a minute."

When Sophie finished her set, Emmy followed her around the corner to a row of elliptical machines facing a window. Ana's body seemed to rattle when she walked. Emmy mimicked everything Sophie did: stepping on the footrests, plugging in a bunch of numbers Emmy made up on the spot for weight and age and finally pumping her feet until the thing sprang into stationary mechanical movement. Americans were crazy, Emmy thought, lurching forward, going nowhere. It was the kind of aggressive stagnation that adolescents suffered, though she had to admit that she herself had succumbed to a kind of paralysis-in-motion over the past couple of days.

Pumping away on the elliptical machine, Emmy

recalled a time when decisiveness came easily, without hesitation. For instance, when she was eleven years old and plotted to get rid of her mother's third live-in "uncle," Rolph after he started sitting her on his lap and rubbing his boner into her ass. The plan took two months to develop, and eight days to implement. First, she had to wait for her birthday, for which she requested the gift of a fish tank. Then she had to wait for her mother to gather all the right supplies to create a healthy aquatic environment in the tank, which Emmy insisted on servicing herself, because she was that kind of kid. Once the alkali levels were balanced, fish were purchased. Finally, after her mother and Rolph had mostly forgotten about Emmy's new fish, but not before he escalated to slipping his fingers under the crotch of her underpants, she switched the powder in his daily heart capsules for the cyanide-laced algae killer her mother had so kindly bought her. She wasted only three heart pills in mastering the opening and reclosing of the little plastic capsules. She could still see them: forest green with white numbers stamped on them. Each morning at breakfast, he ate his toast with butter and chopped chives, drank his black coffee, and swallowed his pill. He came down with something. Got sicker. Keeled over at the office. Died. It was that simple. And that solved the problem of Uncle Rolph. When eventually her mother wanted another boyfriend to move in, Emmy, age thirteen, advised against it—not that her mother listened.

As it turned out, her mother had known all along about Emmy's little murder. Mutti Dearest let decades slip by before pulling out her lethal chit.

Emmy had long doubted that her mother loved her; and this trip to New York, this assignment, underscored that nauseating suspicion. What mother sent her child on a mission like this? Emmy was her daughter, not some competent person who happened to have grown up in her home and now worked for her. She had been a girl, was now a woman, but even at thirty-five wasn't free of her mother's dangerous influence. Emmy's mind swam with fragile choices. Should she carry out Mutti's murderous errand, or simply abandon it and her and never go back?

After thirty grueling minutes, the machine finally declared the workout complete. A waterfall of sweat had drenched Sophie, while Emmy had managed to keep her speed slow enough to incite only enough heat to make it look like she was trying—and even that effort had nearly killed her.

"Always drink a lot of water afterward," Sophie advised, drying her angular face with a towel.

"I will. Thank you. It was very kind of you to take the time."

"Happy to do it. I'm here just about every afternoon. Feel free to ask me how to use the machines. I'm pretty familiar with most of them. By the way, I'm Sophie."

"Hannah."

Emmy smiled and extended her hand. The bones in Sophie's hand felt delicate enough to crush if Emmy wanted to. She gave a friendly little squeeze and released her. For now.

After they traded numbers, Emmy rode the subway downtown, emerging on the edge of Chinatown. Her phone immediately chirped with two missed calls: both from Mutti.

She melted into the clusters of bargain hunters lured by counterfeit hawkers shouting, "Gucci here! Cheap! Prada here! Cheap! Rolex here! Cheap!" When she reached her building on Elizabeth Street she noticed a subtle darkening of the sky, a shiver in the air, and looked up. Her little cloud had followed her, and it looked angry.

TWELVE

Freedom's Just Another Word for Nothing Else To Lose

NEW YORK CITY, May 23, 2013

"Shit this is good cappuccino." A speck of foam nestled in the corner of Artie's mouth when it lifted off the edge of the takeout cup Con had brought him. Artie loved the coffee from this one place down the street, where they still used the old-style containers—blue sky, white Parthenon—and today Con felt a special urgency to please his boss. "Thanks, buddy."

"No problem." Con lifted the cap off his own coffee, inhaling the pungent curl of steam before drinking. It was very hot, scalding his tongue. He set his cup on the edge of Artie's desk to let it cool a minute.

Artie leaned back and winged his elbows behind his head. The view outside his office window showed an unrelenting spring morning: women in pastel blouses, men in just-excavated lightweight suits. Smiling. It seemed as if everyone was smiling. The sunshine was so bright, Con had to squint to read Artie's face. As his eyes adjusted, it was easy to see the glow in his boss's eyes, the thrill of finally being so close to nailing Alexei Dvorshetskii and Pavel Gavrikov to the wall for laundering drug money, and thus closer than ever to ensnaring kingpin Vlad Popov in his big complicated sticky net. Artie had been running the case a long time, assembling evidence, his eyes and ears and nose deep into it, and he was hungry to end it.

Con said, "The sun."

Artie swiveled around, grabbed the cord, and brought the shade halfway down, fragmenting his desk into part shadow, part vivid mess. "So," he smiled, "read any good Dostoyevsky lately?"

"Is there any Dostoyevsky that isn't good?"

"Got me there," Artie said. "All checked out of the library, by the way. No more Dostoyevsky or that other guy...."

"Pushkin."

Dostoyevsky and Pushkin. Dvorshetskii and Gavrikov. It had been Artie's idea once he'd found out about the framed quotations.

Con asked, "How much was bail?"

"A cool mill. Each. They paid up like it was nothing."

"Pavel, one time he says to me they've got a lot of money stored away for 'rainy day.' Not 'a rainy day.' Just 'rainy day.'" Con remembered the second in command's pride in himself: all his money, all his "girls."

"Well, they got their shitstorm now. Here comes flooding and wind, utter destruction." Artie's smile was pure glee.

"I'm going to miss my smarmy pals over at the money factory."

"Not me, can't wait to see those fuckers in prison. Seriously, Con," reaching for his coffee, Artie shifted into a sun-slatted shadow, "the work you did on this case was awesome. You heard what Newcombe said at the press conference? We are to be commended for our work. Case is gonna be a slam dunk, Newcombe thinks."

Con smiled. It wasn't always that way. Sometimes, the spoils of months or even years of undercover work weren't enough to turn charges into a conviction.

"I'm pleased to hear it." Con reached for his coffee and this time took a heady sip, letting it burn his tongue as a reminder not to get too comfortable.

"He specifically asked me to commend you, Con. Called your work in the field 'exemplary.'" Artie grinned. John Newcombe was known for his caution against bestowing accolades to guard against error.

"What was Senator Rapp doing there, anyway? Turned the press conference into a circus."

"That was the point."

"You knew he was coming?"

"You think Newcombe tells me everything?"

Con knew he didn't. Newcombe was a player in the city; to him, people like Artie and Con were replaceable troops.

"I heard from Fire Inspector Bailey last night," Con said.

"Yeah, she called me, too. Listen, I know you're worried how it connects, if it connects, to Dostoyevsky. So am I. And we're looking into it. But right now it could swing yes or no. So what I'm thinking is, and I ran it by Carmel—" Carmel Ollison, his boss "—and what we're thinking is...."

"Artie, I fucked up."

Artie stared at him, waiting for something his expression said he didn't want to hear. In their business, they had more bad days than good ones, and Con hated to be the one to burst the bubble of his boss's very good morning.

Con put his empty cup on the edge of the desk. "It's possible the fire didn't have anything to do with Dostoyevsky."

"I'm listening."

Leaning back, crossing his legs at the knee, folding his arms over his chest, grinding his jaw—he said it: "Yeah, so, the night of the bust, I was celebrating, and I went to bed with this girl, and I had to get out of there in a hurry and left a few things behind by accident."

A lurid grin snaked across Artie's face, igniting a deep dimple on his right side. "Inspector Bailey asked me about a spare set of keys, maybe someone copied your keys, got into your house. We were thinking Dostoyevsky."

"They weren't copies."

"And your phone, she's got that, too?"

"It's been wiped by now, hasn't it?"

"I fucking hope so." Any trace of amusement now gone, a pugnacious silence simmered in Artie's eyes before he spoke again. "Why didn't you tell me right away? You know how many people I've already talked to about this?"

"I'm sorry."

"Not good enough."

"Don't tell me you're not familiar with sexual remorse." Con would never forget how close Larry had come to filing a harassment suit against Artie. But Larry, who always surveyed every angle, had decided not to jeopardize her career or embarrass Artie's family. She'd moved on, transferred to Vice; but it was always there, lingering.

"Who is she?"

"I only know her first name. Emmy. Met her at a bar. Went home together."

"Your place?"

"Hers."

"Why the hurry getting out?"

"I overslept and she had to be somewhere." Another lie, but there were limits to how much of his degradation he could share with his boss.

"How hung-over were you?"

"Enough to not know exactly where I was." Con described his fruitless search for Emmy's building. "Just to be safe, I was planning to get my apartment lock changed."

"Shit."

"I should have told you all this sooner, but—"

"You're right," Artie said. "I'm familiar with shame. So just how crazy is this bitch?"

"Crazy enough."

"Yeah, well, I always said you could improve your taste in women, Con." Artie barked laughter. Somehow, they had navigated to the relatively safer ground of shared sexual mishaps. Con felt a guilty but satisfied relief spill through him. He was pretty sure he'd have been suspended if he'd had this conversation with Carmel Ollison, whom he guessed would never hear about any of it from Artie.

"So here's the thing..." Artie began. "Fresh off a long undercover job...take a few days off before you come back to work. And I think you should talk to someone."

Psych detox. Con had heard it before. "Thanks, but that's not for me."

"It's not a request. And I was planning to tell you before you walked in here. It isn't a punishment."

"You sure?"

"Hear you witnessed a suicide, night of the bust."

"How'd you know that?" Con had only told Larry.

"Word travels. Same bridge your father...well, I don't have to spell it out for you. I'd have hit the bottle, too."

"Thanks for your understanding."

"I mean it, I want you to talk to someone. Get it off your chest. And take some time off—you've banked a lot of vacation days, I noticed. Take it easy for a little while, starting right now. Consider yourself a free man."

A distant refrain from Janis Joplin surfaced, something Sophie used to listen to a lot when she was a teenager. Con low-voiced, "'Freedom's just another word for nothing else to lose.'"

"What?"

"All I'm saying is—"

Artie got that discussion-over look on his face. "Con, I'm not asking, I'm telling. Give yourself a chance to put it all behind you. Come back to work with a clear head."

Con wasn't interested in a therapy session (or two or three). He wanted to move forward, not backward. He wanted to forget about his past. He wanted to get back to work. But clearly, in Artie's mind, this was the path to redemption so Con knew he'd better take it. "How do I find someone?"

"Soon as you walk out of here, I'll zap you a list of in-house shrinks. Choose one. No shame in it—I've used them myself from time to time."

Back on the street, Con checked his phone. Artie's email was already there. So was a text, covered in exclamation points, from Sophie: Called Mom yesterday to tell her about the bridge jumper guy and guess what? She's here!!! She wants to talk to us about Dad!!! Get home quick!!!!!

THIRTEEN

Man and Wife

WEST BERLIN, April 1, 1964

CONRAD AND EMILIE strolled arm in arm along the rutted paths of the Tiergarten, water pooled in potholes where last night's spring rain had failed to drain off. In the twenty years since the war, there had been neither the money nor the will to repair such minor deficits. It had gone on so long, it was rarely mentioned, but Conrad noticed. Since becoming trapped within the suffocating circumference of West Berlin, separated from his family, he'd been aware of everything. Today, for instance, the streaks of blue slicing an otherwise gray sky, the muddy footprints of a dog, a smell of rotting vegetation mingled with Emilie's baked goods scent that only made him miss his mother all the more.

"There's the zoo," Emilie pointed.

A pungent smell of elephant dung grew stronger as they neared the enclosure where one of the giant animals leaned its leathery rump against the fence. A woman in heels and a hat photographed three small children who were touching the elephant's skin.

"Any idea who we're looking for?" Conrad asked.

"He'll come to us, I'm told."

The only instruction Wolf had given them was to appear at the Tiergarten Zoo at the appointed hour. Their new western handler would make the rest clear. For three years, they'd been groomed for this moment, when they would appear malleable and ready to be turned against the HVA. Emilie had insisted that they were capable of pulling it off, though Conrad wasn't so sure.

They found a bench and sat down. After nearly forty minutes, a tall jogger in a dark blue sweat-suit and scuffed white sneakers sat down beside them. Con recognized him: he'd run past their bench twice. The jogger breathed heavily for a few moments before crossing his legs and reaching under his sweatshirt for a pack of Marlboros. His dense brown hair was cut close to his head, but his brows were untamed, spiky caterpillars over smallish eyes.

"Smoke?" The jogger offered one to Emilie first.

"No, thank you."

Conrad waved his hand when offered.

The man lit up, sucking on his cigarette and exhaling through his nose before turning to them again. "You're German?" he asked, and this time Conrad detected a slight American accent.

Emilie's mouth twitched on one side. "Of course we are—we're in Germany."

"Fair enough." The jogger nodded. "Married or engaged?"

This was the question they'd been told to expect: Their American handler would light a cigarette, and casually inquire as to their marital status.

"Neither, exactly," Conrad ventured to answer; but Emilie corrected him.

"Engaged."

It was the first he'd heard of it. Conrad's pulse fluttered with an urge to jump up and run away. He stayed where he was, paralyzed. "That's right," he dutifully agreed. "How could I forget?"

They all laughed. "Cold feet," the jogger diagnosed him. "It's only natural."

"You're an American, am I right?" Emilie asked.

"Correct." He extended a hand. "David Call."

"I'm Lena Froebel," Emilie introduced herself using her official cover.

"Pleased to meet you." David Call shook her hand. He then extended a greeting to Conrad, who grasped the man's cold palm with a spike of adrenaline, and introduced himself:

"Julian Wimmers."

It went without saying that David Call wasn't the jogger's real name, either.

Call remarked, "Nice day for a stroll."

"Or a run," Emilie added.

"It's good to get out of the church now and then." Rotating his wrist, as if offsetting a sudden pain, Call's cigarette dragged a circle of smoke that brought to mind a lasso.

"The church!" Emilie didn't even try to mask her surprise.

"I'm the American chaplain at the Herz-Jesu-Kirche, over in Templehof. Not as glamorous as working in radio."

Trying not to appear rattled, Conrad snuck a deep breath to calm himself. They had told this man nothing about themselves other than their cover names and that they were engaged. He was definitely the one they had come to meet.

Conrad wondered if David Call really was a chaplain, though didn't doubt that he worked for the CIC. It was well known that the Allied forces, and the U.S. Counterintelligence Corps, in particular, were sopping up as many West German agents as possible in their quest to short-circuit the Soviet hold on the GDR. But double agents like Conrad and Emilie, bonafide Stasi operatives willing to betray their country, were the real prize.

How, though, did Call plan to test their dubious loyalty? A sensation that he was about to suffocate crept through Conrad at the thought that they all navigated each other's treachery with open eyes and knives behind their backs.

"You know," Call uncrossed his legs, leaned forward, and looked Conrad right in the eye. "I could marry you today if you'd like."

"How kind of you," Conrad lied, "but we don't have a license."

"Do we even need one?" Emilie asked.

Conrad pressed out a pleasant smile. "The truth is, I have no idea."

"It's all taken care of," Call said, as casually as if he'd told them lunch was ready. With that, all pretense dropped. "This living together business, it doesn't sit well with us. We'd feel better about things if you were solidly committed —you marry each other, and you marry us, so to speak. We have to know you're in for the right reasons. What do you say?" He stood up and waited for them to follow suit.

Conrad knew that this was the moment when he might have objected, found some way out of it, but how could he? It would create suspicion on all sides—the Allies wouldn't trust him, Wolf wouldn't trust him, Emilie would turn against him. It was a test, and failure threatened to bring unpredictable consequences.

"We're eager to serve," Emilie answered for them both.

They walked alongside David Call to the U-Bahn. Twenty minutes later, they alighted from the subway into the neighborhood of Templehof-Schoeneberg, quiet except for the occasional roar of a plane close overhead. The American ignored the epic rumblings of the nearby airport, apparently used to it; when the quiet returned, he engaged Emilie in conversation about something innocuous, weather or food, but Conrad's thoughts were elsewhere.

Did he love her? He wasn't sure. He felt as if he was being led to a gallows, not a church wedding. It was one thing to live with Emilie, to sleep with her and eat with her and even work with her; but to marry her would only hurl him farther away from his parents and the life he'd left behind. The official nature of marriage would solidify the impulsive mistake he'd made, three years ago, when he leaped from east to west, and the series of mistakes that had followed: staying with Emilie, allowing himself to get drawn into her world instead of finding his way back home. But each time a low flying plane roared through the quiet on its way to or from the airport, a claw of reality descended into his consciousness, separating his feeling of despair from the rationalization that his choices were limited and had been for some time. He reminded himself that he was far from the only person whose life had been affected by the Cold War. He would soldier on, and do his best.

Herz-Jesu-Kirche was a quaint church in the Bavarian style, made of brick and whitewash, with heavy ornamental doors and a spire topped with a Catholic cross. Emilie was Catholic; Conrad knew this must have pleased her. They held hands as they followed David Call into the cool, hushed interior.

A mottled rainbow from the rounded stained-glass windows lapped over the empty pews and threw color onto the white walls. Call led them through a door at the right of the nave, and into a small office. On the wooden desk were two mugs: one holding pencils and a miniature American flag, the other containing the dregs of cold coffee in which the stub of a Marlboro floated. From a locked drawer in his old wooden desk, Call brought forth three pieces of paper, and swiveled them to face Conrad and Emilie. He then placed a pair of gold wedding bands beside the papers.

They stood facing the desk. There were no seats other than the straight-back chair in which Call made himself comfortable while they looked over the paperwork. The first was an application for a marriage license, the second was the license itself, and the third was a marriage certificate. All had been filled out and notarized, and only lacked the signatures of the happy couple.

"You first." Call pushed a pen in Conrad's direction.

The cap was off, and he had to scratch on the border of the license application before ink appeared.

Signature by signature, he gave himself to Emilie. She followed.

And then, standing in front of the chaplain's desk, without so much as the overhead light turned on and without a single witness, the American chaplain-jogger— who Conrad presumed would now become their puppet-master on one side while Mischa Wolf pulled their strings on the other—declared that the startled young spies were now man and wife. Conrad and Emilie slipped the rings onto their own fingers; incredibly, they fit.

In place of celebration, they returned to the nave and

followed Call to a pew farthest back on the right side of the church. He grasped the knob of what appeared to be a solid armrest, squeezed something with his middle finger, and then abruptly drew his hand away to repeat the rotating gesture of earlier. "Old war injury," he explained. He tried again, and this time a plank of wood fell onto the cushion, revealing a hollow narrow cabinet.

"This is our drop. Anything for me comes here, and vice versa. We won't see each other often. When you come here to make a drop, do it quickly, do not look for me, just say a few prayers and leave."

FOURTEEN

Truth and Consequences

NEW YORK CITY, May 23, 2013

"CON, HONEY!" Ruth had her arms around him before he could close the front door.

"Mom...you're here."

She pulled away to shine one of her smiles on him. She looked a little older each time he saw her, but that was because when they weren't together he always thought of her as the young, vibrant mother he'd trailed around the city growing up, the lady who taught him how to live. She had stopped dying her hair, which was now frosted with a distinguished gray. Her lipstick was a brighter red.

In the dining room, Con found Sophie at the table, set for three, covered in food still in its plastic Zabar's containers. Even if he hadn't seen their mother first, he would have known this was her doing; an impromptu gathering in her home had always meant a trip to Zabar's with predictably lavish results. There was a roast chicken already carved up, potato salad, three kinds of cheeses, sliced roast beef, smoked fish, crab salad, celery root slaw, brown bread, rye, knishes, chocolate babka, a variety of dried fruits, and Con's all-time favorite, cinnamon rugelach, which he knew his mother had bought with him in mind as if he were still a boy tamable with a treat. There was an open bottle of wine. Sophie had an array of food on her plate, barely touched.

Ruth patted an empty chair. "Sit right here by me. Eat something, and we'll get started."

"Mom brought slides," Sophie told him.

"I already dug out the old projector," Ruth announced.

Sophie rose abruptly, clearly eager to put some distance between herself and her plate. "I'll get everything set up." She disappeared to the living room.

Con leaned close to his mother, and whispered, "It's a job getting her to eat anything if you didn't notice."

"That's the other reason I'm here," Ruth whispered back. "I saw her pictures on Facebook—I was shocked. I'm going to try to get her some help. But first, there's a lot to talk about. It's time to get this family centered, though I warn you, sweetheart, it's going to hurt. Forgive me?"

"For what?"

In the semi-darkness, the old projector shone a dusty beam at a white wall, where one of Ruth's paintings now leaned off to the side. Con could see the rectangular ghost of the frame where dust had collected over time. His mother held an old notebook on her lap, her veined hand resting on top of the torn leather cover. "This was your father's. He specifically asked me to hold onto it until, well, this moment. He knew it would probably come eventually, though he hoped it wouldn't. But first...."

A slide flashed onto the bumpy over-painted wall.

Conrad Sr., as a young man, riding a bicycle. Con felt something flip inside him. He'd never known his father to ride. This was news.

"Wasn't he handsome?" Ruth cooed. "Of course, by the time I met him he was almost forty. But look at him here when he was nineteen years old."

"What brought this on, Mom?" Con asked.

"You've both had a lot of questions about Daddy over the years, so here I am. It's time."

"Are those his parents?" Sophie asked of the couple smiling behind Conrad Sr.

"Yup. Erich and Bettina. Soon after this picture was taken, he left East Berlin and never saw them again."

"Why did he leave home?" Con thought: East Berlin: the German Democratic Republic, after the war. At last having a geographic, and socio-political, focus for his father's youth.

"He didn't want to go." Ruth's voice rose. "He loved his parents. He was working as a guard while they were building that God-forsaken wall. He was only a teenager and it was a lot to process. The world he lived in had gone through a lot of trials and tribulations, you have to remember that."

"How did they end up in the east after the war," Con asked, "instead of in the west?"

"It happened to be where they lived."

"That simple?"

"Nothing was simple then, not in Germany."

Sophie reached over Ruth's lap and pushed a button on the projector. The next slide cranked into position. Conrad Sr. as a baby, cradled in the arms of a youthful Bettina.

"Keep going," Ruth told her. "They're all out of order, but there's a lot there."

Sophie flicked through the slides and they watched

images from their father's life like puzzle pieces scattered against the blank wall. There he was as a young boy, again on a bicycle. There he was as a toddler, smiling uproariously. As a teenager, all awkward limbs and ruffled hair. Younger again, doing his homework with a pencil squeezed between his fingers, a crumbly plate of cookies at his elbow. Again, as a young man, this time in uniform, guarding the border.

"That was taken when the Wall was going up," Ruth said. "It separated families, depending on where they happened to be. Some people didn't see their own children, their own parents, for years. I remember seeing a picture once of someone holding a baby up over the Wall for its grandparents to meet."

"Why didn't Daddy ever talk to us about this part of his life?" Sophie asked.

Ruth turned to her. "Shame."

"For?" Con asked. The crux of all his questioning, all this time. If only he could talk with his father now about shame and how to not drown in it.

The slide changed.

In the next photograph, with its Technicolor brightness that didn't look fully real, a fit and handsome Conrad Sr. sat with a woman with a striking resemblance to Emmy. Con's stomach tightened. The woman had the same heart-shaped face, the black hair, but instead of blue her eyes were brown. There were two babies in the photo with the smiling couple. One was a boy dressed in yellow, goofy baby-grin on a chubby face, little fingers hooked onto the collar of the woman's shirt. The other baby, a girl, was smaller, wearing a little white dress with her roly-poly legs loose on Conrad Sr.'s lap. Black hair fluffy as a duckling's. Dramatic blue eyes.

Con glanced at Ruth in the glowing darkness, the

projector whirring, that picture frozen on the wall. He looked back at the bright flickering photograph and saw the sapphire gaze he'd luxuriated in, the mouth he'd kissed, the face he'd been so close to while they fucked that he could still smell her peppery breath. Could still taste her.

Vomit rose into his throat. He swallowed it back down, unable to look at either his mother or sister. This had to be some kind of cruel joke.

"Your father was married before," Ruth said, plainly, as if giving them a bitter medicine she believed would help them. "He had another child. And he was a spy."

Con and Sophie looked at each other in disbelief. She said it first, "A spy?"

Ruth nodded.

Con stared at his mother in the glowing darkness, the projector whirring, that picture frozen on the wall. He asked her, "Is that me in the picture?"

Ruth nodded again, stoic, regretful.

"That other baby—is she my twin?"

"Yes."

"You're kidding, right?" He smiled, but she didn't.

"I'm sorry, sweetheart."

"Why didn't I know this?"

"Oh, Con…it's a long, long story."

"I've had thirty-five years to hear it." A twin. There was no way to justify that kind of omission.

"I'm so sorry." She reached for his hand and squeezed. "This is how your father wanted it. It was his choice."

"And you—you're not really my mother?"

"I am your mother." Her voice was firm. "She was your birth mother. I as good as adopted you and I raised you, Con."

"How old was I?"

"When I first got you? Almost one."

"So she..."

"She had you for around three months, that's all. There were the two of you, the twins, and when that marriage broke up I mean it blew up. By then, they were undercover agents working for the GDR, living in West Berlin. I still don't get how they brought themselves to make such a decision, separating twins, but they did. Don't forget, they were used to making ruthless choices."

"What about me?" Sophie asked. "Am I—"

"Do the math, Soph." Con immediately regretted his bitter tone. "Mom and Dad were married for eight years before you were born. You're safe."

"You're safe, too, Con," Ruth tried to comfort him with a touch of her hand.

When she moved she must have pressed the button because a new slide slipped into position and there, on the wall, was his nineteen-year-old father, wearing the uniform of an East German border guard, leaping over a tangle of barbed wire into West Berlin. Helmet askew. Machine gun strapped to his shoulder. Jumping straight into a photographer's lens.

Con shook off Ruth's hand. "So, what else? How fucked up does this story get?"

Ruth sighed. "Conrad wouldn't talk about it, but there's something in this notebook about..." She thumbed through the pages. "Here it is. 'Later I helped U.S. intelligence with active measures.' But it doesn't say when, and I don't know about you, but I have no idea what he meant by active measures."

"Disinformation." Con knew all about active measures; he employed them all the time at work, and sometimes in his life. A logic was beginning to take shape. The pain in his stomach deepened. "He was a double agent."

Ruth's eyes widened as she took it in. "That's hard to believe."

"But that's what it means. Is there any mention of when? Before he left Germany, or after?"

"Daddy wasn't a spy over here." Ruth was adamant. "I'm sure of it. He worked as a journalist." Her words hung in the room, her tone of certainty chopped into bits by the swift rotations of the projector's fan. "He was a journalist," she repeated. "I know he hated being a spy. Hated it. He left it behind when he came here with you, Con. It's why he came. He wanted to raise you away from all that."

"Dad wouldn't have told you if he was still spying," Con said, gently. "Especially if it was true." Working as a journalist while he cooked up stories to mislead the enemy. It was a perfect cover.

"The Cold War was over," Ruth argued. "They were reunified over there."

"It wasn't over for years after it was supposedly over." Con stopped himself. He didn't want to rake her over these coals, but he doubted the spying would have just suddenly ended. It never did. It sickened him to think of his father trapped in that murky transitional space between undercover work and so-called real life, when you've ruined the boundaries of your identity by pretending to be someone else for too long.

"He was scared," Ruth went on, "that much I do know. Here, let me read you something else. 'When my name was erased from the Rosenholz files, and the other ops started dying, I knew the time had come. I would never get away from them.' What did he mean by that?"

"Who's 'them,' Mom?" Sophie asked.

"That's the thing, I really don't know."

"Do you think that's why he jumped off the bridge?"

Con asked. "Because he was afraid of something from his past?"

"I hate to keep saying I don't know, but I don't know."

"He died pretty soon after I told him I was going to work undercover for Rackets," Con said. "Right?"

"All that fighting," Ruth remembered. "It was awful."

"Why was it so awful?" Con leaned toward her. "Why did it upset him so much?"

"All I knew was that he wished he'd never become a spy. He thought it ruined his life until he came here," Ruth said, "and met me, and we were a family. Then he was happy. Things got better for him."

CON AND SOPHIE lay together on top of the nubby white bedspread belonging to a roommate away for the week, passing a bottle between them and gazing at the dazzling nightscape of New Jersey from Riverside Drive. This had been Con's room growing up, his view of the real world outside his window, the future that awaited when a boy grew his wings and flew the nest. Lush and absorbing. Penetrable. All his.

Throughout his life, he'd been secure in who he was and where he came from. And now. And now. He finds out he's someone else. A man with a twin sister, and no boundaries. A man with a father who'd been a spy, a father he didn't really know. A man with a mother who wasn't his. He took the bottle from Sophie's hand and finished it in one long swallow.

He slurred, "It's going to take some time to get used to all this." And then he thought of Emmy. "Oh, God." And how while they fucked he'd believed he was in love with this woman who would be his life partner. He'd felt that they were meant for each other. Felt it. And he'd been right: the way they'd clicked, it had been real, but only because they were twins. Why was she even in New York? How was it they'd even met? He wanted to talk to Sophie about it, but how could he? It was too awful, too strange.

"I can't believe you're only my half-brother," Sophie said.

"How do I stop thinking of Mom as my mother? This is so confusing."

"I don't think you have to. She raised you. She loves you. She's your mother."

Con lurched off the bed. "I gotta puke."

But in the bathroom, hunched over the toilet, nothing came at first except more tortured thoughts. Had Emmy known all along who he was? Was that why she'd behaved so strangely? His body lurched and finally, his stomach relented, emptying itself into the porcelain basin in a bathroom in an apartment in a building on a street in a city he'd known and understood for thirty-five years until suddenly, now, he understood nothing at all. Except for one thing: Emmy had sought him out. She must have. She'd known who he was, even before they met. And she'd come for him. But why?

Empty and sour, he returned to his old bedroom, where Sophie now sat alert on the edge of the bed. She said, "I just realized something."

He settled miserably beside her.

"This woman I met at the gym yesterday, Hannah, looks like the woman in those old pictures. Your real mother…I mean your other mother…I mean—"

"She'd be old now, you realize."

"No, the woman I met is more your age." Sophie described her encounter with Hannah. "And she kept talking to me and following me around. Wow. I thought she was just friendly, now I don't know what to think."

Bile crept up his throat at the thought that Emmy had found Sophie, found her, and called herself Hannah. This nut job, his sister, had seduced him; she'd bitten into his flesh; she was probably the one who'd burned down his apartment. What was she up to, now? How had she found out where Sophie exercised? Coming so close to his real family…this had to stop.

Con wished he could tell Sophie and Ruth everything, but how could he? He'd need to do this carefully…it felt like revealing to a peaceful village that there was a vampire in their midst. "I may have met her just like you did, without knowing I was meeting her. She's...complicated."

"We traded cell numbers and everything."

His pulse jack-rabbited. "Give it to me, Soph. Give me her number right now."

In seconds, a reverse directory on his phone matched the number with an address on Elizabeth Street.

FIFTEEN

The Window Shatters

NEW YORK CITY, May 23, 2013

EMMY OPENS HER EYES SUDDENLY, her mind bogged in a dream: She needs to pee, but can't, and then she's being chased by someone, a man, a man with an ornate facial tattoo, a man whose face turns into a butterfly but is still part of his head, and she still needs to pee, but she runs instead, runs and runs to get away from butterfly man. But he's too fast for her. Because she can't run. Because she has to pee. But she can't pee because she has to run.

Blinking, her vision adjusts on the window across from her bed. Streetlight filters through the curtain into her dark bedroom, throwing abstract shapes across the ceiling and floor. A band of light bends over the foot of the bed. Her heart flutters and she pushes herself up, sitting now with her back slumped against the headboard. She feels confused. Butterfly man. The window. Why is she even awake?

Outside, the headlights of a middle-of-the-night driver illuminate the front of her building. Suddenly, she sees it.

In the window, a masked face. A real person in a balaclava with slits for mouth, nostrils, eyes. Watching her.

And then the window shatters. The man hurls himself into the room. She rolls off the side of her bed and runs for the door.

But he's faster and strong. He holds her against the door with such force that pain flowers instantly. He's so close she can smell him, she can smell him...the boozy sexual tang…and suddenly she knows who he is. And in the violence of the moment, she decides. She will handle this. Suddenly, she knows exactly how.

She tells him, "Take it off."

When he doesn't, she claws under the mask, feeling her fingernails scrape off skin, his flesh giving in with the acquiescence of a supple cheese. The momentary pleasure of having hurt him evaporates when he pulls back a hand and slams it against her cheek.

LIGHTHEADED, Con tasted something salty, blood, crawl into his mouth. He'd pounded on her door for a while before she finally woke up; and when she answered, she attacked him. So he hit back.

"You're going to keep away from my family." He found the light switch in the dark and turned on the overhead.

Her eyes blinked, shaking off disorientation—what a crazy dream.

"Take it off and we'll talk, or whatever you want."

"Take what off?"

"You can fuck me again if you want to."

He wanted to slap her face again for that. "Don't even

suggest it." Instead, he punched his fist into the door beside her head and felt something burst inside his hand.

He stepped back, putting space between them while pain consumed him. There was a chair nearby and he sat on it, holding his bleeding face in his uncrushed hand, the other one pulsing on his knee. When his head stilled, he glanced up. She was standing there, against the door, watching him. Bruises were already appearing on her face.

She squirmed away from the door, moving her jaw, rubbing her shoulders. Stooping to pick up a robe from the floor, she said, "It's cold in here."

"Want to know how I found you?"

"I could guess."

"Hannah. From the gym." With his tongue, he inspected a cut on his lip. It didn't feel very deep. Whatever she'd done to his cheek felt worse.

She stretched out on her bed and patted the mattress. "Come to mama."

Con used his good hand to flip the chair around and sat facing her. Beside her, on a nightstand, was the detritus of lone hours: a folded-open magazine, a bottle of nail polish, a glass of something, an iPad oozing a blackish light, a box of tissues. His watch. A quick tempo of pain danced between his fingers and wrist as he snatched the Junghans and slipped it into his jeans pocket.

"You're my sister," he said.

She rolled her eyes like it was old news.

"What are you up to, Emmy? I want the truth."

"Who doesn't?"

"You went to my apartment."

Her eyes darted away.

"You set it on fire."

She looked back with a grin that was cold, sly, seductive, ugly in her rapidly swelling face. She was a different person than the one he'd met at the Mercury Lounge, or thought he'd met. He could feel a rivulet of blood coagulating on his cheek, tightening the seam of injury, promising a nasty scar if he didn't get it looked at soon.

"You knew who I was from the beginning. You always knew I was your brother. Why are you doing all this?"

"I didn't always know. This was news to me, too."

"When did you find out?"

"Oma Bettina called me out of the blue. A few days ago. Before I left Berlin."

Their grandmother. Con shivered to think how much trouble he might have avoided if he'd gone ahead and sent the email, though what were the odds that she would have answered him, and what were the odds that her answer would have been coherent?

"So you did know before we met." Confirmation made the fact of what they'd done even more awful.

"There were two of us, and two of them." Emmy pulled the sheet up to her chin, covering herself. The contour of her stomach beneath the sheet was a soft mound. She would have been lovely if she hadn't been his psycho sister. "He took you, and she kept me. You got the sane one, I got the crazy one. You went off to the golden land, I stayed behind in a broken-down war zone after everyone was gone."

"How do you know our father was sane? He killed himself. How sane is that?"

"I looked him up on the Internet. He looked pretty sane to me."

"If I had found out about you first, I wouldn't have gone and tried to hurt you. I would have met you. Talked to you."

"I talked to you."

"No, you...." There she was, lying on the bed, the very bed. "You didn't talk to me, Emmy."

"I wanted to get to know you quickly."

"Like that?"

"I don't know what I wanted," she tried again. "I wanted you to suffer, like I did, left over there with her." She tapped the side of her head with a chipped red fingernail. "The things I remember. The stories I could tell you about our mother."

"Is she really that bad?"

"Am I really that bad?"

He looked at her. Yes, she was.

"You have your answer, Conrad Jr."

"Listen, Emmy—please. Stop all this bullshit. Leave me alone. Stay away from Sophie. Do you understand?"

"She's my sister, too. Half-sister."

"This is not a good time for her—she's fragile."

Emmy yawned. "I'm tired. You woke me up."

"If you don't, I'm going to arrest you for stalking. Ever been to prison?"

"You wouldn't."

"Try me."

"I'm your sister."

"Try me."

"You want everyone to know you fucked your sister?"

"Try me."

She whipped the sheet off and sat up. The whites of those showy eyes glittered through the darkness as her pale skin seemed to drink in shadows. "There's something I want you to do."

He stood, body shaking, face bleeding, hand throbbing. He needed to get to a hospital.

"Our mother wants you to go to her in Berlin. She can't travel. She's ill."

Heading for the door, he asked, "Can't she dial a phone?"

"She wants to see you. She's your mother."

"My mother is right here in the States."

"Your real mother."

"My real mother is the woman who raised me. She's the only mother I've ever known, and I love her."

A few moments of silence stretched between them. Con got the feeling Emmy was processing the idea that he could love someone, that anyone could love a mother.

"I'm flying back to Berlin tomorrow," she said. The news sent a fizz of relief through Con. And then she added, "You should come with me. You can meet your real mother in your natural habitat."

"I'm in my natural habitat here."

"You can meet our father's family. We have aunts, uncles, cousins. Don't you want to?"

Did he? "Dad told me he didn't have anyone left over there."

"He was a liar."

The hard truth of that hovered like the ghost of their father. He had to admit there was a temptation, and he had the time right now, a vista of unplanned vacation days that stretched purposelessly before him. But no. He stopped that nib of possibility before it dug any deeper into his imagination. He opened the door.

Emmy touched her iPad to wake it up, swiped it, and tapped it. It emitted a sound like a spaceship taking flight, and then a voice: "Wo bist du?" A woman's voice, light yet churlish, foreign…familiar.

Emmy answered, "Ich bin hier mit ihm. In meinem Schlafzimmer. In New York. Mit meinem Bruder."

"Oh!"

"Ja, mein Zwillingsbruder."

"Er spricht Deutsch?"

"Nein."

"Du kleines Miststück." Laughter. "Zeig mir."

Con knew who the woman was before Emmy angled the iPad so he could see her.

A frazzle of short gray hair framed her face, making it look less oval than it had in Ruth's slideshow. She was considerably older now, jowly, with only an inkling of her former beauty. The collar of a worn chenille bathrobe gathered loosely below a sag of mottled skin that looked as soft as well-loved suede. The top of a yellow mug edged into view when she moved, smiling now, making eye contact from a continent away with her long-lost son. She looked like a nice older lady, not the nightmare Emmy had described. Had his twisted sister lied about that, too?

Weak light from a window behind Emilie suggested early morning. It would be about six a.m. in Berlin. She looked at Con with hungry eyes and he looked back. He couldn't help himself. He wanted to know her. He wanted to ask her questions. He wanted to turn away.

Hunger and Thirst

"Democracy means that if the doorbell rings in the early
hours, it is likely to be the milkman."

--Winston Churchill

SIXTEEN

The Picnic

—————

WEST BERLIN, July 26, 1970

"I've invited Monika and Kolman to join us at the lake." Emilie stood at their cramped kitchen counter, arranging a portable meal.

"Grunewalsee again?"

"Why not?"

"It's a good idea—it won't be nearly as hot by the water."

"Find my swimsuit, will you? It's probably in my third drawer."

When Conrad's hands came from behind to cup her breasts, she wiggled away. He kissed her salty neck. This time, her knife swung up from the sausage she was slicing to rest against the back of his hand.

"Watch it, I'm busy here."

Conrad pulled his hand away from the blade. "Do you think Monika and Kolman would be scandalized if we swam naked?"

"She might be. What do you think of them, really?"

Conrad shrugged. "They seem nice."

"I'm not sure I trust them."

"They're kindergarten teachers."

"Exactly—impressionable young minds, you know?"

"Seriously….Emilie…"

Monika and Kolman Walz had moved in down the hall from them just under a year ago, but already they were good friends. As he did with everyone these days, Conrad had started by speculating as to whether they, too, were somehow embedded in a cause—in fact, his conscience would have rested easier if he knew that they were at least informers—but with the Walzes he'd quickly discounted the possibility. In any case, he didn't care. The only thing he personally had to hide was the fact that he was an informer, and a double agent—absolutely not to be trusted —but so long as the Walzes did or said nothing worthy of his special attention, he wouldn't pay any. Unlike some operatives, he didn't seek to cause trouble, only identify it, and even that he undertook selectively.

In the nine years he'd been with Emilie, he'd had to forge a truce within himself or he'd have gone mad. He was a husband. He worked in radio. And, oh yes, he was watching. One learned to be as many people as necessary in order to survive. It was a matter of adaptation. Conrad had surprised himself with his flexibility.

Emilie turned to him with a tight smile that told him to leave it alone. She thought what she thought; they both knew that he would never change her mind.

The straps of her sleeveless shirt clung to her sweat-glistening skin. It was hotter than yesterday. She wrapped waxed paper around the sausage coins and placed them into Conrad's backpack along with a container of the pickled potato salad he had made last night and half a dozen bottles of Krombacher. He knew, from the backpack, that they'd be riding their bicycles and he'd be hauling their portion of the food.

Conrad and Kolman rode ahead of the women, both laden with supplies, while the wives kept a lax pace behind them. Eventually, Emilie and Monika fell behind. It didn't matter; everyone knew the way to the lake. The men arrived first, laid a blanket, arranged the food, and started on their beers.

Kolman—a small, hairy man with a bald pate and youthful face—peeled an orange with his teeth and spit the rind onto the roots of the tree beside which they had settled themselves. "It's good fertilizer."

"Emilie tells me that you and Monika want a farm someday."

Kolman looked surprised. "I hadn't realized anyone else knew about it. I think of it as a daydream, you know, the kind that will probably never happen."

Swallowing a spicy taste of sausage with a swig of cooling beer, Conrad said, "Life feels like a daydream sometimes. All of it."

Kolman smiled: white, crowded teeth. "We spend too much time trying to figure things out. That's what I love about working with five-year-olds—they live in the moment, without a worry."

"You don't seem like a man with worries."

"I'm not, really. Well. Monika isn't ready for children, but I'd like some. I suppose you could call that a worry."

"Ah, now I understand our wives' bond. Emilie's also against the idea of a family."

"But not you?"

"Actually, we agree about that. She's enough for me to handle."

Just then, the women rode up, laughing. Monika was as

light as Emilie was dark. Fair and green-eyed, with freckled cheeks. Conrad wondered why a woman who worked with children was against having any of her own. He understood Emilie's desire not to have any: she was inherently selfish and knew it. But Monika, with her characteristic tenderness and patience, struck Conrad as a natural mother.

The food and beer disappeared quickly. The sun moved up the sky and brought with it the worst of the heat, shimmering through the speckled shade afforded by their tree.

Emilie stood up abruptly, pulled her shirt over her head, and dropped it beside a pile of empty bottles. They had brought their swimsuits, but she had chosen to ignore that, which pleased Conrad. He loved looking at her.

Apparently, so did Kolman. Their neighbor's gaze stayed glued to Emilie's breasts a moment too long, but he avoided staring as she peeled off her skirt and underpants and ran naked into the lake. Conrad pretended not to notice the swiftness with which Monika's face turned red when Kolman stood and stripped and followed Emilie into the water.

"Well," Conrad said, "what do you think? Do we join them, just to be friendly?"

"Maybe." But Monika didn't make a move to undress.

Conrad picked up the box of melted chocolates that Monika and Kolman had brought. They both ate one, watching their spouses swim and laugh. Finally, he couldn't resist fishing his suit out of his backpack. Hiding behind a tree in deference to her discomfort, he shimmied out of his clothes and into the swimsuit he hadn't wanted to bring in the first place.

The water was refreshingly cool, an immediate relief.

Monika stayed onshore and watched from a distance.

· · ·

THE COUPLES SPENT MORE and more time together, either all of them as a group or Emilie alone with Monika or Kolman. Conrad knew what she was up to—she was a dedicated spy—and left her to it; complaining would have caused more trouble than it was worth. The dinners and coffees and movies were otherwise enjoyable, and Conrad began to think that, despite Emilie's hidden agenda, the friendship was real.

One evening, he'd been preparing himself a simple dinner of boiled eggs and buttered bread when Monika tapped on his door. Emilie had told him she'd be working late, and he'd come home from the office without her. Conrad opened the door to find Monika already crying.

"What's wrong?" He ushered her to the living room and sat down beside her on the couch.

"Kolman went out for cigarettes two hours ago."

"Maybe he stopped for a beer."

"Where's Emilie?"

"Working late."

"Conrad—doesn't it bother you about Kolman and Emilie?"

His impulse was to offer her some wine and tell her everything—they were spies from the Ostzone, the dreaded Soviet-occupied east, and Emilie seduced men as part of her work as one of Mischa Wolf's infamous swans.

Wolf had once joked, obtusely if you didn't know him, that the Cold War could be won by sex. For those who moved close within his many overlapping circles, like Conrad and Emilie, he couldn't have been more clear. If you were a good-looking operative and had a strong stomach, sooner or later you'd be expected to open your legs or drop your pants in service to the GDR. Conrad was in no way a bad-looking fellow, though he'd never been asked to trade affection for secrets. Ever since Emilie lured him into the west, Wolf hadn't fully trusted him. It was just as well. Conrad had learned that he could toe the line so long as too much wasn't asked of him. Sometimes, working at the radio station, he almost forgot that his real work was espionage.

Another thing Conrad could have revealed to Monika was that, if he hadn't learned to turn a blind eye to his wife's activities, he would have lost his mind a long time ago. But the truth wasn't a good idea. Instead, he feigned surprise.

"You're imagining things, Monika. Emilie's at the office, I left her there just a little while ago. And Kolman's not the unfaithful type."

"How would you know?"

"Don't you?"

"I never distrusted him before." She managed a deep breath and started to calm down.

"Look," Conrad smiled, "I admit that Emilie's a handful, but she's your friend. She wouldn't do anything to hurt you two." That such insincerity could spill so easily from his lips no longer troubled him. He had decided, years ago, to hide behind a generous protective layer of wishful thinking. The useful skill of active denial had kept him alive, and he didn't see why he shouldn't share it with Monika.

"I never would have thought it of her, but…"

"Then why start now?"

She wiped her tears with her hands. "I'm sorry I barged in like this. Kolman always tells me I'm over-sensitive."

"I was just about to eat something. Since he's not home, why don't you join me? Let him worry when he gets back and doesn't find you."

She laughed at that. "Yes. Thank you. I like that idea."

They had eggs, bread, and wine at the kitchen table. She chatted about her young students with such enthusiasm that he couldn't resist bringing up the question of children, though he deliberately phrased it so as not to betray his previous conversation with Kolman.

"When do you think you'll start your own family?"

Her cheeks blushed violently. "We haven't made up our minds about that yet."

"I think you'd make a good mother. Do you mind me saying that?"

"No. It's just that my own mother scared me off. She was so unhappy."

Three hard knocks on the front door announced the end of their conversation. Conrad let Kolman in. He smelled of beer and was repentant although Monika didn't say a word about her reaction to his unexplained absence earlier. The couple went home together as if nothing had happened.

The rest of the evening was quiet until Emilie came home at a quarter past two in the morning. Pretending to be asleep, Conrad listened to her slip into their room. He kept still as she settled into bed.

She was already gone when a commotion outside their apartment woke him early in the morning. He stepped into yesterday's clothes and entered the hallway to find a beehive of police and neighbors clumped at the Walzes' open door.

In the hall, Kolman's hands were restrained behind his back; he stumbled forward between a pair of officers who led him roughly by the elbows in the direction of the stairs. Conrad's pulse jumped when he saw the bloody footprints his friend was trailing.

"What's happening here?"

Kolman turned around, his face disordered by agony, and cried, "Monika!"

A pair of officers blocked a clear view through the doorway to the Walzes' apartment, but Conrad saw enough to suggest a violent tumult. A chair was overturned. A vase was broken, white carnations strewn in a pool of water. And there was blood; a lot of blood.

Conrad watched his friend's retreating back, wishing he could promise to find him help, a lawyer, something. But he knew immediately that he mustn't involve himself in this. Light-headed, he found his way back to his apartment, closed himself inside, and sank to the floor.

Kolman Walz didn't have it in him to hurt his wife, Conrad was sure of it. The man had loved her.

He would never see his friend again. He was sure of that, too.

Lifting his eyes, he scanned the sunlit floor of his living room, searching for traces of Monika's blood. Emilie always kicked her shoes off by the front door. Whatever she'd worn in last night must have gone back out with her this morning. If there had ever been a hint of blood on them, he would never find it now.

Conrad sat forward on his knees, gazing over the apartment he shared with the only lover he'd ever known. The woman who had lured him past a series of outer and inner boundaries. Who had stolen him from his home and his parents, ripped out his heart over and over until he'd locked it away so tightly she could no longer reach it. He looked at the walls they lived within, the furniture they sat on, the floor they walked across together. Outside, a cloud shifted, casting their home in a steely metallic light devoid of color. Flattening it.

He felt ill.

A storm was coming. A hostile inner wind that lifted

the fallen leaves of every doubt he'd managed to suppress about the limits of his wife's deceit, exposing a brutal awareness.

Was Emilie more than an informer? More than a swan? More than a double agent? Was she also one of Wolf's assassins?

He closed his eyes. And like the magician he had learned to be for the sake of his own survival, he willed away the possibility that Emilie had been responsible for this horrible thing.

SEVENTEEN

A Ticket to Berlin

NEW YORK CITY, May 24, 2013

EMMY TRANSFERS her clothes piece by piece, and then grabs clumps by the handful, flinging them into her suitcase. She hasn't been here long and didn't bring much. Toiletries. Shoes. Chargers for her cell and laptop. The new purchases are folded carefully but ultimately crammed on top of her regular junk.

She looks forward to getting home, where she can crawl into her own bed in her Prenzlauer Berg apartment and stay there until her bruises fade. The pain is worse this morning. If she so much as blinks, hurt radiates across her face.

Closing her eyes, she thinks of Mutti. Opens her mouth, tries unsuccessfully to fill her lungs with air but manages only a few thin sips.

She thinks of the man she was sent here to eliminate—some old defunct spy called Don Fennell—clueless that his days are numbered or how her distraction has bought him more time.

She thinks of Con, how knowing him has made her newly prone to a raw kind of loneliness only Mutti was able to inspire in her before, an unrequited yearning to be appreciated by someone with a unique inability to see you for who you are.

She thinks again of Mutti, and wonders if her mother is even capable of love.

Emmy goes to the desk by the window and taps an addition onto her list, hide gun, beneath cancel sublet. She has a seat on a red-eye to Berlin. She picks up her phone and, while it rings, reviews the remaining items on her list: tell Con; send ticket.

He answers, "What?"

"Mutti bought you a ticket on my flight," she lies. If he knew that Emmy bought it, he would never agree to come. She needs to see them together: mother and son. To gauge Mutti's reaction. To find out just how heartless her mother really is.

"Who's Mutti?"

"Our mother."

Silence deadens the line between them until finally he responds with a deep sigh. "Why doesn't she come here if she wants to meet me so badly?"

"I told you, Mutti can't travel."

"What's wrong with her?"

"The flight is tonight, out of JFK, the six-fifty on Lufthansa, direct to Berlin Tegel. You can stay in the spare room in my apartment."

Another of his silences swallows the conversation, until finally he mutters, "I don't know."

"She won't live forever." The bitter edge of Con's laugh cuts Emmy with delicious precision. He's her brother, all right. "I'm only reminding you that a person in her seventies has a limited lifespan. This is your chance."

After a pause, Con says, "I'll think it over."

Emmy emails Con his electronic ticket, knowing that he'll at least look at it. Hoping that he'll do more than that. Betting that he might.

When she's all packed, she puts the gun in her purse, walks to the Canal Street subway station, and stands on the uptown platform. She recently noticed a broken padlock on the chained door handle of one of the public bathrooms no one ever seems to use. As soon as a train whisks away all the people waiting with her on the platform, she lifts off the lock, pulls out the chain, and lets herself in.

The smell is fetid, and there is no light. Illuminating the abandoned room with her phone, she enters a doorless stall and tucks the gun into a crevice behind a toilet smeared in ancient shit. If someone finds it, so be it. If not, then she'll know where to look when and if she comes back to New York to finish Mutti's treasure hunt.

Con put down the phone. A ticket to Berlin. Tonight. To meet his birth mother. It was a ridiculous idea, this invitation into a long-lost past he hadn't known existed.

On the other hand, he had the time now. Reluctant days forced on him by Artie.

He looked at the gold watch strapped to his wrist and thought of his father. There was still so much he didn't know.

EIGHTEEN

The Anniversary Gift

WEST BERLIN, March 6-16, 1977

CONRAD WATCHED the on-air light blink. It was his first time inside the booth during a broadcast, this close to a live mic.

The moment the light held steady, Barry leaned in and announced, smoothly, as he'd done a hundred times before, "This is the Barry Graves show. Are you ready to get your mind blown? Good, because I'm giving you something different today. Introducing my buddy, my pal, my producer and Dylan freak…Julian Wimmers!"

Conrad brought his lips an inch from the mic, the way Barry had shown him, and said, "Hello Berlin, this is Julian, live from the RIAS studio. Barry asked me to do my Dylan riff today, yeah, we got a little drunk the other night and I went off on Dylan and next thing I know, here I am. Bob Dylan's got a new one for you. Cover your ears, east-ies, because this one's verboten in the zone." He lifted his chin to the show's producer, Fred Hicks, seated in the control booth beside news announcer Don Fennell—two tall, strapping Americans, always ready to comment or advise. Hicks, with his unusually narrow face and kind eyes, encouraged Conrad with a smile. Fennell was the more handsome of the two, and Emilie, who was also there, leaned in his direction. She didn't smile. Conrad couldn't tell what she thought of his stint announcing, but knew he'd hear about it later, at home.

Dylan's "Forever Young" took over. Conrad was sweating now, his pulse racing. While it was easier, quieter, and safer on the other side of the Plexiglass, where he usually sat, he liked this. The exposure of live broadcast felt like being bathed in light.

"You did good, Julian." Barry's mustache twitched over a wry smile. "Four minutes and you're back on the air. Ready?"

Conrad nodded. Smiled. Cleared his throat.

"Happy Anniversary." Emilie set a long jewelry box beside Conrad's morning coffee. She'd had her bath while he was eating his breakfast. She broke a piece off last night's stale loaf and spread on a thin layer of margarine.

"What's this for?" he asked.

"You've been on the air a solid week without being canceled." She laughed sarcastically. "Congratulations." In her moment of humor, a new spate of wrinkles appeared around her eyes. They'd been together sixteen years now, they were in their thirties; it shouldn't have surprised him that they had aged, that time had passed so quickly, while their youthful choices had grown around them like old trees blocking the horizon.

He opened the box. Inside lay a handsome gold watch on a brown leather strap, stretched long on a bed of velvet.

It was a Junghans, not the fanciest watch but certainly beyond their means.

"This is ridiculous," he said.

"Don't you like it?"

"Of course I like it. How much did it cost?"

"It's a gift, Connie." The way her dark eyes glimmered, he knew she hadn't paid for the "gift" with her own money.

"What's is for," he put the watch back in the box, "really?"

"It's a gift. Really." Her lips stretched into a wry smile. "But you're right, it isn't exactly from me."

He waited. She had a tendency to be full of surprises, though he no longer found them in any way charming. They'd passed a point in their relationship when the love affair was dead and buried; what was left was familiarity and tolerance. He often wondered why he'd never cheated on her, why he took the gold ring on his finger so seriously. The gold watch that wasn't "exactly" a gift from her would complement the ring with precision.

"Herr Lehmann told me to give it to you."

"Ah, that makes more sense." Oskar Lehmann was Mischa Wolf's handle for all matters related to RIAS.

Conrad picked up the Junghans and examined it from every angle. It looked like a watch, nothing else. Emilie observed him as if waiting for something. He could practically hear the sharp words dancing on her tongue, but she said nothing. Finally, she padded away on bare feet. When he heard the hairdryer turn on in the bathroom, he picked up a butter knife, wiped it clean on his napkin, and ran the blade along the lining of the jewelry box until the edge lifted easily.

Nothing was hidden, which surprised him.

He strapped the watch onto his left wrist.

When Emilie emerged from the bathroom, her sleek black hair now dry and swinging at her shoulders, she wore her customary blood-red lipstick and acted as if nothing had happened.

"Emilie—"

"Shall we go?" she said, moving their morning forward as if it was just another day when it wasn't. Something had shifted. He had been given something by Wolf, and she had been left out. Her jealousy chilled him.

He wore the Junghans every day, receiving compliments whenever it peeked out from beneath his cuff. Conrad decided to express his gratitude to Wolf for the generous gift, and so, after a week, he left a note of thanks with the executive secretary, sealed into a plain envelope, asking her to get it to Herr Lehmann.

Three days later, the secretary handed Conrad an envelope addressed to Oskar Lehmann at an address in Kreuzberg, and asked him to hand-deliver it. It was close enough to walk, and he set out right away. Not knowing in what capacity he was being summoned—as East Berliner Conrad Schumann or West Berliner Julian Wimmers; as a spy or a radio producer/announcer—he made the delivery in the guise of a blank slate.

Wolf-Lehmann occupied a fourth-floor office in a nondescript building rented mostly, it seemed, to travel agents and insurance brokers. A sign on the door read Lehmann Travel. The large, sun-filled office was decorated with tasteful art.

"Come in, welcome! Thinking of a trip?" Wolf spoke rather loudly, making sure that anyone who might happen to be in the hall could hear. In this case, a woman in a tight dress, her high heels clomping noisily on the tiled floor. She paid no attention to Conrad or the raucous voice spilling into the corridor.

The HVA spymaster dropped the act as soon as the door was closed. Conrad had met with him a few times since his recruitment in '61, always in a different location, always with Emilie. The man had so many handles, you couldn't know where he'd turn up next, or as who.

Leaning stiffly against the edge of his massive desk, arms folded over his chest, Wolf asked, "Enjoying your gift?"

"Very much so."

Wolf strode across the office. He was considerably taller than Conrad and smelled vaguely of grapefruit. His fingers felt damp on Conrad's hand when he turned it over to unclasp the watch. "And how is Lena these days?" Here, Emilie was Lena Froebel. They spoke for the benefit of possible wiretaps; there was no point in taking any unnecessary risks. Whatever this conversation was really meant to be about would have to be read between the lines.

"No children yet?" Wolf commented, pulling the watch off Con's wrist. "I hope it's not too personal to say that I'm surprised."

"Not at all. I'm more eager on that front than she is." A pleasant lie. Neither he nor Emilie had expressed any interest in having children together. "You know how women are these days," Conrad went on, "enjoying their careers."

Wolf turned the watch over atop his desk and reached for a letter opener. "I suppose I'm lucky that my wife came from an earlier generation. Always a hot meal on my table when I get home in the evening."

"Lucky man. Though it doesn't bother me, to be honest. It's all really a matter of generational perspective."

Conrad watched as Wolf pried the tip of the letter opener into the seam circling the back of the watch. The backing popped off and tumbled soundlessly to the carpet.

"Perhaps you and Lena would care to come to dinner chez Lehmann one of these nights?" Wolf asked, insincerely. They both knew that such an invitation would never happen in reality. "My wife can make her famous wiener schnitzel."

"It would be our pleasure. Name the date."

Wolf indicated the floor. Conrad bent to retrieve the gold coin of the backing. He placed it in Wolf's open palm and watched as it was turned over. A tiny piece of metal, shaped like a bolt of lightning, was embedded in the gold. Wolf chipped it loose with his fingernail. He then extruded a small, flat key from his pocket and fitted the lightning bolt into the key's stem. Hammered into the key were the numbers 357.

There was no way Conrad could ask questions, not here. Wolf could have arranged to meet him somewhere safer to talk; that he hadn't, indicated that Conrad was expected to pay close attention and await further instructions. He watched as Wolf returned the tiny piece to the back of the watch, which he reassembled and handed over. Wolf then pressed the key into Conrad's palm.

"Shall I mention the dinner invitation to Lena?" Conrad asked.

"No." Wolf was definite. "Why not let it come as a surprise?"

That night, over supper at the kitchen table, Emilie took Conrad's left hand. Her skin was cold. "What did he have to say?"

So she knew he'd been to see Wolf. He shouldn't have been surprised.

"Dinner invitation, he claimed."

Emilie laughed. "Seriously? Is that what he said?" In the harsh light of their kitchen's overhead, the lines on her face reappeared, tracing shadows where flesh once softened her cheeks, and she looked old, older than he'd ever imagined she could.

Conrad's appetite vanished.

The topic was dropped between them.

A month would pass before he would learn where to find the lock that fit the special key.

NINETEEN

Thirst

BERLIN, May 25, 2013

EMMY LED Con along the memory-laced early-morning streets of her Berlin. Coffee-pungent cafes threw open their doors to spring, yeasty bakeries raised their windows, yelping dogs had their morning walks. Somewhere nearby, a mother cried, "Hurry or you'll be late." It felt surprisingly good to be home.

Trudging along these familiar streets in her new bomber jacket, she wondered why she had thought America and specifically New York would be a radical upgrade when in contrast these streets were perfectly nice. How was it that she'd held so tightly to her memories of a bygone place that time and capitalism had mostly expunged? Berlin was undoubtedly fancy now; she knew that: she'd lived here all her life, watched and absorbed the city's transmutation from broken to thriving. Even so, that wasted place shimmered through the renovations; for her, it would always be there, a menacing illusion.

She had come to hate herself for the seeds of her childhood, hate her mother for nurturing those seeds, and hate (now) Con for escaping all of it, as if in his infancy he had deliberately left her alone to suffer the national pride of relentless thrift that had defined her upbringing. But it struck her that the thrift had been more than material: it was an emotional thrift, specific to the way Mutti had raised her.

And she knew something else: Her posh jacket was lovely, substantial, the leather pliable and soft—but she hadn't earned it yet. She still had to face her mother, and her own hunger for the money being dangled in front of her, and her yearning to be transported out of her past into an idea of an alternate future she wanted to deserve. Nothing was simple. She had been sent to New York to kill a stranger and found another one instead. No, she had found two: Con, and herself. Walking the old streets with her newly discovered brother, Emmy felt skinless, naked, exposed.

Mutti had told her that if she did this one thing—accepted the assignment, got the job done—an easy life would be hers. Well, her mother was wrong about that: it would never be easy.

Con followed Emmy through the streets of her neighborhood, intrigued by a strange familiarity. He knew little about his earliest life other than that he had been a baby when he was taken out of Germany.

"Is this where you grew up?"

"With Mutti, in her apartment, yes. This is her street, right here."

They turned down a dead-end street lined with eighteenth and nineteenth-century apartment buildings, their decorative facades worn by time. Windows adorned with flower boxes looked down on him and he imagined himself a boy returning home from school along this very route. Would flowers have been allowed, or affordable, during the socialist years? The dress boutique that looked like something from New York wouldn't have been there then. Neither would the hip restaurant beside the faded green door where Emmy stopped. She rang their mother's bell.

Walking up two flights of stairs behind his prodigal sister—decked out in a pricey leather jacket, crisp designer jeans and trendy sneakers whose American price sticker ($220!) flashed each time she raised her rubber sole to the next step—he struggled to see her as anything but a disaster. At the same time, for now, he decided to believe that she really was his sister, his twin. And that, despite all the trouble she'd caused him, she was about to demonstrate her until-now unrevealed compassion, her humanity, by leading him to the person who could elucidate his father's past.

The apartment door was cracked open when they reached the fourth floor. An eye peered at them through the gap, dark pupils embraced by soft, wrinkled skin. The door swung open and Con's heart leaped into his throat, because he knew this woman, he recognized her like he'd recognized Emmy the night they met at the Mercury Lounge. The bottomless sense of familiarity snatched him out of his body for a moment before he harnessed himself. When he'd met Emmy, he was blasted drunk. Now, cold sober, seeing Mutti in the flesh, he knew better than to succumb to a blind thirst for her.

The envelopes containing two buccal swab kits—which he'd picked up from the lab at Hogan before setting out—had shimmied up the back pocket of his jeans while he'd walked up the stairs, reminding him now to slow down, to take everything that happened with a dose of skepticism until he could get the Emilies' DNA processed. He pushed the envelopes back down and put on a smile.

Leaning on a pair of crutches, their mother was medium height, lean, her sinewy arms pale in a short-sleeved blouse, her hipbones sharp under black slacks. One foot was manicured, shiny with a bloody maroon; the other was encased in a plastic medical boot.

Emmy announced, "This is Con."

Mutti's face froze; she seemed surprised to see him. She asked Emmy, "Was machst du?"

"Spielen nett. Ich warne Sie."

MUTTI ASKS EMMY, "What are you doing?"

"Play nice. I warn you."

Emmy is practiced at reading the sparks of fury in her mother's eyes. And her words: her words are as sharp as ever. "You little bitch. I told you—"

"That I was an only child. You didn't mention that I had a brother. Who's the bitch, mother dear?"

"WILLKOMMEN, WILLKOMMEN." Emilie's arms opened like sails to wind, and without a moment's thought, Con was hugging this stranger, a tangle of arms and crutches, and just as quickly pulling away. Her smile faded, looking him over. "Du bist verletzt."

"Speak English, Mutti," Emmy reminded her.

Mutti surveyed the rainbow of her daughter's face. "You're hurt, too. What happened to you both?"

Ignoring her mother's questions, brushing past her into the apartment, Emmy asked, "Do you have anything to eat?" From Con's doorway vantage point, the place appeared large and airy.

"Please." Mutti waved him in. "Let me see what I have for you."

"I'll give you a hand," Con offered, as this woman-who-was-his-mother hobbled toward her kitchen.

"Thank you, but no—Emmy will help."

While the women rummaged in the kitchen, Con located the spacious living room: broad, undressed windows; mismatched chairs; an afghan-covered couch; walls lined with bookshelves. On a mantle above a fire-place, half a dozen library books were stacked. A glass of water, its rim ghosted with lip prints, sat near the edge of a coffee table where an ashtray overflowed on top of another pile of books. So she was a reader. And she didn't bother keeping house. But mostly she was a stranger. He had no sense of having been here before, as an infant; if he had, the memory was too deeply buried to conjure any feeling at all.

In the cramped, inglorious kitchen of Emmy's youth, mother stands propped on her crutches while daughter hunts through cabinets. As usual, there is very little here. She settles on an open box of crackers, emptied onto a plate along with the decimated contents of an old package of figs.

Mutti shuffles on her crutches, a storm glowering in her eyes. "Why did you bring him here?"

"Right before I left, Oma Bettina called and told me."

"That old fool? She can't even think straight, and you listened to her?"

"What she told me turned out to be true. What do you say to that?"

"Why didn't you talk to me before you went and found him?"

"I didn't want to talk. I wanted to see for myself."

"What do you expect me to do with him now?" Mutti's face is blank. Cruel and empty. The leading edge of a terrible loneliness that has haunted Emmy all her life.

"I guess that's for you to decide. The guy's got a beating heart. Hot potato, Mutti. Catch!" She tosses a hard fig at her mother who doesn't so much as lift her hands. The fig tumbles to the floor, landing beside Mutti's boot.

"Don't be an idiot, Emmy."

"Why didn't you tell me about him?"

For a moment, Mutti almost seems to feel something, but just as quickly the mirage vanishes. "I didn't think it would help you to know."

"Help me what?"

"Live with the consequences."

"How did Vati get him out of the GDR, anyway?"

"It's complicated."

"Shit, Mutti, why does everything always have to be so fucking complicated."

"Your generation with your cursing." Mutti shakes her head. "The world is built on complexity. It isn't a cartoon."

"Believe me, I know that."

"Why are you putting me in this position? It changes things."

"Yes, it does, doesn't it? I've gotten to know him a bit and he isn't all that bad."

"He's handsome." Mutti smiles.

"Why don't you fuck him? I did." She waits for shock to cross her mother's face, but Mutti's features don't shift. Instead, she sighs, and a foul but provocative odor reaches Emmy.

"I sent you to New York for a specific reason." Mutti

crutches forward to shake a finger in Emmy's face. "I should have known you couldn't do the job. You're a follower, a greedy follower, I knew that and I made a mistake trusting you with something so important."

"Why is it so important to eliminate this Fennell? Who is he? Why can't I just ask him for the key you're after, threaten him if I have to, and get out?"

"Just tell me—are you with me or against me?" The coldness in Mutti's eyes startles Emmy. In the chill of her silence, her mother continues, "Well. Now that your brother's here, let's find out if he can get the job done since you're obviously useless."

Against you, is the answer that rip-roars through Emmy's mind. But beneath that thought is a powerful, contradictory sensation she is helpless against. What she craves, despite her better judgment, is evidence of her mother's love. The money from Mutti's mysterious donor —or victim, depending on what the monster has planned; she still hasn't divulged whether Fennell is the man with the money or a target who has to fall first—won't mean anything without it. What Emmy wants is both.

After a moment, they returned, Emmy carrying a plate of crackers and dried figs. It seemed a strange, paltry snack, especially compared with what Con was used to from Ruth's kitchen. He thanked them and popped a fig into his mouth. It was so dehydrated, it was almost impossible to chew.

Mutti leaned her crutches against the wall and situated herself on a worn but comfortable-looking chair with its back to a bright window, beyond which a springtime tree bloomed with clusters of new green leaves. The paint was chipped all around the windowsill. In the harsh light that poured through the glass, Mutti's eyes appeared sunken in charcoal smudges. Again, the tremor resurfaced in Con's chest. This was a woman who could choose between children. Who in fact had made such a choice. Her bare foot tapped the wood floor. "You resemble your father," she said.

"I've heard that before. And Emmy looks a lot like you."

"Like I used to. Yes."

Con took out the envelopes containing the swabs. He asked, "Would you mind?"

"No, not at all. I understand. But not quite yet."

Emmy said, "Mutti likes to know someone better before she exchanges bodily fluids." Her foot rhythmically kicked the underside of the coffee table, knock, knock, knock. Con refused an urge for nervous laughter and glanced at Mutti, who didn't appear at all shocked.

"Con." Mutti turned back to him, smiling. "I'm so glad you came to see me. You've come a long way. You must have many questions."

He put the swab kits on the table beside the snacks. "To say the least."

"Here I am, and here you are. So...." She shrugged her shoulders, just a little; a subtle invitation. He pulled a chair beside her and leaned in close enough to count the lines on her face if he'd wanted to. Beneath a generous amount of perfume, he detected an acridity, maybe garlic. "You came so you won't have to rely on what others tell you, am I right?"

"Basically, yes."

"At heart, your father was a good man."

That took him by surprise; he wasn't sure exactly what she meant by at heart. "I know he was a good man. But

I've often wondered if he was running from something when he came to America."

He read her slight nod as affirmation.

"I loved Dad very much," he began carefully. And then, like a hastily turned-on tap, words flowed. "He never talked about the early part of his life. Now, I find out he was a spy. I find out about you. I find out I have a twin. What else is there that I need to know?"

Mutti's hands fanned open, revealing craggy palms. "Will you mind if I speak frankly? This is not an easy business, but here you are, asking, and I can see how badly you want real answers."

"Please do."

"Your father was a double agent. You know this. But the truth is, he had no core. No beliefs. He served everyone and no one. He came to hate himself. Eventually, he hated me."

"That doesn't sound like him."

"Perhaps he changed in America, but I doubt it. People rarely do."

"Why did he hate you?"

"Because I knew who I was; it was both my strength and my weakness. Conrad was different. Softer. I shouldn't have recruited him and we probably shouldn't have married."

"You recruited him?"

"He was weaker than I'd thought."

"But you had children together."

"I was getting older, and I thought, why not?"

Con glanced at Emmy. She had lain back as if resting and the domed lids of her closed eyes registered not a flutter. Apparently, none of this surprised her; she must have grown up on a steady diet of these pellets of hard truths. Her detachment appalled him. He wondered how he'd ever thought he could love her. But then, to his surprise, he felt a ripple of pity. Something about the way she lay there passively, pretending not to care.

"I never should have let him take you," Mutti said. "I've regretted it ever since."

"Why did you let him?" Con asked.

"It seemed to me at the time that he had a right to one of you." She shook her head as if disappointed in the cold calculations her younger self had been capable of. For a moment, Con felt trapped between two Emilies, two Emmys, at opposite sides of a lifetime; one seasoned, the other ruthless; both somehow coexisting with, because of, and in spite of the other. Their dynamic baffled him. At any given moment, it was impossible to know which one to trust less.

"What happened to your hand?" Mutti asked in a voice so tender, Con found himself leaning closer.

"I punched a door."

"Did it solve your problem?"

"No."

"You're sure you didn't hit your sister? Your hand, her face." The blend of irony and remorse in her smile startled him. What he felt, more and more as the meeting progressed, was that he wanted to open up to this woman who had (allegedly) given birth to him but couldn't, or shouldn't, trust her. At that moment, he understood with force his father's urgency to stop him from working under-cover, effectively becoming a spy; to keep him away from the kind of work that, over time, destroyed your ability to both trust others fully and trust yourself to read them accu-rately. So you held back. You watched. And when the moment was right, you slithered away, if possible unharmed. Mutti had been a spy, too. Con could imagine the impossibilities of that marriage.

Emmy shifted onto her side and opened her eyes, facing them now, and as if tuned into his thinking blurted, "Con's a spy, just like you and Vati."

"I'm not a spy, exactly. I do undercover work for the district attorney."

"You sound so much like Conrad." Mutti smiled wistfully. "Do you want to know why he first went to work for the Stasi?"

"Something about a family friend," Con answered, "and a bicycle?"

Emilie nodded. "That was all it took. Luring him over the border was just as easy. Do you want to know how we did it?"

"We?"

"I worked for Wolf by then. You've heard of him?"

Con nodded. Markus Wolf was the legendary spymaster who led the HVA, the foreign branch of the Stasi, running the German side of the Cold War against the west.

"I was just a girl, and I was in pretty deep. I decided I wanted Conrad with me, but I knew from my sources that he was angry at how I'd left him back home. I'd simply disappeared, you see. It wasn't very nice of me."

Amusing herself now by erecting a tower of figs on the coffee table, Emmy laughed. "Du warst eine Hündin, Mutti, wie du jetzt bist."

Mutti ignored her. "It was decided to tell him that I'd given birth after I left him. He came running."

"That was over fifty years ago," Con noted. "Are you saying we have an older sibling?"

Mutti pressed her lips into what was meant to be a smile. "No, my dear. It was a...story."

Con felt stupid for having asked. He wondered why his father had believed in the lie wholly enough to have jumped a very dangerous border with that look in his eye: the young man of the photograph, mid-leap, face flickering with a youthful elixir of hope and anarchy.

"Wolf ran both of us," Mutti continued. "We were a team. For a while, we were the best. And then, Conrad...."

"What?"

"I told you. He was a coward from the beginning."

"He wanted to stop working for Wolf, didn't he?"

She nodded.

"And you didn't."

Again, a simple nod.

Con's thoughts returned to that night on the Brooklyn Bridge, seeing a man who was-but-wasn't his father throw himself into the river, rewinding his father back up onto the tower to the moment just before he leaped and begging him to focus on now, his second family, all the love, begging him to release his misbegotten history, and to understand that Con was never going to relive his father's mistakes. That there was hope. There was always hope.

But Con sensed that the story was more complicated than that.

"Before he killed himself, Dad wrote in his journal about something called the Rosenholz files, that he'd never be able to get away—from what?"

"Ah, yes." Mutti shook her head. "Rosenholz."

"What is it?"

Emmy explained, "It's kind of an old-style database identifying Stasi undercovers."

"Your father was afraid," Mutti said, "but not of Rosenholz, exactly."

"Then what?"

Mutti nodded, her eyes on his face. "Conrad killed a woman, and—"

"Killed?" The word reverberated through Con. His father, a killer? It wasn't possible.

Even Emmy seemed surprised, sitting forward now, alert with curiosity. "Why did you never tell me this?"

"He was one of Wolf's assassins. But Ilsa Vogel, the last one—she was a friend of mine."

Con said, "It doesn't sound like Dad, not at all. I just don't understand."

Mutti placed her hand on top of his; her skin was ice cold. "I know this is difficult for you to hear, but it's the truth. Ilsa didn't go well…he was sure he'd be caught. So he fled."

It was impossible for Con to believe. "With a baby?"

"We were out at a café all together, me and your father and Ilsa. Emmy was fussy, we'd forgotten to bring a bottle, so I took her home. Conrad stayed out with you. I never saw either of you again. And Ilsa was dead. Now here you are, and you tell me that he took his own life, and you ask me if he was afraid of Rosenholz." In the window behind Mutti, what had remained of the afternoon suddenly faded, replaced by a glowing half-darkness.

"He wrote about Rosenholz," Con argued. "He never mentioned running from a murder."

Mutti shrugged. "Well, maybe he was afraid of Rosenholz. Plenty of the operatives from back then didn't survive the publication of those files; the minute they were released to the public, in 2003, anyone who wanted to could find out what we'd done for our country at a time when it seemed to matter more than anything else. Quite a few old patriots have been hunted down by relatives of the traitors they now call victims. Your father may have worried that Rosenholz would connect him to activities he would have liked the world to forget about. Not just the people he spied on, but the people he killed."

"People?"

"He worked for Wolf. He crossed boundaries, often. We all did."

"But why would he kill himself? Why wouldn't he just run away again?"

"I can only guess."

"What about you, Mutti?" Emmy asked. "Aren't you afraid?"

"No. I searched for my name in the files several years ago, and it wasn't there. Apparently, Rosenholz isn't complete. I've often wondered about the names that were held back."

"That's the thing." Con tried to recall exactly what Ruth had read aloud from his father's journal. "Dad said that his name was erased from the Rosenholz files. Wouldn't that have made him safer?"

Mutti shrugged her shoulders as behind her the window's darkness swallowed her almost completely. "He was a coward; he was probably afraid he'd be found out sooner or later and dragged back here to face the music. You say he jumped off a bridge? Yes. That sounds like Conrad to me."

"Not to me," Con said. Something felt wrong. Not just the information Mutti was offering, but the quality of her self-assurance. He stood up, turned on a lamp, and got the swab kits from the coffee table. "Any objections to getting this done right now?"

When Emmy appeared to bristle, Mutti volunteered. "Start with me."

She held open the cavern of her mouth while he pulled on latex gloves he'd brought from the lab. Following the instructions the tech had given him, he rubbed the swab end of the long stick up and down fifteen times in Mutti's inner cheek.

He repeated the procedure with Emmy, who endured it with obvious annoyance. Both swabs sealed into their respective envelopes, Con decided he'd better hold onto them for the rest of the visit. He didn't trust Emmy, and he didn't know what to make of Mutti yet.

"I'll put on some coffee." Mutti leaned forward, reached for her crutches, prepared to stand. And then, as if upgrading the proposition to a meal, she asked them both, "How hungry are you to know about your father? I can give you the name of someone who can tell you even more than I can."

"Yes," Con said. "Please."

"Don Fennell—he was an American spy, during and after the war. That wasn't his real name, of course." She struggled to her feet. "I'll make coffee, and we'll talk some more. I'll try to remember as much as I can that might help you find him."

STARTING the coffee while Mutti sits at the kitchen table and lifts her boot onto a chair, Emmy turns to her mother and asks, "Was any of that true?"

"Most of it."

A thought crystallized for Emmy. "You think Fennell is the one who held back part of Rosenholz, don't you? You want to stop him from ever releasing your name—that's why you sent me to off him."

"More or less."

The thought of her mother dying, being murdered like some of the other old spies who had suffered retribution since the release of the Stasi files a decade ago, surprises Emmy with a clear, simple dread. "Why didn't you tell me that before?"

"I didn't want you undertaking the assignment in rage. I wanted you thinking clearly. It's easier that way."

As the coffee drips, Emmy is caught between a desire to warn Con not to take Mutti's story at face value, and the surprising look on her mother's face. When she was growing up, Emmy had upon rare occasion seen that very expression: the fragile lines bracketing a maternal gaze, lines that are deeper now, more like cuts in the skin. There it is now, perplexing, irresistible, hotly desired: a mother's concern. But is it real?

Against you, Emmy silently repeats her mantra, trying to hang onto her anger, though she's no longer so sure. Alone with the woman herself, the powerful woman who raised and trained her—who as a child Emmy loved and whose approval was almost more essential than air or food or sleep—the determination that propelled her here begins to dissolve.

"You didn't answer me before," Mutti says, "when I asked if you were still with me. Because I'm willing to give you another chance."

"Yes," Emmy hears herself mutter, reflexively, "I'm with you."

"Good. Then trust me." Close now, Mutti's familiar scent, a reduction of sweet and sour, is calming, providing a dissonant undercurrent to her powerful, confusing words: "By the way, I'm sorry."

"Are you?"

"It's been so long, well… I'd lost touch with the reality that I also had a son. I should have given you the full picture."

"Told me the truth, you mean."

Mutti's eyes smile. "Come here."

Emmy crosses the small kitchen.

The weathered hand that Mutti places on her daughter's cheek is unexpectedly soft. Tears gather in Emmy's eyes as it occurs to her that it's been years since her mother ventured to touch her. "You are mine. I lost the chance to know him a long time ago."

"Don't you want to now?"

"I kept you because I wanted you. I chose you. I still choose you. You have always been enough for me."

"I might have liked to grow up with a brother."

"I see that now. And I'm sorry, but it's too late. We can't turn back, we're set on a path." The sublime conflict of her mother's arms around her radicalizes the moment for Emmy, makes her starving for more of what she's always yearned for but never fully possessed. Something warm and good and dependable. Love, probably, but she's no longer sure. Mutti whispers, "We can't change the past, but we can control our future," and it's true, it's true.

The devil you know, Emmy reminds herself.

And yes, she is, she is with Mutti.

Soon, when they have their money, real money for once, and life eases, all the trouble it will have taken to get there will have faded into a distant oblivion.

Emmy's heart jumps when Mutti looks into her eyes, and says, "Con is a problem—he's too curious. But he's an experienced investigator so let's use that against him. Let him think there's something to find. He'll look for Fennell, too—you'll let him lead you to him—you'll find the key, and then you'll finish them both at once. Leave no witnesses. Come home to me, and we'll take the final step together. You'll have such a future, Emmy. You'll never have to work again if you don't want to. You'll have anything you want. Your life will open up."

"You mean…?" Does Emmy understand her mother? Is she now being asked to kill her brother, too?

"We do what we must in life," Mutti says. "Even if it's hard."

"But I—"

"You're much stronger than you think," Mutti whispers, her breath hot on Emmy's ear. "I raised you to be strong. Decide. The uncertainty ends right now."

"Just tell me, please, who he is—the man with the money. The reason we're doing all this."

"The reason is so that we can both be free in our own way. Trust me, Emmy. You'll know everything when the time is right."

The coffee sputters to a finish, filling the room with hints of chocolate and hazelnut, though Emmy knows it's just cheap grocery store coffee. She pours out three mugs and sets them on a tray.

TWENTY

The Gun

WEST BERLIN, *April 14-22, 1977*

CONRAD SAT in the broadcast booth, preparing to go on the air when producer Fred Hicks hurried in with a slip of paper. "A bit of news," he said. "Read it with the opening headlines." Hicks leaned in to add, in a whisper: "This comes from the top."

Conrad glanced at the typed sheet. It was a short announcement, a small pebble that might have sent ripples through a large pond thirty years ago. It seemed an odd bit of news to read decades after the fact; but "from the top" could have meant any number of people, all of whom were to be obeyed.

When the time came, Conrad read aloud to the listening world:

"In a blow to the international effort to restore Nazi-plundered art to its rightful owners, the widow of art dealer Leopold Sommer announced that her late husband's extensive collection of paintings, thought to include looted masterpieces, was destroyed in the fire-bombing of Dresden in 1945. Asked why she waited so long to make her announcement, she replied, 'No one asked.'"

Turning the page over to make sure that was all for the announcement, he saw it: VB10961, scrawled lightly in pencil as if left behind by mistake. He immediately knew it was meant for him. He memorized the cipher, folded the page, and placed it in the pile to be shredded at the end of the day.

First thing the next morning, Conrad visited the Volksbank branch in Kreuzberg, in district 10961. He presented himself to the female guard who watched over the bank's vault, using his Julian Wimmers credentials and his friendliest smile. The key Wolf had given him was in his pocket. His work bag was slung over his shoulder and he made a point of checking the time to indicate a hope that he wouldn't be late for the office. He was a husband on an errand before work. There was no reason for this woman to think otherwise.

Conrad followed her into the vault, the open door like a huge and exuberantly round sun, its steel and brass mechanisms at rest. Using her own key, she released the largish drawer numbered 357 and set it on a table in the center of the room. Then she left him alone with his key.

The quiet in here was perfect: the vault's thick walls denying any sound whatsoever. He tried his key, to see if it would open the double-locked safe deposit box without the tricky little lightning bolt inserted into the stem. The lock didn't turn.

He unbuckled his watch and lay it on the table beside the box. Then he snapped off the heel of his shoe and removed a retractable flat-headed screwdriver, minus a handle, that had served various purposes over the years. In this case, the narrow edge easily dislodged the back of his watch. The lightning bolt edged out of the gold disk with some difficulty but slotted easily into the key's stem. The lock now popped right open. He hinged open the top, letting it fall behind the box, and looked inside.

It was empty. But the point was made: he had a new conduit for the items he moved to and from the church in Templehof. It was not the first time, but it was by far the most secure and yet insecure location to which he'd been directed. A bank? Operating right under the nose of the authorities? Conrad wondered what Wolf was up to now, or if this was, somehow, David Call's operation. Lately, it had been hard to know where the interests of one ended and the other began.

He locked the box, reassembled his watch, and called the guard back in.

THE OFFICE WAS QUIET. Emilie had left over an hour ago with the American announcer Don Fennell, and Conrad didn't expect to see her at home until late. The affair had been going on for months. Nothing had been spoken, but clearly, Wolf had sanctioned it; he probably suspected Fennell of working for the CIC, the U.S. Army's Counter-intelligence Corps, and aimed to find out. Wolf had always worried most about the Americans under his nose, thus he brought them in closest, especially lately as a threat of nuclear engagement had been rumbling between the two sides.

"Drink?" It was Fred Hicks: big and sturdy as a farm boy, blond hair hiding threads of silver. The able body, light hair, and substantial, razor-sharp nose might have marked him as a German of an earlier era: an example of Aryan aspiration. Luckily those days were over, and Hicks was nothing but an aging American who had found himself in the postwar menagerie of allied and not-so-allied spies at RIAS.

It was late and Con was tired. But a drink with a colleague, and possibly an opportunity to sweep up some harmless dirt? "Why not?"

There was a bar two streets over. They found a quiet table at the back of the smoky room and sat quietly together until well into their first pints. A small black-and-white television perched behind the bar had lost its reception; Fassbinder's Frauen in New York rolled up the screen in incoherent frames. Conrad had seen it advertised lately but wasn't sorry to miss it. It would be broadcast again next year, certainly, and the following year, and if he never managed to catch it, well then, the world would somehow go on.

Conrad went to the bar to fetch a second round. When he returned, an envelope lay on the table. It looked as if it had been passed around, or carried around, for some time.

"Put it away," Hicks said, quietly. "I'm told you'll know what to do with this."

"You, too?" Conrad was always disappointed to realize it when a friend revealed a secret agenda. "I'd know what to do with it if I knew who you'd been talking to."

Hicks whispered, "Lehmann."

Another missive from Mischa Wolf to David Call.

Conrad slipped the envelope into the inside pocket of his jacket. In doing so, he felt something hard inside.

They didn't mention it again. After another half hour, they parted ways.

Conrad wasn't surprised to find the apartment quiet; Emilie hadn't yet returned. He considered having another beer but opted for a glass of water, instead. Seated alone at the kitchen table, the square of the curtainless window beaming dark night into the cold, white room, he reached into his pocket and withdrew the envelope. It was sealed. Nothing whatsoever was written on it. He lay it flat on the table and with a fingertip traced the edges of the hard object inside. It was a key. Another key. From its shape, he could tell that it was one of the old-fashioned skeleton keys that still floated around; the front door of his parents' East Berlin apartment took one just like it. He felt a wave of despair at the thought of his parents, whom he missed with a simmering desperation.

Lights off, Conrad lay on the couch watching shadows drift across the ceiling. He understood that he was to place this envelope, and this new key, inside box 357.

Emilie slipped into bed at three a.m.

At eight, he got up, showered, had his coffee, walked through a cold rain, and took the U-Bahn to Steglitz.

This time, the box wasn't empty.

A canvas sack, cinched at its neck by a drawstring, was nestled into the corner. He placed the key, still sealed inside its envelope, beside the box and picked up the sack. Whatever it held was solid and heavier than he'd expected. He pried open the knotted drawstring and stole a look.

A Soviet Makarov semi-automatic pistol sat in the sack as innocuously as if it were a can picked up from the market.

He didn't know why he was surprised; it seemed absurd to be. So he was to be a gun runner now, was that it? Or maybe even worse—a killer, like his wife? Had he graduated to something more lethal than parsing secrets?

The look of shock on Kolman Walz's face seven years ago, and the trail of bloody footsteps that marked the kindergarten teacher as the prime suspect in his wife's murder, swam vividly into Conrad's consciousness. And then wave upon wave of the tortured minutes that followed

—his friend being taken away, the awful realization that Monika was dead, Conrad shutting himself inside his apartment where he pulled all his most reliable rationalizations to the fore of his breaking consciousness as he struggled to suspend his disbelief long enough to maintain his survivalist's frame of thinking. He couldn't have allowed himself to think that Emilie had been involved in the murder. How could he live with her if he'd allowed himself to think that? Dissolving the marriage was out of the question; Call had made that clear from the beginning. Conrad and Emilie were a team. The strength of their covers lay in the misdirection of each other's differences.

Seven years ago, an investigation had revealed that Monika had been killed by a Tokarev pistol. Kolman had been found guilty not just of her murder but of prolonged and systematic espionage, against the Allied Forces, on behalf of the GDR, which of course was utter nonsense. During his trial, he'd denied all of it. His lawyer had waged a solid argument that Kolman had been born and raised in West Berlin and had never shown so much as an interest in socialism. Even so, the GDR won his extradition. Within a week, he was executed.

The Makarov, still in its sack, settled its weight into Conrad's reluctant hand. This wasn't the gun that had killed Monika or gotten Kolman executed. No. It was a different gun. But a Tokarev or a Makarov on German soil, east or west—didn't it all amount to the same thing?

Fingers trembling, Conrad struggled to pull closed the sack's drawstring and buried the pistol back in its corner of the box. No—he wouldn't deliver the goods to Templehof. The thought of more death sickened him.

He hurriedly locked up and called the guard before noticing the envelope Hicks had given him lying on the table; he'd failed to deposit it alongside the gun. Next time, maybe. The truth was, he felt a sentimental attachment to the idea of the old key he'd been carrying in his pocket. He'd resisted the urge to open the envelope and take a look, but maybe now he would.

He slid the envelope into his jacket pocket and left.

That night, when he was sure Emilie was asleep, he crept into the kitchen to make himself some tea. Once the kettle had boiled, he held Hicks's envelope over the steam until the glue let go. He dumped the key into his hand.

It was exactly like the keys that opened the doors in the building where he'd grown up: the rounded crown on top, the tubular stem ending in a rigid double-pronged foot. It had always amazed him that these keys weren't good for opening any old door, but somehow they weren't. He hadn't seen one for a long time and it felt good in his hand.

He slid the key into the pocket of his robe, hid the envelope at the bottom of the trash, and placed it outside the door to be taken down in the morning.

"Getting hot in here." Don Fennell stood at the urinal, waiting for Conrad's response. Two men, alone in a room, members exposed to the chilly air.

"I don't feel it," Conrad answered. He couldn't look Fennell in the eye, knowing that he'd slept with Emilie last night. In his heart, he didn't particularly care; but it was wrong. He hated this game. He thought again of Monika Walz, of her sweet freckled face, of her concern that she wouldn't be a good enough mother, of her murder.

"Your wife is…" Fennell couldn't, or wouldn't, in any case didn't finish the thought. Conrad knew what Emilie was. He knew her through and through. Nothing Fennell or any man could tell him would come as a surprise.

Conrad zipped up. Turned to face the blue-eyed American whose thick brown hair was still damp from his morning shower. "How's your show going, Fennell?"

Fennell didn't respond until after he'd closed his slacks and washed and dried his hands. Then, skin clean and pink, he reached into his pocket and produced a slip of paper on which he'd already scripted a message. Conrad could see, from the length and position of the string of digits, that it was an overseas phone number.

"Show's going well." Fennell pressed the paper into Conrad's hand. "Though lately, I wonder if my voice is going. I may be out of here soon. Well. If you ever need help with your show, let me know. I'm your man."

A week later, when Conrad returned to the bank at Steglitz on schedule, the gun was gone.

Silence is Suicide

"I have had to eat my own words many times, and I have found it a very nourishing diet."

--Winston Churchill

TWENTY-ONE

Where Are They Now?

NEW YORK CITY, May 26, 2013

THE BELLS of the Most Holy Redeemer resonated with eerie clarity. Larry stood on the threshold of her apartment, front door swung open, apricot sunshine bathing the wood floor. Listening. She'd spent the afternoon in the deep quiet of New York's satellite office of the National Archives, housed in the cavernous old Customs House grand with the luxuries of extraneous space and carved marble. She seemed to have carried the echoes home with her. Though the church bells had rung often during the years she'd lived here, the chiming now swung through her consciousness with subtle harmonies she'd never noticed before.

She carried her backpack over to the coffee table and emptied it. The flurry of paperwork she'd brought home from the archives fell like confetti over the low table, notes and photocopies settling among takeout containers and smeared dishes from last night's dinner. Her laptop, open where she'd left it on the corner of the table, had died in her absence.

Setting down her takeout coffee, she pried off the lid as carefully as she could, and took a long drink of it. Sat on the couch. Leaned back. Closed her eyes. The final bell transmuted to a memory of her phone ringing late that morning, just when she was waking up and starting to think about how to spend her day off. The surprisingly far away sound of Con's voice.

"Where are you?" was how she'd greeted him. It was Tuesday, and they hadn't spoken for a few days.

"Berlin. Long story. I'm about to get on a flight home and I need your help."

"You're in Germany?"

"Larry, just listen."

And then he'd told her everything he thought she'd need to know to wreck her head for the day. An insane mother-load about his life that had left her, still, to this moment, reeling in near disbelief. His father had been a spy. He had a birth mother. And a twin sister. It was a lot to take in all at once.

She kicked off her clogs, sending them flying halfway across the small living/dining room. Peeled off her socks and dropped them on the floor. Reaching down, she grasped her left foot in both hands and pressed her thumbs into the pad beneath her toes, trying to pressure some relief into a swollen bunion she'd earned from all those nights on stilettos. Whoever had decided that high heels were sexy was a sadist.

Barefoot to the bathroom, she stepped over a fallen towel to get to the medicine cabinet, and swallowed an Adderall; more coffee alone wasn't going to subdue the pinball machine of her brain for the rest of what promised to be a long night. She found the laptop charger flopped under her bed, still plugged into the wall behind her pillow, and yanked it free.

Con had told her that his father had been a Stasi agent during the Cold War—a spy and (supposedly) an assassin. Heady stuff. He'd instructed her to "Find out as much as you can about the Stasi, the Rosenholz files, and the US Army Counterintelligence Corps—the CIC, predecessor of the CIA. Specifically, see if there's any evidence that some of the Rosenholz files were missing when they were returned to Germany by the CIA. We'll go over it as soon as I'm back." His plane was due in at around ten o'clock that night.

"That's it?" She'd laughed. "Seriously, Connie, people get their PhDs in that stuff. You want it in one day?"

"Please," he begged; actually begged. That he didn't call her an asshole for calling him Connie meant he was dead serious. "And while you're at it, keep an eye open for the names Don Fennell, Lena Froebel, and Julian Wimmers."

She'd jotted it all down. "Who are they?"

"Froebel and Wimmers were covers for my real...my birth parents. But Don Fennell—he's the big question mark. We need to find him."

She'd sighed then, and promised, "I'll do my best." And she sighed now, looking at the mess she'd generated in the course of an afternoon.

While the Mac rebooted, she got down onto her knees and gathered all the papers into a single pile. The banner of the National Archives materialized like magic on her screen, landing her on the last page she'd visited under the subcategory Research our Records.

The archives contained a ton of information about World War Two and its aftermath and how all that had evolved into a broken and paranoid Germany. Stimulantcharged, Larry managed to focus on Con's specific mandate of Rosenholz, the CIC, and whether all the files were intact when Germany got them back from the U.S. in 2003. Right away, assumptions she hadn't even known she'd made started falling away.

Rosenholz, for instance, wasn't the name of a person— it meant Rosewood, and was the code name for a project by the Stasi to create a detailed record of its undercover agents working in West Germany under the auspices of Markus Wolf's counterespionage organization, the Hauptverwaltung Aufklärung, or HVA. Stasi chief Erich Mielke was worried that the United States might launch a nuclear assault in which case, in the chaos, they could lose track of their many agents. With good record keeping, they could know who was where and why and prioritize whose services were the most essential in the case of a crisis that, it turned out, never happened.

The files were comprised of three sets of information —the person index, detailing names and personal facts about individuals who might make good operatives; the operation cards, on which registration numbers identified specific operations along with the type of operation it was; and the basic agent statistics cards, bearing personal information about operatives, but not their real names. Together, the three sections of the Rosenholz files presented a puzzle that someone very determined might piece together with an eye to identifying agents. The files didn't make it easy, but they made it possible.

Rosenholz presented a mosaic of the activities of at least thirty thousand West Germans who had worked for the GDR's secret espionage service over the course of forty years, spying on neighbors and coworkers, serving as couriers, operating safe houses, even infiltrating the highest levels of West German government. It was incendiary stuff. In the chaos of the GDR's disintegration in 1989, the Stasi destroyed as many of its records as it could. But somehow, a copy of Rosenholz survived and fell into the hands of American intelligence.

Larry looked and looked, but found no evidence that the entire Rosenholz file wasn't eventually returned to Germany. She wondered why Con was so interested in a possible lapse. Glancing at her watch, she discovered that it was getting on seven o'clock and there was still lots to do before his plane landed.

As her findings accumulated, Larry composed a (long) sentence to share with Con about Rosenholz: It was a collection of information about Stasi counter-espionage operations and undercover spies working in West Germany; it was obtained by the Americans during the Cold War; and it was held by the CIA until 2003, when it was returned to Germany, apparently intact. She reached for her laptop to type it up, lest she forgot her sentence, the fruit of her haphazard labors.

Now she had to find out if his birth parents' names were included in the files.

Then she had to dig into the CIC archives looking for Don Fennell, Lena Froebel, and Julian Wimmers. And the RIAS radio station...while she was at it.

She felt the stirrings of hunger and thought of eating something, but decided to continue her research instead.

The archivist on duty had led her to the work of Germany's Birthler Commission, which had been tasked with literally piecing together tons of documents the Stasi had shredded during its last gasps of life. A group of women who spent their days puzzling the papers back together—they were actually called the "puzzle ladies"— had managed to reconstruct some of the Rosenholz files, linking operations with their code names, and cover names with an agent's real identity. Larry had been shocked to learn that those sensitive connections were being shared online, though the archive didn't make it easy to access. The archivist explained that it had been a subject of national debate in Germany up until the decision was made to risk exposure of former spies in the name of truth. As an undercover agent herself, Larry felt a jolt of desperation on behalf of those Cold War operatives whose covers were being unceremoniously divulged. The publication of an agent's real identity, in any form, at any time, was treason in the undercover world, potentially a death sentence outside it.

None of the covers Con had asked her to look for came up in the reconstructed Rosenholz files available online.

She wrote another, simpler sentence for her report: Don Fennell, Lena Froebel, and Julian Wimmers do not appear anywhere in the Rosenholz files.

Time was hurrying past, and since she was in the groove of it, she dipped into a few web pages about RIAS, the radio station, and came out with this to add to her notes for Con: RIAS stands for Radio in the American Sector. Based in West Berlin, it was operated by the US government from 1946 until the fall of the Wall in 1989, reporting on events as they unfolded. It was recast in 1993 as a German/American exchange program for radio journalists and is still operating today. Fennell, Froebel, and Wimmers were all employed by RIAS at various times between 1961-1978. After 1978 there is no record of any of them, anywhere.

It was dark out by the time Larry turned her attention to reading through issues of The Golden Sphinx, the newsletter of retired CIC operatives that the archivist had pointed her to. She organized her copies chronologically, starting with an issue from 1984.

The earlier issues were typed and photocopied, the later issues growing snazzier in their design and layout as the veterans got their hands on computers. They ran about twenty pages of fairly dense text, interspersed with photos of grinning seniors, sometimes (intriguingly) alongside grainy black-and-whites of their younger selves. Larry challenged herself to read every word and kept an eagle eye trained for those three names which, as she read, seemed unlikely to materialize in the sea of alphabet soup. Mostly the newsletters were bleak documents filled with veiled memories that, like inside jokes, were barely intelligible to Larry. The old spies kept it close to the vest. As she read forward, the obituaries increased—only in death were the former agents' real names revealed. The reminiscences grew bolder.

By nightfall, Larry had scrounged an old slice of pizza she'd had the foresight to store in the freezer and devoured every last crumb of the microwave-toughened crust, washed down by a tumbler of tepid tap water. She returned to the newsletters.

Her pulse thumped as her eye stumbled on something, in the winter 2003 issue, tucked into a bottom corner of the very last page:

Where Are They Now?
Jonas Heusler
Conrad Mathis, Sr.
Simon Engemann
Valerie Marin
David Volz
Maximillian Haberfelt
Reply: editor@cicrp.org

The boxed announcement startled her. First, because it

included Con's father's name in the raw, without the Julian Wimmers handle he'd hidden behind during his undercover days. Second, because if there was a group of names missing from Rosenholz, revealing their identities would be one way to tease old spies out of the shadows.

TWENTY-TWO

The Blue Letter

WEST BERLIN, January 9, 1978

CONRAD'S HAND rested between Emilie's breasts. Small and lovely, they'd grown softer over time. When they'd met, as teenagers, her breasts had been so firm they would spring back at the smallest pressure. Now, she gave way to him; when he touched her, when he entered her, her flesh conceded. Their bodies had learned to fit, just as their minds had learned to forget everything else when they were together, or at least pretend to forget.

He leaned over to kiss one of the pink starbursts of her nipples. Under his fingers, he could feel her ribs. They'd been lovers eighteen years, married sixteen. He had never known another woman, and so the gypsum coolness of her skin felt only natural. For a moment he wondered what the other men in her life thought of her body, and quickly forced the thought away.

He rested his face in the warm crest where his hand had been. He inhaled her vanilla scent.

She pushed him off. "I promised to meet Carla this morning. For breakfast."

The part about breakfast had been unnecessary. "Go ahead."

Carla was one of Emilie's West German "friends" who were either unaware that she was being spied on or preferred not to know. They met frequently for meals, discussed books, saw movies, took walks. Carla worked at the United Nations outpost in Berlin, and so was of particular interest to Emilie. As far as Conrad knew, his wife had no real friends.

Emilie walked naked to the bathroom and let the door slam shut behind her. Conrad lay on his back and glanced at the clock: it was not yet seven. He decided that he may as well get his day started, too.

He always visited Steglitz first thing Monday mornings, to deliver to the safe deposit box whatever was on his agenda, retrieve whatever his invisible contact had left for him, and deliver it to the drop at the church in Templehof, all before work. The relay took well over an hour.

He was at the bank by eight, flirting with the Monday morning guard, who no longer bothered to check his credentials as he was such a regular customer. He imagined that the bank was used to it; he couldn't have been the only one. For all he knew, she could have been an agent, herself.

The first thing he noticed, when he lifted the top off box 357, was the aroma of vanilla that wafted up at him. That he could still smell Emilie on his skin pleasantly surprised him.

He flipped over his necktie and pried apart the magnetized strips that held the fabric folded in shape. The negatives Hicks had given him scattered out of their waxy sleeve; there were four strips this time, six frames apiece. He slipped them back into the sleeve without bothering to look at them. Why should he? He was just the messenger. He placed the negatives in the box and picked up the items that had been left for him.

A bar of soap wrapped in green paper—something undoubtedly embedded inside.

A small plastic bag of fake wood buttons—for obscuring hidden camera lenses, he guessed.

A rubbery mound of something brown—crap, undoubtedly—that didn't look real enough to fool anyone.

An eight-by-ten manila envelope, clasped and sealed.

A blue international envelope—the kind of onion-skin stationery that folded over itself to seal with scant adhesive edges—which had been opened and clumsily reassembled. When he picked it up, the scent of vanilla grew stronger. It was as if Emilie was in the room with him. He thought of her breasts under his lips, just over an hour ago, and a shiver of pleasure ran through him. At the same time, he felt nothing for her, not in his heart, a dichotomy that always left him unsettled after they'd made love.

The blue envelope was addressed to him at his home address. The handwriting looked familiar—it was his mother's writing, he was sure of it. How long had she known where to find him?

His hands shook as he unfolded the fragile paper, flattened it on the table, and lifted it to the light to read.

My dearest Conrad,

I don't know if you'll receive this letter. How can I know? You haven't answered me in all these years you've been gone. I won't give up hope, though, and so I write to you again.

My darling son. I have the worst possible news. I am sorry.

Your father is gone.

A heart attack.

Mercifully, it was quick. But cruel. He was just sixty.

Your father loved you. He understood why you left us. I struggle with it more than he did. He knew you are a good boy. So do I—but why did you have to go?

I am still living at home if you want to find me some-day. For now, at least. Lately, I worry that my mind is slip-ping. More than that, I worry that we've wasted so much time.

Your loving mother

CONRAD PRESSED the letter to his nose, inhaling his wife's scent.

Emilie had touched the letter, held it, just as she'd touched and held him this morning. Sickness crept from his stomach into his brain.

She had put this here.

How long had she been intercepting his mail?

Why had this been left for him to find?

His father—dead.

The letter floated to the floor, making not a sound as it landed by Conrad's feet. He collapsed into a heap of little-boy and wept. He hadn't seen his parents in seventeen years. Why, why had he been so sure he'd somehow find them again? As if time and circumstance didn't devour you when you weren't paying the right kind of attention. As if you could call for a re-do. Take me back! I am better than the choices I have made!

The love he felt for his father was a hot, sharp knife pulling through his body. How could he get to his mother in time, before she also evaporated?

But he knew the answer. The Wall loomed high and

mighty in his mind. Wolf was powerful; he would have Conrad killed before he'd allow him to abandon the mission. It wasn't as if Wolf's reach didn't extend through both halves of Germany.

Conrad wept, the letter ruined in his hand, radiating vanilla.

CONRAD WATCHED his wife day and night. He needed to know how fully she had turned against him.

Emilie would leave the apartment first in the morning, and he'd be right behind her. She would leave work before he did, and he'd shadow her and her lover. Still Don Fennell, a fact of life Conrad despised all the more as he recognized and appreciated the bridge out that his rival had offered: an American phone number to be used if ever in need. But if he couldn't trust Emilie, how could he trust Fennell?

Conrad would make sure to get home first, so as not to arouse her suspicions. All these years, Emilie had had the upper hand in their marriage and their work. Now, convinced that she didn't suspect what he was up to, he experienced a trickle of unfamiliar power.

He surveilled her constantly but, to his surprise, never once did she visit the bank in Steglitz. And yet, on the following Monday, more items were waiting for him in the box. Nothing personal this time, and no more weapons, just more flotsam to be moved to Templehof.

Day to day, the sensation of power diminished, replaced by a fog of helplessness as he was reminded that no aspect of his life would ever be his own.

He went about his business. Worked. Ate. Slept beside Emilie. Sought, and failed, to sustain a rickety faith in his long pretending. But the seed had been planted. He had never nursed an illusion that he himself wasn't being watched or manipulated. They all were. But suddenly he felt plotted against, the paranoia moving through him with the force of a terminal growth.

On Monday morning, he paid his usual visit to the bank at Steglitz. This time, inside box 357, he found a bulky envelope spilling sheets of microfiche in clear wax sleeves. The package was marked Rosenholz, in Emilie's hand.

Conrad had picked up some chatter recently about an operation code-named Rosenholz, something about a collection of data which, pieced together, would reveal the identities and locations of every Stasi operative working in the west. It had instantly worried him. The implications of what might happen to covert operatives—like himself, like Emilie, like all of them—if such a trove of information fell into the wrong hands, were immense. He could begin to imagine who would want to gather such an incendiary collection of information into a single file, exposing true identities, putting all their lives in instant danger. But now, this morning, his concern wasn't so much about who had placed it here as what, exactly, he was supposed to do with it.

Was he actually expected to transmit Rosenholz to Templehof, right into the Americans' hands? Reveal to the enemy the secret identities of his fellow agents?

The scent of vanilla that lingered in the box resonated with Emilie, and Conrad suspected that his wife's hard-fought loyalty to her beloved GDR had been genuinely breached. He never would have expected it of her.

But then again, from the moment his father had sat him down all those years ago to lecture him about the improprieties of owning a bicycle when owning a bicycle had seemed like the most innocent of desires, nothing had been as he'd expected. Nothing.

Conrad took the envelope and stuffed it into his satchel. He locked the box, left the bank, and proceeded to the radio station. But, as with the gun and the key, he had no intention of running Rosenholz over to Templehof.

Later that night, while Emilie was out, he emptied the cabinet under the kitchen sink and, through the opening where the water pipes emerged, hid the file between the back of the cabinet and the wall where it could wait while he made up his mind.

THE BLUE LETTER lay open on the kitchen table. Conrad sat in his customary chair, sipping the bad red wine that he and Emilie bought for its cheap price. Food and drink for them had always been more about sustenance and effect than pleasure. The only real gratification they'd shared was sex, but now, ever since finding the letter, Conrad found that he had no desire for his wife. The scent he used to enjoy now repulsed him. It had taken a long time for their solipsistic marriage to die completely if it had ever truly been alive.

The apartment door squealed open. He heard her kick off her shoes. She walked into the kitchen and glanced at him. She had to have seen the letter but she didn't acknowledge it. Without asking, he poured her some wine in the glass he'd had at the ready.

"Long week," she said lazily, cringing at the first bitter taste of wine. "Trying to get the hang of the new show." Emilie had recently been transferred onto the production staff of the wildly popular comedy The Islanders, which Con found ironic, as she had no sense of humor.

He waited. Finally, her red-enameled fingertip wormed over to touch the edge of the letter.

Conrad asked, "What else of mine have you stolen?"

Her dark eyes snapped at his face. "Nothing." A horrid lie.

"I don't know how this is done in a situation like ours," he kept his tone calm in a hedge against a bubbling rage, his and hers, "but we won't be the first conscripted couple to call it quits. Will we need a lawyer, do you think, or can Wolf take care of it?"

"You want a divorce."

"I've never known you to state the obvious, Emilie."

She picked up the letter and read it carefully, as if for the first time. When she was finished, she put it down, and said without a trace of emotion, "I'm sorry about your father."

"Do you remember him?"

"He hated me." She smiled. "So did your mother, for that matter. What was I, seventeen?"

His parents had warned him against her; somehow, they had known she was bad news.

"I could move out," Conrad offered, "or you could go stay with Fennell until we get our living arrangements organized."

"I'm pregnant."

The words landed in a tangled lump in his brain, as the past echoed through him.

"Tell Fennell, not me."

"You're the one who needs to know."

"Are you joking?"

"Don and I haven't…" She waved her slender hand in the air. "I've been much more loyal to you than you realize, Conrad."

When she said this, her gaze was on a high corner of

the kitchen ceiling, not on him. He joined her in looking at an intricate cobweb woven at some point in the distant past. She was his wife, yes, but how could they possibly know whose baby it was? If she was even pregnant. If it wasn't another one of her deadly lies.

"This has to end, Emilie."

"You'll want to know your child," her tone hard, but persuasive, "and not from a distance. I know you, Conrad. You'll want to be fully immersed in his life."

"His?"

"Or her." Emilie's smile seemed genuine. A mirage. He remembered seeing her for the first time when they were teenagers: the surprise of her quick smile. He was thirty-seven years old now. She was thirty-six. It was late to start a family…and yet.

"How far along are you?" he asked.

"Two months. I wasn't sure until this morning."

Interesting timing. But he didn't say so. It didn't matter how long she'd known; what mattered was if it could possibly be true.

TWENTY-THREE

The Golden Sphinx

NEW YORK CITY, May 26, 2013

THE BUZZER BLASTED into the midnight quiet of Larry's apartment, startling her. She capped the lime-green highlighter and set it on top of the obituary she'd just printed for former CIC operative Jonas Heusler, a.k.a. Leon Jost. Navigating with only the anemic light from her two lamps (the overhead bulb had blown out a month ago), she sidestepped the gridwork of papers she'd assembled on the floor.

"Hey." Con's cheerful smile, when she opened the door, was betrayed by the dark crescents underscoring his eyes. The end of an angry scrape crawled out from under a crosshatch of Band-Aids on his cheek, and his hand was wrapped in an Ace bandage.

"What happened to you?"

"Long story. I'm fine. Did I wake you?"

"Are you kidding me? I'm neck-deep in your research. I thought you'd be here sooner."

"I dropped the buccal kits at Hogan. Kartara said he'd process them stat."

"He's fast when he wants to be."

"Listen, Larry, I'm sorry I threw all this at you like I did."

"No need to apologize. It took a while, but I get it now. Come." She held out her hand and led him inside to her masterwork. These last few hours, she had started to understand the source of his urgency, why he'd traveled so far on a moment's notice, and what he was after now. "I think that Emilie—"

"Mutti—her nickname's Mutti."

"I think Mutti might be onto something. Check it out."

Con stood in a puddle of darkness in the lamplit room, focusing not on the mind-boggling mess she'd made of her place but what she was telling him, what she was showing him. Printouts of obituaries were tiered across the floor beneath a single color-coded page of a Golden Sphinx newsletter dated winter 2003. In the middle of the chaos of dishes and paperwork, she had managed to create an island of organized clarity.

Kneeling, she picked up the newsletter. On the open page was an inset box containing a list of names, each of which she'd highlighted in a unique color that matched the highlighted headline of one of the obituaries. "Every one of them worked as an operative at RIAS during the Cold War. It starts with Jonas Heusler, then there's your father, then Simon Engemann, and then—"

"Larry, I can read." Con started out of order, picking up Engemann's obituary first. His frozen expression reflected the same surprise she'd felt upon first discovering the list and matching it to the obituaries. The vulnerability of the printed names. The certainty that death would follow.

There was so much to tell him, she couldn't wait. "The names are published and then, in this case, four weeks later, Engemann and his family perish together in a house fire, middle of the night. Your father is listed second, but he died third. So I'm not sure the order means anything."

Con raised his eyes off of Heusler's obituary from a 2004 LA Times, dated three weeks after The Golden Sphinx in which the list appeared, and looked at her, startled. "He also killed himself."

"Gunshot to the head. Con, everyone on the list died." She handed him Valerie Marin's obituary; she'd died of an overdose of sleeping pills. "She was an American, so was Engemann, but the rest were German. A few settled in the States, one was still in Germany, one was in Buenos Aires."

"And they all worked for U.S. intelligence?"

"Probably, otherwise why would their names be published in the CIC newsletter? Someone was looking for them, using their real names. None of them show up in the reconstructed Rosenholz files—I've checked every one— but the names all connect with an obituary. Look." She handed him another printout. "Volz was murdered in his sleep during an unsolved home invasion. Marin and Heusler were suicides, but this one, Haberfeld, died in a hit and run accident, driver never identified."

"There's no pattern to how they died."

"Nope. The names appeared all at once, but the deaths are spread out through the years after publication. I emailed the contact in the box. It bounces right back."

"That doesn't mean someone isn't making a connection with whoever tried to answer," Con said.

"Exactly." It was easy to hide in a maze of IP addresses; if you knew what you were doing, you could quickly drive the communication underground. "I was just about to put it all together in a single list with the names and dates and manner of death."

"A hit list." The way he said it. "It's even worse than Mutti thinks."

"I'd say so."

"What about Don Fennell—dig up anything about him?"

"Not yet."

"I'll take over," he said. "You get some sleep. Mind if I hang out here and keep working on it?"

"I'm staying up with you. I didn't come this far to not find out how it's going to turn out."

He threw an arm around her, buddy-style, and kissed the top of her head. The affectionate gesture pleased her. True to form, she pretended it was nothing, and asked, "What exactly does Mutti expect you to do when you find this guy Fennell?"

"Talk to him," Con said, "so he can fill in the blanks. Seems there's a lot she's not aware of. It's going to be an interesting conversation."

HE HAD A DEEP, creamy, sexy voice, Larry thought, lying on the couch and listening to Don Fennell read the news first in German and then in English. She hadn't thought of checking YouTube for archival material from RIAS, but Con thought of it right away. Interspersed with grim news from the east/west standoff were chirpy German songs. Larry couldn't tell what Fennell was saying in German, but his English sounded perfect.

"Which is he, do you think?" she asked Con, "German or American?"

"Mutti said he was American." He sat cross-legged on the floor, reading the last of the obituaries she'd linked to a

Golden Sphinx Where Are They Now ad. She checked through other RIAS samples, and, not finding another with Fennell announcing, clicked on an old television interview with Markus Wolf, the Stasi chief of counterintelligence in West Berlin.

"Con, look."

Wolf was a gray old man at the time of the interview, neatly dressed in a suit and tie, with a new haircut. "For those of us out in the cold, it was a battle to the death," he reminisced with a smile. Proud of turning politics into a war? Certainly not ashamed to call it one.

Larry searched for a clip with Julian Wimmer—Conrad Sr.—announcing, and, after nearly ten minutes, found one that lasted all of twenty-seven seconds. "Hallo Berlin, das ist Julian, live aus dem RIAS-Studio. Barry hat mich gebeten, meine Dylan-Riff heute, ja, wir haben ein wenig betrunken die andere Nacht und ich ging auf Dylan und nächste, was ich weiß, hier bin ich. Bob Dylan hat einen neuen für Sie. Bedecken Sie Ihre Ohren, easties, weil verboten in das hier ist die Zone." The voice was a little reedy, and a little cavernous, resonant, much like Con's.

"Do you have any idea what he's saying?" Larry asked.

"No. Play it again." He listened, gaze frozen on nothing.

She replayed it four times before he'd finally had enough. He was lying on the floor now, eyes closed, and she wondered if he'd fallen asleep. But then he rolled over and faced her and said, "Mutti was right about one thing: Dad didn't kill himself for no reason."

"Absolutely—that's clear."

"You know what I'm thinking?"

She did. "He was murdered."

They stared at each other, eyes locked in a click of recognition.

"I'm going to go see Artie in the morning," he said.

"I'm going with."

"You don't have to, Lar."

Because Artie was a scumbag. Because she'd left a job she'd liked at the DA's Investigation Division thanks to his obnoxious daily harassments. Because she'd often said that if she had to lay eyes on him again she just might slap that lawsuit on him after all.

"No. I want to."

Con smiled. "Good. And I swear, if he so much as makes an off-color crack about what happened between the two of you, I'll break his fucking neck."

Larry liked the sound of Con jumping to her defense. She played the Don Fennell clip again so they could memorize his voice: his round, deep, ice-cream-on-a-hot-day voice. When they faced Artie with the proposal to turn a suicide into a cold-case homicide investigation, they would have to do it with conviction.

TWENTY-FOUR

Facts Admissible in a Court of Law

NEW YORK CITY, May 26, 2013

"Yo, Con, wait up!"

Footsteps echoed off the hard surfaces: pale gray walls, darker-gray checkerboard linoleum, lit unkindly by cheap fluorescent tubes. And the wet cardboard smell that permeated the massive building. Even with your eyes closed, you would know that One Hogan Place housed a government bureaucracy. Con had long stopped noticing the smell, but since returning from Berlin his senses had been heightened, and now, his inner axis tilted, he was aware of everything. For instance: Larry. Her willingness to return to this place she hated; walking beside him, projecting a tranquility he was sure she didn't feel.

Con turned around to see Kartara step-slapping forward in his leather-soled shoes. He had on jeans, as usual, a paisley button-down, and translucent tortoiseshell glasses distinctly different from the boxy black ones he was wearing last night when Con dropped off the swabs. Definitely the most stylish tech in the lab.

"Get my message?" Kartara asked.

"Phone's out of juice." Con and Larry had fallen asleep, she in her bed, he on the couch, having reasoned that it was best to confront Artie without the delirium of exhaustion. "I was going to pop in to see you in a little while."

"I ran all the tests last night and double-checked them first thing this morning." By which Kartara meant afternoon, as he worked the night shift; about now, three o'clock, was when he started his day.

A knot of voices preceded a trio of agents making their way to Investigations.

Con, Larry, and Kartara stood against the wall to let them pass. Quietly, Con asked, "And?"

"Positive matches, all three. Definitely closely related, on the maternal side."

The news fell heavily; it was not what Con had hoped to hear. So it was true. Evil Emmy was his twin. Mysterious Mutti, his mother.

"You okay, buddy?"

"Fine. Just tired. It was a long night working this mother of a case—no pun intended."

"I hear you," Kartara said. "Hey, you know what they say: 'I'll sleep when I'm dead.' Fits this place. Who said that, anyway?"

"Warren Zevon," Larry answered, "I think."

"Thanks again." Con and Kartara pumped a quick handshake. "Much appreciated."

"Anytime."

Alone again in the hall, nearly at the door into Investigations, Larry whispered, "You didn't tell him the third swab was yours, did you?"

"Didn't want to complicate things. Said it was for a case."

"I would have done the same."

He opened the door and led her inside the bullpen she used to call a "rat's nest" before making her departure for the relative safe haven of a demotion to Vice.

"Ready?" he asked her.

She nodded, briskly, once. "Let's do it."

THE FIRST THING Larry noticed was that, in the year since she'd moved to the Vice Enforcement Division, which these days was just an offshoot of Narcotics, there were noticeably more women working here at Hogan. Nine now, maybe ten, in the Investigations Division. A sweep of her eye across the space informed her that most were riding desks, but still, it was a start. Investigations couldn't avoid deploying undercovers; common sense dictated that like it or not, some had to be women if you wanted to reflect the real world. Not Artie's big strength, reflecting reality. Thinking of him, she forced a deep breath and tugged Con closer to her side. She wouldn't have done this for anyone else.

Voice low, she asked, "You tell him I was coming?"

Con grinned. "Nope. Couldn't resist a chance to see the look on his face. All I told him was that I had something I needed to run by him, in person."

Artie blanched when Larry followed Con into his office. Afternoon sunlight bled through the slatted blinds, throwing bars of darkness across the desk. The shadowy stripes contorted their way up and over Artie's bulky shape, entangling him in a ghostly set of prison pajamas. An image that Larry thoroughly enjoyed.

"Hey!" Artie, sporting a sudden, plastic smile, stood up

and hurried around his desk. He reached both his hands to grasp hers as if she were a visiting dignitary. "Wow, great to see you."

"Hi, Artie." The flat tone was all she was willing to offer.

"What brings you… You know what? Never mind." He settled his hip on the edge of the desk and shielded himself behind crossed arms. Hairy, beefy arms protruding from nerdy shirtsleeves…stop. This was business; she had to try to discipline her thoughts, not drift back to the final moments of their last confrontation. But it wasn't easy. She could still see his sausagey finger, stiff in her face, and hear the sizzle of rage in his voice when he said…when he hissed….

"If you ever, ever—" he'd threatened on that crucial morning a year ago. Turning red. Realizing she had him if she wanted him.

"Ever what, boss?" That single word. He'd been her boss and he'd been smarmy with her one too many times. She wasn't the only woman in the office to have attracted his inappropriate attention, but she was the only one who'd dared to ply her trade and gather evidence.

Facts admissible in a court of law:

"Take it down a coupla buttons," he'd whispered in her ear, alone in his office one evening, touching his fingertip to the top button of her blouse, bringing his flesh this close to hers. "You're a lot sexier than you think."

That was her first bit of evidence. The second was an email message he'd sent her, using his personal account, when they were the last two in the office late one Friday night. "How about that drink you promised me? We can talk about your work. Or we could lighten up and have some fun. Your call."

Larry had never promised him a drink. It was obviously manipulative, the threat barely veiled: Come and get it; if I can't screw you, I can screw your career.

The morning she'd confronted him, after another night of beating her dilemma to death instead of sleeping, he told her, "Go ahead, show them what you got." And then, leaning closer, his breath hot on her face, he added the addendum of a whispered promise, "But trust me, when word gets out, no one's gonna hire you in law enforcement. Ever. Again."

The problem was that she knew he was right. She had him, but he had her, too. Larry loved her career and didn't want to see it end, so she'd settled for a transfer to the VED where she could work undercover from another angle. Theirs was a brokered peace. It had helped not to have laid eyes on each other since.

"So...what can I do you for?" Artie asked now. Producing the imitation of a smile. Lizard-eyes slithering between her and Con, who as agreed would do the talking until the whole story was told.

They sat down, and Con began.

Emmy. Mutti. The possibility that Con's father had been murdered. The hit list. Everything.

"THAT'S IT," Con finished. "The entire story, beginning to end, based on what I know right now."

Artie had moved behind the bulwark of his desk; Con guessed he felt safer the farthest he could get from Larry and the hate-rays she was beaming at her old boss. He knew how hard it was for her to be here. But having her with him, knowing the truth (or most of it: he hadn't told her about his first night with Emmy because how could he?), had made it easier for him to spell it out to Artie.

"That's a lot of heavy shit." Artie leaned back, elbows

perched on the arms of his chair, and steepled his fingers thoughtfully. "The autopsy they did on your dad didn't catch anything suspicious?"

"Broken bones from impact, death by drowning. Open and shut suicide."

"Nine years ago…who was the M.E.?"

"Tim Fisher," Con answered. Fisher had run a famously disorganized (in retrospect) medical examiner's office.

"Fisher—right. Not a stellar reputation. DA's had to reopen a few cases he botched."

Con leaned forward to make his pitch. "Let's reopen this one, Artie."

"I don't know, pal."

"We think my father was murdered. The two of us, last night—" Con tilted his head in Larry's direction. "We mapped it all out. Larry, show him."

She lifted her shoulder bag to her lap and removed the folded wad of highlighted pages. "Mind?" she asked, sweeping clear his desk with an aggressive gesture Artie didn't dare complain about beyond a limp, "Whoa there." Con sat back while she arranged her paperwork.

"It's all there," Con told Artie. "The whole picture. Take a minute—you'll see."

Larry narrated while Artie read through the documents. After, he swung back in his chair so hard it creaked. "You want to open a serial murder case."

"I want to reopen the file on my father's death, reclassified as a cold case. Yes."

"I'm not so sure this is a thing for our division. Shit, you've got people dying all kinds of ways, all over the place. Your dad alone…what tower did he, you know?"

"He was pushed off the west tower, landed on the Manhattan side of the bridge."

And as simply as that, in that single word—pushed—Con owned the new story of how he'd lost his father. The DNA had linked him to an unexpected parentage and a surprising past. What was printed on those pages were facts, hard pieces of correlating information that supported a different narrative than the one he'd retold himself a thousand times.

"I'm pretty sure Chinatown has jurisdiction over the west tower," Artie said. "But I dunno…the captain over at the 5th's a sonofabitch about his CompStat numbers. Guaranteed, he won't like adding a case like this."

"Who cares if he likes it?"

"That precinct banked zero homicides last year, it was a big fucking deal for them. He won't like the smell an old, complicated case like this is gonna leave on them."

"So what?" Con forced his voice out of the hot zone he was edging into, faced with Artie's objections, into a simmering compromise between insistent and angry. "If the murders are scattered, then everyone gets involved if they have to. You know that."

"Thing is, it's gonna be a bitch to coordinate. Ollison's gonna have a calf. And Newcombe—just last week he told us he's thinking hard about the cases we take on because our budget sucks and he might have to cut back. I don't even know when I could get his attention on this, anyway; he's been doing a shitload of fundraising for his BFF, Senator Rapp. Fucking Republicans. Suffice it to say, this isn't the best time."

"Am I really hearing this? We're talking about retired intelligence officers, some of them from the old CIA." Con shot up out of his seat, and Larry stood with him in a strange, gorgeous piece of choreography that bolstered his confidence like nothing else. "I'll take it to Ollison myself if I have to, Artie. You know I will."

"No need, Con." Larry's voice was admirably measured. "Sit down. Artie's going to make this happen."

Artie finally unzipped a raucous laugh. "Am I?"

"Matter of fact," Larry said, "you are. I can still file that harassment case in state court; there are two more years on the clock." Con was well aware that she knew exactly what the statute of limitations was on filing a sexual harassment suit—three hundred days in federal court, three years in a New York state or city court—because they'd discussed it enough times when she was toiling through her decision last year.

"You wouldn't."

"Wouldn't I?"

"You don't remember our conversation?"

"Sure I remember it. But you know what, Artie? After a year in stilettos, I don't give a crap anymore. Screw my job. This is more important."

Con was floored by the abandon of her promise that now, suddenly, after all this time and trouble, she was willing to walk away from her career. "Larry," he said, "don't."

"She doesn't mean it," Artie said, his tone unctuous with forced calm.

"Oh, I mean it. I've had enough. I'll do it in a minute. I'll do it right now." The way she stood there, her arms relaxed at her sides, cool as a breeze while Artie was sweating in the vivid bands of light dropping off his window. Either she meant it, or she was very good under stress—the latter, Con decided, because he knew she loved her job. He realized that he had never actually seen her working undercover until now; he was witnessing a truly great performance.

"Yeah," Artie rubbed a palm across the weed-swept dune of his balding head, "well," his eyes darted away from Larry onto something, or nothing, on his desk. "It'll be one whopper of a cold case, but I guess I can see what I can do."

By morning, a task force had gathered, and Con felt a wind at his back—the hot, glorious wind of Artie's fear—though maybe calling it a task force was grandiose. Chief of the Investigations Division (and Artie's boss), Carmel Ollison, in cahoots with the Captain of the 5th Precinct, had decided that they could afford (financially, politically) to throw a few people at it and see what stuck.

They were fixed up with a conference room at the Puzzle Palace, otherwise known as OPP or One Police Plaza—a brutalist concrete lump of a building that might have been thrown up by the GDR if they'd gotten their hands on New York in the seventies. Worn brown industrial carpeting. Smudged beige walls. Dropped ceiling mapped by a rusty water stain the shape of California. Table. Chairs. Triptych of dry erase boards bolted to the wall. They brought their own laptops.

And so, with five investigators of various stripes, it began.

The 5th sent over the original file from Conrad Sr.'s death in the hands of Yep Hong-quan, aka Tony Yep, a Chinese-American homicide detective assigned to the case for the rest of the week (two days) or as long as it took ("We'll see," Artie). Yep didn't look old enough to shave, but with a deep-barreled voice that could rival Johnny Cash's ooziest bass tones and his Chinatown-lifer slangy patois, he grew up leaps and bounds after a sentence or two.

The FBI contributed Special Agent Jace Suarez, clean-cut, thirtyish, soft-spoken, polite. He exuded hints of private school entitlements, though Con recognized that it was too soon to see behind the armor of the standard-issue uniform of dark suit and white shirt and tie that all the feds wore. Special Agent Suarez was charged with coordinating the jurisdictions that were implicated in the wide-ranging investigation and covering any federal aspects of the case. He would also serve as a liaison with the CIA, if necessary since some of the alleged murders had taken place overseas.

And then there was Homicide Detective Trinity Vandyke from the 61st Precinct in Coney Island, where one of the deaths—a bona fide murder—had occurred. Without meaning to, or wanting to, Con found himself peeling off layers of her appearance; not to get her naked, it wasn't that, but because there was something about her he couldn't quite place. She wore a noticeable amount of foundation on her brown skin, and whenever she blinked, a trace of gold eyeshadow sparkled on her lids. Her lips were glossed bubblegum-pink. Most of the female cops Con knew didn't pretty up for work, and he couldn't understand why Vandyke bothered; she was unusually good looking and certainly could have done without makeup on her worst days. Tall and stick-lean, a cascade of braids was braced behind her neck with a hairband. And then, in a flash, he caught what looked like the possibility of an early five o'clock shadow. An Adam's Apple swiveled up her throat when she spoke.

Con and Larry rounded out the five. Larry had strong-armed Artie to arrange her temporary transfer from the VED to Homicide in the 5th precinct, where she would team with Tony Yep.

As the day wore on, as the fledgling task force wired up and the story was told and retold, the pieces were put together and strategies and tactics were tossed around. By afternoon, they'd managed to identify three detectives, representing the farther-flung jurisdictions in which U.S. deaths connected to the names in The Golden Sphinx had occurred, who were willing to be Skyped in as needed.

They made slow, steady progress until the end of that first day when the investigation lurched forward in exactly the way you hoped an investigation would.

Suarez put down his phone and addressed the group. "A pal over at the Company dug into old CIC archives—Don Fennell was the Cold War handle for an agent named Lukas Blume. Guy worked as a radio jockey in New Jersey until he retired. Collects his government pension at an address in Princeton."

TWENTY-FIVE

Unambiguously Sharp

PRINCETON, *May 27, 2013*

THE LAST OF the three roommates finally leaves. Emmy throws off her covers and emerges, naked, from the tiny bedroom she had sublet from an economics major who'd left for an internship. Alone, at last, the apartment is quiet save for the chirping of birds outside. Occasionally, a car whooshes by on the suburban street. She stops in the shared bathroom, takes what she thinks is her toothbrush, and cleans her teeth. Splashes some bracingly cold water on her face. Surveys the cacophony of bruises that continue to mutate a rainbow across her face. The swelling is starting to go down.

In the slip of a kitchen, she opens the refrigerator and scans for breakfast. Her assigned half-shelf on the bottom right, helpfully labeled Hannah by the cheerful "Clara, I'm doing pre-med" when she arrived yesterday, is empty except for the remaining part of her wax-paper-wrapped sandwich she'd picked up at the airport along with two disposable cell phones, an international calling card, a bottle of peroxide and a box of hair dye. A strawberry yogurt in Mindy's corner catches her eye.

Sitting with her laptop at the dining nook table, Emmy savors the sweet yogurt on the tip of her tongue before swallowing the first spoonful. She clicks open YouTube and pulls up the two radio clips that led her here: one an old RIAS clip of Don Fennell speaking German in a deep, velvety voice; the other, a newer WNJT clip of a man with a different name but the same voice. Mutti thought Emmy couldn't find him herself, that she would need to follow Con. Well, Mutti was wrong. She found Lukas Blume a.k.a. Don Fennell—Fennellblume, as she's come to think of him—all on her own.

Emmy gets up to make some coffee, using grounds from a bag labeled Christine. While it brews, turning the air delicious, she examines the knives sheathed in a countertop butcher-block. It looks like something one of the roommates' mothers bought to outfit the student kitchen: six cooking knives with a variety of blades, each one unambiguously sharp. She pulls one out and runs her finger along the blunted top edge of the cold steel, wondering what it would be like to plunge it into someone's flesh. Gruesome, she imagines. Luckily, she was able to retrieve her gun from the subway bathroom, undisturbed, and won't have to resort to the theatrics of a slow kill.

By noon, her hair is blonde, orangey in spots, but she's transformed and thus pleased. She even lightens her eyebrows. She'll have to dye it all back to black before leaving the country as the dark-haired Hannah Treppel pictured in the passport Mutti gave her.

Christine has a fitted white blouse that looks great on Emmy with a pair of skinny jeans she finds in Clara's laundry hamper. Mindy has a big pair of camouflaging sunglasses tucked into her underwear drawer that will nicely conceal Emmy's eyes.

It's warm and breezy out, a pleasant walk along Witherspoon Street. She stops in at the Moon Doggie Cafe for a double espresso to give her jet-lagged brain another bump of caffeine for her visit to Town Hall to research voting records in the hope of finding the most recent home address for the man with the radio voice.

TWENTY-SIX

Unnecessary Deaths

WEST BERLIN, November 19, 1978

CONRAD LOOKED UP WHEN "MUTTI" swung open the bedroom door. Emilie had taken to referring to herself in the third person as Mom, a common nickname for an uncommon mother.

She asked, "Ready?"

"Just about." In the middle of changing little Con's diaper, the boy had almost gone to sleep. The plan was to let the babies nap in their strollers while the parents visited with Emilie's new friend Ilsa at a nearby café. Ilsa's son was just a month older than the twins, and the mothers had quickly grown close.

"Hurry. Emmy's about to blow." At three months old, the twins hadn't yet fallen into a regular nap schedule. You could hear Emmy fussing in the next room, winding up for the solid cry that generally preceded the little catnaps she took while her brother tended to sleep heartily.

"Why don't you go ahead?" Conrad suggested. "We'll meet you there."

She considered it a moment before agreeing. "Café Heisenberg. Don't take too long."

He listened to the whine of Emmy's pre-hysteria fade when Emilie wheeled her out and closed the apartment door.

Ten minutes later, Conrad was pushing Con in his stroller along the winding streets of Kreuzberg. He found the café on a garish wreck of a cobbled street, rough with graffiti, where he'd seen children in heavy makeup parading around at night. He was grateful that Emilie had chosen this spot for its proximity to their apartment, and was glad that his babies were young enough that they would never remember having been here.

Inside, the café was furnished with ratty mismatched chairs that looked like relics from the second world war. The place smelled deliciously of good, rich coffee. Ilsa and Emilie had taken over a pair of loveseats facing a chipped, over-painted table stained with coffee rings. Conrad saw that his wife had already bought his espresso, which he wished she hadn't, because it wouldn't be hot. He said nothing. Emmy was asleep in her stroller, but Ilsa's baby was nowhere in sight.

Ilsa sprang up smiling when he walked in. Tall and plumpish, with graying brown hair although she was barely into her thirties, she greeted him warmly with a kiss on both cheeks. They had met only once before, but her closeness to Emilie made it a given that they, too, ought to be friends. She fell to her knees to inspect Con, who slumped sideways, drugged by sleep.

"So handsome," Ilsa looked up at Conrad with a friendly wink, "just like his father."

"Watch it," Emilie laughed. "That's my husband."

The feigned jealousy was a joke he tolerated with a grin. He was the one who had cause for jealousy if only he'd cared enough. They were bound together by their children now, nothing else. He parked Con beside his sleeping sister, removed his jacket, and sat with his wife on the tattered loveseat facing their friend.

"I'm afraid I'm solo today," Ilsa apologized. "Wolfie fell asleep before I could get him out the door, so he stayed home with Papa."

"Unlike ours," Emilie said, "Wolfie's already a regular napper—guess we should have done this an hour earlier."

"Another coffee while I'm already up?" Ilsa asked Emilie. The women had already finished their first espressos.

"They're bitter here, don't you think?" Emilie complained.

"A bit. A little extra sugar did the trick."

"All right, then."

Ilsa waited while the counterman got to work.

Conrad tasted his coffee before deciding whether to sweeten it. "Mine's not bitter at all." He finished the rest in a single gulp.

"Another for you, too?" Ilsa asked, returning with two tiny steaming cups.

"No, thanks."

The women chatted, with Conrad listening, and the babies sleeping. He admired and loathed Emilie's facility to get people talking, and wished he could have warned Ilsa to hold back when it came to gossiping about her husband's brief association with Willy Brandt after he'd been elevated from mayor of West Berlin to chancellor of the Federal Republic of Germany—how frightened her husband was when Brandt's associate "turned out to be a Stasi rat." Emilie lapped it up. Conrad knew that she would report everything to Wolf. Conrad wouldn't; it wasn't his case, and anyway, Ilsa was a new mother… wasn't it right to show some mercy?

It couldn't have been ten, twelve minutes before little Emmy's blue eyes sprang open, as if alarmed by a noise, though the place was quiet. Conrad leaned in close to his daughter with a tender smile. He rocked the stroller with his foot and reached in to smooth a finger along the soft, agitated face. But he couldn't calm her. In moments, her mouth was wide with high decibel screams.

"Did you bring the bottles?" Emilie asked Conrad.

"Didn't you?"

Emilie caught her friend's eye and pursed her lips in the old female conspiracy about the shortcomings of men. Conrad ignored it, as he always did.

"I'll take her for a walk." He stood, about to put his jacket back on, when Emilie stopped him.

"Let me run her home and give her a bottle. I'll calm her down in half the time it takes you, and then I'll be back."

It was true: Emilie was better with Emmy. It had been that way from the very beginning.

Left alone, Ilsa checked her watch; he was sure she was about to make an excuse to leave now that her friend was gone. It would be awkward, just the two of them, given the way Emilie had elbowed them at the first suggestion of an imagined flirtation. But then Ilsa surprised him by touching her stomach with a grimace. A film of perspiration appeared on her forehead.

"I don't feel quite right," she said. "Shouldn't have had that second coffee. Be right back."

He watched her disappear down a long hall, toward a bathroom in the back. He looked at his son sleeping peacefully, drool threading down his chin. After a minute or two,

Conrad found himself beginning to doze, pulled irresistibly into a dream about…about…

"Excuse me." A sharp voice interrupted. Conrad startled awake to see a woman with glittery orange eye-shadow addressing the counterman. "I've been waiting for the bathroom for nearly half an hour. It's locked and no one answers. Do you think the door is stuck?"

"That's funny." The man dried his hands on a dishcloth tucked under his belt and followed the woman down the hall. Conrad heard the rattle of a locked door. When it refused to open by force, and when no one answered from inside, the counterman went to find some tools.

Little Con was still sleeping. Emilie and Emmy had not returned. Ilsa's wool coat was still draped over the opposite loveseat, but she was nowhere in sight. And now, Conrad was fully, electrically awake.

He stood up, feeling dazed, and started down the narrow hall. The walls were plastered with hand-written signs of offering and protest: people were looking for jobs, or organizing against the oppressiveness of the GDR, or hoping for love, or questioning the Allied occupation, or seeking homes, or trying to elect a new councilman, or searching for lost pets. The human drama went on and on. Hovering, he watched with unvarnished interest as the counterman put a screwdriver into the lock, unsuccessfully trying to open it from the outside. Conrad had a bad feeling about this. He should go, he knew he should go; he should take the baby and run, but something drew him forward.

"Let me help; I'm pretty good at that," he offered.

Conrad didn't dare reveal the miniature tools hidden in his shoe and struggled instead with the counterman's screwdriver until the telltale pop told him he'd found the sweet spot. The bathroom door sprung open.

Ilsa lay on the crusty tile floor, wet with vomit and water from the overflowed toilet. She must have struggled mightily in here, alone, before passing out.

"My God!" the orange-eyed woman shouted.

The counterman ran to call for help while Conrad entered the narrow bathroom to check for a pulse—he found one, though it was weak. A metallic chlorine smell hung like a fog in the bathroom. Was he insane, or did he also detect a faint scent of vanilla?

Conrad's pulse hammered at his ears, warning echoes that burst through his consciousness. He didn't have to be told what had happened, or who had done this. Emilie had poisoned her so-called friend. Ilsa was guilty of nothing. Monika had been guilty of nothing. They were bookended murders, unnecessary deaths, between which lay Emilie's inscrutable blood-lust of an agenda.

He wondered how many others she had killed. And why she had allowed him to glimpse this side of her.

It was a taunt, he was sure of it. Possibly also a warning.

His thoughts swung to Kolman, falsely accused of treason by both sides, and then railroaded into a swift execution. Conrad saw his future unfold in the school-teacher's fate. Cold nausea swept through him as he realized that the odds were against him.

Did Emilie know about his sequestration of the Rosenholz files? Did she know that he'd never passed along the envelope containing the key that Hicks had given to him? Was he to be her next victim in punishment for his transgressions?

The counterman was sweating when he returned with the news that help was on its way. Little Con had woken and was crying alone in his stroller.

"She's alive," Conrad told the man, "but only just. Did you clean the dishes from my wife's visit?"

"What?"

"If you haven't, don't. Evidence. Explain every detail to the police—remember, I arrived at least ten minutes after them. Sorry, but I have to go."

"Hey—"

Without pausing to console his son, Conrad pushed the stroller into the cold outside where, raw with agony, the thick skin of his denial finally ripped off.

It was over.

He should have escaped years ago, after Monika and Kolman Walz.

They never should have had children.

He shouldn't have come to her in the first place.

He should have known she'd turn her sights against him sooner or later.

CONRAD SLOTTED coin after coin into the payphone until he'd deposited enough for an international call. The baby had finally worn himself out with crying and fallen asleep again in his stroller. He probably needed a fresh diaper, a bottle, perhaps a change of clothes. Conrad had nothing left to offer his son but a difficult refuge with the long view in mind.

Don Fennell had gone back to America ten months ago. In all the time that Conrad had fantasized about dialing Fennell's number, which he'd carried with him as a pressure valve against hopelessness, it always rang through to an announcement that it had been disconnected. Of course, it would be. Why would Fennell want to help him? Only a truly desperate man would reach out to his enemy.

Indeed, it rang and rang. Conrad was about to hang up when an American voice came on the line.

"Hello?"

Conrad suddenly realized that, without knowing Fennell's real name, or whatever handle he was now operating under in the States, he didn't know who to ask for. And so he rather lamely said, in English, "I'm sorry."

Fennell switched to German. "Yes, Wimmers, I recognize your voice. Are you all right?"

"I'm calling from a payphone."

"Good man."

"Listen, I—"

"There are several flights a day out of Tegel through the Allied corridor. Fly straight into New York. You don't have to tell me you're coming, just let me know when you arrive. I'll help you get settled somewhere. That's the most I can do."

"I don't know how to thank you."

"Do you have the microfiche?"

Conrad answered, "Yes." There was no point asking how Fennell knew. They were spies, both of them—untrustworthy and untrusting—and they traded in each others' secrets as a means of survival. But handing Rosenholz over to the Americans was a terrifying prospect. "What will you do with it?"

"You have to work with me if you want me to—"

"I'll bring it," Conrad interrupted. "Do you also want the key?"

"Key?"

"Never mind. Just get me out of here."

"I can guess what you're up against," Fennell said. "Better get out fast."

He made it sound so easy. He didn't seem aware that Conrad and Emilie were now parents. It was true that

Conrad could quickly get his hands on the documents he'd need to travel…but how could he move so far from his mother, leave her in East Berlin? If he did, he was certain he'd never see her again. And what about his daughter? How could he possibly abandon her?

But Emilie had left him no choice.

He lurked half a block from their building until he saw her pushing Emmy in her stroller in the direction of the café, making her appearance for the final act. When she was out of sight, Conrad parked the stroller in the hall, carried his son inside, and gathered what he could.

Hurrying, he removed the skeleton key from where he'd taped it into the back of a bible, a book he knew Emilie would never open, and retrieved the damp envelope containing the sheets of microfiche from behind the kitchen sink.

He thought of Kolman, grabbed his son, and ran for his life.

TWENTY-SEVEN

Lair of an Old Spy

PRINCETON, May 27, 2013

FOOTSTEPS APPROACHED SLOWLY on the other side of the door. A plank of shadow had removed the sun from Con's face and, waiting, his skin began to cool. He flicked away an insect that landed on the back of his neck, and mentally rehearsed his cover: he was Walter Connelly, a volunteer. At the crack of a turning lock, Don Fennell's front door began to open.

Fennell a.k.a. Lukas Blume wore natty brown slippers, thin at the heels. The sleeves of his crisp yellow shirt were rolled up over knotted elbows. Tanned skin evoked a man who got out every day unless the ruddy face was a hallucinatory effect of the white hair and the youthfulness of his blue eyes. The long sinews of his neck, disappearing under his collar, reminded Con of puppetry.

"Come in." Blume pulled the door open, revealing the dark mouth of a downward stairway.

"I work with Cause for America," Con offered, despite

Blume's lack of inquisitiveness. "We're collecting data on gun control, and I'm assigned to interview veterans if you have a minute."

"I thought you'd cover as a reporter." Revealing the tombstones of his teeth, Blume smiled. "Or you could be with the Census—that could work, except you don't have any paperwork with you. A location scout would also work. But if you want to go with…what was it? Cause for America?"

Suddenly naked, Con willed himself steady, put out his hand, and introduced himself sans bullshit: "Okay. Con Mathis." Cold traveled up his spine; this felt like a ruinous exposure. Obviously, Blume had heard he'd be coming. Once a spy, always a spy; the grapevines never stopped circling.

"Lukas Blume." The hand was firm and dry. He opened the door all the way. "I've been expecting you."

EMMY UNFOLDS TO STANDING, her legs aching with relief, and leaves behind a rump-shaped indentation on a neighbor's freshly mowed lawn. The verdant scent of just-cut grass has lodged inside her nose—she stifles a sneeze. Only when Con is fully out of sight will she allow herself to disturb her carefully crafted quiet. External quiet. Inside her mind, it's all noise.

The long wait for him to appear has made her prolix with cooped-up words, swirling thoughts unmolded by decision. Mutti's proclamations of weakness and love echo and obstruct and complicate her thinking.

She notices a twitch at the back of Con's neck a moment before he appears to feel it, slapping at it from behind as if an insect has landed on his skin. But no: what he feels is her presence. She watches from around the side of the neighbor's house as he vanishes through Fennell-blume's door.

AN OLD MOSS-GREEN rug loped down the narrow staircase, its claustrophobic walls lined with the kind of grim wood paneling popular in the seventies. A door at the foot of the stairs opened into a large English basement, high, short windows like hooded eyes. Living room, dining table, discreet kitchen, all combined in a single room much like Con's incinerated apartment in Brooklyn. On a neat desk, the kaleidoscopic elements of a laptop screensaver continuously rearranged themselves without adherence to either gravity or logic. So this was the lair of an old spy.

Blume settled himself into one of a pair of facing couches, long legs crossed at the knee, slipper dangling off a raised foot. Nearby, on the floor, sat some kind of medical equipment, a tangle of plastic tubes. A silver canister that Con guessed was an oxygen tank leaned against it.

With a tone that put Con on guard, Blume asked, "So, Con Mathis, who do you work for?"

"Since we're cutting to the chase, why don't I ask you the same thing?"

"I'm retired."

"You said you were expecting me."

"I still have friends. When I hear someone's asking about me, I ask back, but I only got the broadest outlines. Something about an old case and a new task force. So… you know a little something about me, but I don't know anything about you. We should start on equal ground."

"What," Con asked, "do you think we're starting? Just so we agree."

"Sit down." Spoken like a mildly disgruntled teacher.

And like a chastened student, Con complied, occupying the couch opposite Blume.

"I'm an investigator with the New York District Attorney's office. I work undercover for the Investigations Division." Con was sure he had never spoken so plainly to an outsider about his work. Modulating his breathing, he vanquished the trickle of anxiety that threatened to redden his face and drench him in sweat. Blume watched him closely, and Con sensed that the older man knew what he was experiencing. Blume had been there, done that, and now he was retired except that you could never actually retire from this kind of work.

"White-collar crime?" Blume said. "I wonder if you're barking up the wrong tree—in whatever forest you're in."

"What forest are you in?"

There was little humor in Blume's laugh. "I'm a retired radio announcer. I worked at WNJT, a local NPR station out of Trenton."

"Retired how long?"

"Six years."

"Ever married?"

"Not really."

That answer could have meant anything. Con let it go. Sat forward. "I know that you worked for RIAS during the Cold War. How long were you with the CIC?"

He was sure he saw a quick mobilization occur behind Blume's eyes: the rejiggering of strategy that went with a newly defined understanding. Which was essentially what Con had just gone through, moments ago, at Blume's door. The old man hadn't expected this, either. "Ah," he said, at last.

"You were Don Fennell then."

Blume's eyebrows lifted, mouth pursed. "So, Con

Mathis. I knew a Conrad Mathis once, a long time ago, when he went by another name."

"Julian Wimmers," Con said.

"That's right. Or Conrad Schumann, depending on the day. He moved here and changed his name to Mathis, with my help. And you're Con Mathis. Yes, I see."

"How well did you know my father?"

"Julian Wimmers was someone I worked with in Berlin, after the war."

"He died nine years ago."

"Yes, I heard he committed suicide. I'm sorry for your loss."

A long exhalation ended in a spate of violent coughing. Blume plugged a plastic cannula into his nose, turned on the machine, and for a minute or two just sat there, breathing. Con disliked the motorized humming that had replaced their conversation. At first. Until he understood that Blume was still communicating with him.

"Emphysema?" Con's maternal grandfather, Ruth's father, had gradually suffocated from the disease until it killed him.

Blume nodded.

"I'm sorry."

"But this isn't a sick visit. I could die in front of you, so you better get to it. You came here for something, didn't you?"

"I did." Con leaned forward and looked Blume in the eyes. "Do you remember Lena Froebel?"

THE EDGE of the house where Blume rents a basement apartment is seamed with bricks, affixed to the side of the foundation with cement, in what looks like a jerry-rigged effort at keeping natural life at bay. Thanks to this anomaly, all four windows peeking into the English basement are sealed at the bottom, where brick cements to rotted frame. By the look of it, the windows would open from the top only four inches or so. All the windows are closed and Emmy can't hear a thing, but she can see through the murky glass.

She kneels beside one of the windows. There they are, across the apartment: the back of Fennelblume's white head and Con sitting on the facing couch, elbows on knees, body pitched forward, talking with an energy that disturbs her. His existence disturbs her; the mere fact of him. Her tendency to like him. How he clearly thinks little of her.

Hesitation rears up. She steels herself with thoughts of Mutti and the promise of what lies ahead if she does this. All the money. A better future. Love, maybe.

"Yes," Blume answered. "I knew Lena."

"Emilie Schumann, that's her real name. But you must already know that, too."

Blume nodded.

"She told me to find you."

"I hadn't realized...well."

"What?"

"You won't possibly remember, but I met you once before. When you were a baby. Your father reached out to me for help. He needed to get out of Germany, fast."

"Why?"

"You've heard the phrase 'Silence is Suicide'?"

"Of course."

"Any idea what it means?"

"I've never really thought about it."

"It was the slogan of the KgU—the Fighters Against Inhumanity. The founder of the KgU was Rainer Hildebrandt. He was an anti-communist resistance fighter, and as soon as I met him, so was I. Hildebrandt was my hero. He was the reason I went to work for RIAS. The CIC collaborated with the KgU on all kinds of projects aimed to free East Germans who were being trapped by what Hildebrandt, and I, and many others, deeply believed was a dangerous shift away from democracy, in a country that had just been devastated by a cruel war. It was a ridiculously bad time for people who happened to live in the east. RIAS was one of Hildebrandt's and the CIC's hubs for real information, but also disinformation."

"And the Stasi's, too, from the sound of it."

"We were all there. Yes. Hungry rats in the same nest."

"What was my father running from—exactly?"

"How well do you know Lena?"

"I only just met her."

"Do you trust her?"

"Should I?"

Blume stared at Con for a moment that stretched too long. "I worked and lived in the cold for many years. The CIC was and is a brotherhood, but no one trusted anyone. You couldn't. We worked together, we worked apart, we worked with each other, against each other. It was each man, and woman, for himself. The only person I trusted was Hildebrandt."

"What was my father running from, exactly?" Con asked.

"How about a drink?" Blume removed the cannula, crossed the all-purpose room, and returned a few moments later with a bottle of vodka and a pair of scratched water tumblers. He poured two fingers each. "Prost."

"It's still morning, and I have to drive back to the city."

"And you're working. I know, I know. Do whatever you want."

Con ignored his drink while Blume settled into his, wheezing after the first swallow, reaching for another hit of oxygen.

"You okay?"

"Lena worked for Mischa Wolf—"

"Yes," Con interrupted, "I know."

"Good. I'll get right to the point then." Another sip of vodka, the glass now balanced on the old man's knee. "Lena did a lot of things for Wolf. They were close. She was one of his moles at RIAS—so was your father. This is how I knew them. I was there too, as a swan."

"A swan?"

"I was to woo her, romantically. It was part of my assignment."

Con listened. Mutti had failed to mention that.

"Ostensibly, she didn't know that I worked for the CIC, and I didn't know she was with the Stasi. But, of course, as it turned out, we both knew. She was also a swan. We tested each other constantly, and at the same time it was a perfect affair; we were willfully blind to each other's weaknesses."

"How long did it last? Between you two."

Instead of answering, Blume said, "Mutti was also one of Wolf's assassins, and she was said to be good."

Con's pulse jumped. He sat forward. "She told me that my father was an assassin for Wolf. So they were both—"

"No. Not your father." Blume reached for a sip of air, a gulp of drink. "Lena pushed things too far with her last hit. A woman named Ilsa…can't remember her last name. A young mother."

"Ilsa Vogel. She told me my father killed Ilsa, and that's why he ran."

Blume shook his head. "I'll ask you again: Do you trust

your mother? Right now, that's probably the most important answer you'll need."

Emmy hunches down at the rumble of a car passing, and
then the street falls quiet again. She shades her eyes against
the bright sun, assessing the situation.

No car in the driveway. Not a sound coming from
inside the house.

She can see into the landlord's kitchen from where she
stands: outdated, all white, meticulous.

A small porch leads to the back door, secured with a
flimsy lock. Using a stone from the garden, she breaks a
low pane of glass…and waits. Sure enough, out here in the
middle of suburban nowhere, nothing happens. She is
careful not to cut her arm, reaching in to twist the pinch-
hold. The door falls open.

Worn linoleum squeaks underfoot in the antiseptic
kitchen. A neat stack of mail sits on a Formica table. A
matching pair of small cat dishes are parked beside a
refrigerator whose buzz is the only sound.

Vaporous male voices rise through the floor and she
freezes, listening, but Emmy can't make out their words.
Quietly, she proceeds, searching for an inner door that will
lead down to Blumc's basement apartment. She locates it
easily. This time, the pinch lock is already broken. She sets
her purse on the floor and fishes out the gun. Pushes the
door open until it gapes onto a dark stairway that smells of
mold and dust. Slowly, careful not to provoke complaints
from the old wooden steps, she takes her first step down,
underwater voices swimming closer.

Con sipped his vodka, despite his better judgment.

"Lena was a master assassin. But her weakness was hubris—she finally took things a little too far."

"What happened to Ilsa?"

"Your mother had worked out a pretty good m.o. that kept her clear of a lot of trouble over the years. That's one of the reasons Wolf liked her so much—she'd get in, and she'd get out. Neat and clean. But Ilsa…Ilsa was a mess." Blume paused for oxygen. "Lena would only do a hit once she knew someone else would be held accountable; she took down two birds for every stone, and she was a sure shot, regardless of the weapon she chose. She was that good. But Ilsa turned into a mess when your father saw what Lena was trying to do to him, and he got out. He took you and ran."

Con's throat warmed from the booze. He took another sip. A buzz was clearing space in the bracken for his mind to process what Blume was telling him. "She was going to frame him for murder?"

Blume nodded. Finished his drink. "You wouldn't be sitting here right now, to all appearances a full-fledged American, if not for your father's quick reflexes. The moment he saw that she was turning against him, he got the hell out."

"Mutti didn't tell me any of this."

"You actually call her Mutti?" Con couldn't read Blume's reaction: grimace, or smile. Whatever it was, it was packed with unmistakable irony. He repeated, "Mutti."

"It's what my sister calls her."

"Yes, I heard. Twins, born in the west, and Lena kept the girl. When Wolf got wind of your father's defection, Lena caught hell. Wolf stationed her back in the eastern zone, he couldn't trust her anymore because all of the Allied operatives knew exactly what went down with Ilsa, Julian, the marriage, all of it. After that, from what I heard, Lena worked as an IM—a run-of-the-mill informer. It was a big step down. She couldn't have been happy about it."

Born in the west? The words ring in Emmy's ears.

All her life, Mutti had painted quite the bedtime story about the meager circumstances of Emmy's birth, bedecking both of them in accolades for the valor of their mutual sacrifices. The underequipped birthing room at a subpar hospital in the eastern zone: how the mother, weak, collapsed with exhaustion, had managed one more push to expel the baby; how this squall of a newborn had landed on a cold metal table and after a brisk slap started wailing; how this harsh entrance into a difficult world had only strengthened the mother's resolve and straightened the baby's spine. That was how Mutti put it: "straightened your spine."

Born in the west? Had she, in reality, landed into the warm hands of a doctor? At a decent hospital? Had she been cleaned up and swaddled in warm flannel? Had her mother's pain been anesthetized? Had Mutti even been awake for her birth, or had she chosen from a menu of palliatives that included oblivion?

Born in the west. And then smuggled into hardship, her story rewritten, before memory could argue otherwise. Separated from a father apparently generous with his love, from a twin who might have kept her temperate; ripped from a soft landing and hurled into the cold.

Had Mutti really been prepared to frame her own husband, the father of her babies, for a murder that she herself had committed?

A red-hot fury blooms in Emmy's naval and spreads, luminous, throughout her body. Fills her mind.

Her life, sacrificed then for her mother's mistakes, sacrificed now for her mother's ambitions.

Rage uncoils as she listens by the door. Word by word, she is reinvented.

"ONE MORE THING," Con said. "Rosenholz."

"Yes, of course. Rosenholz. Your father brought a copy of the files out with him. It was his price of admission. He handed it over at the airport, and I gave him his new name and an address where he could stay. It was the last time I saw him."

"How did he get hold of the files in the first place?"

"My guess? Your mother was passing it to David Call, one of my CIC colleagues at RIAS, and your father somehow got his hands on it. I still don't know Call's real name. I had my suspicions that he was doubling for the GDR. He was also a swan, and let's just say that he knew your mother pretty well."

Mutti certainly got around; she hadn't mentioned that, either. "This David Call, what happened to him?"

"That's a good question. I've been trying to figure it out, myself."

"So, once you had the Rosenholz files—"

"I immediately handed them over to the CIC. But I was no fool: I made a copy for myself and stashed it away."

"What did we do with it—the Americans?"

"They were held on account for future negotiations that never came to pass." Blume sat forward to put his drink on the table with a punctuating slap of glass on wood. "Things move on. Change. What you know as your life settles into history. The CIC was turned into the CIA and eventually the files were like a denuded bomb. So we returned them to Germany in 2003. As it happens, the real value of Rosenholz is to the German public. People who remembered, thousands of people whose lives were destroyed by the Stasi or whose families were hurt, used the files to look back and find out who betrayed them. Names—covers, real identities. It was all there."

"Was it?"

Deep wrinkles fanned across Blume's face. He sipped his oxygen, sipped his drink. Eyes clouded, he asked, "How did you know?"

"My father wrote something in his journal about his name not turning up in Rosenholz, how because of that, he knew he would never get away. The other ops were dying, he wrote."

"Julian was always clever."

Con received that as a compliment on behalf of his late father. Maybe this tough old man had been a friend.

"After I retired and had some time on my hands, curiosity led me back to the files. The Germans were piecing Rosenholz together and putting it online, and so I paid attention. I began to realize that there was nothing about our operation at RIAS—no names, no references, nothing at all. It was a blank. The only thing I could think of was that the CIA had deliberately withheld that part of the files. Naturally, I wondered why."

"So it was you who published the names in The Golden Sphinx."

"I hoped to find my old colleagues, to talk to them. My only goal was to get the history right before I die. I put my life on the line to serve my country. The truth matters to me."

Blume's search for truth resonated with Con; after all, he was here for the same reason. But something wasn't sitting right.

Deaths had followed the publication of the names.

"What's the point of killing them all?" Con asked.

The blue eyes ignited. Shaking his head, Blume yanked the tubes out of his nose and breathed on his own. "So that's what you think. You said your father died; you didn't say he killed himself. I like your precision. You believe it wasn't suicide."

"He was murdered. But I think you know that."

Wheezing, Blume plugged the cannula back in.

Con forged ahead. "In 2003, his real name was published in The Golden Sphinx along with a list of others. Soon after, one of them, Jonas Heusler, puts a bullet in his own head. Then another one, Simon Engemann, dies in a house fire. Then my father jumps off a bridge. And the list goes on. You publish, they die."

A haze seemed to pass over Blume. "Yes," he said quietly, "I'm aware of that."

"Why didn't you just try to contact them privately? Why publish their names?"

"I tried, briefly, and got nowhere. I thought I might have better luck if I reached out through the newsletter. It was a mistake."

"I'd say so."

"I had nothing to do with those deaths. In fact, when I saw what was happening, I deliberately withheld the other names as I decoded them."

"There are more?"

"Let me tell you," Blume leaned forward, sharp gaze intent on Con, and spoke fiercely, "who I believe is behind all the deaths."

.   .   .

Emmy's ears ring and ring with the layering of truths upon truths. Accusations upon accusations. The cacophony of everyone trying to get what they want.

She knows what Fennellblume is going to say before he says it: "Your Mutti."

She figured out long ago that her mother was and is an assassin; but now, fit into this new framework, that knowledge takes on a different shape.

The possibility that there is no money crystallizes in Emmy's mind; that, once she's completed the "job," she'll be allowed at best to walk away into the chill of her own remorse, or at worst her own name will appear on the list and Mutti will have her twisted world all to herself.

A world in which you forfeit one child and ruin another.

In which you frame your husband for your own crimes.

The gun grows warm as it settles heavily in Emmy's hand. Mutti asked her if she could do it, if she was ready. Her finger twitches into the trigger.

Yes, the answer is yes.

She can do this thing for which she has been preparing her entire life.

"Your mother was a double agent," Blume told Con, "just like so many of the 'weak fools' she despised. David Call broke her. She hated him. If I know her, she still hates him."

"You're sure about this?"

"This is not a woman who goes easily into the night."

Con thought of his father escaping Mutti. And then thought of himself, now, writhing in her net.

"Your mother's strategy was always to eliminate obstacles so she could reach her prey. Two birds with one stone, remember. In this case, several birds have gone down."

"You really think she's the one who killed all those old operatives?"

"It's my best guess. Until I put those names out there, as far as she knew, her past was safe from scrutiny. There was no public record in Rosenholz of Lena Froebel, of any of our old covers at the radio station. None of us would ever be asked any questions. No one would ever talk. She was going to get away with everything."

Con felt sick to realize that he had been manipulated by his own mother. They all had, even Emmy—confused, angry Emmy. If Blume was right, everyone was fodder for Mutti's larger agenda. "Why am I really here?"

"You're her son, but you only met her recently."

"That's right."

"What else did she give you, other than my old handle?"

"She told me that my father was an assassin. And then she gave me Don Fennell—she gave me you."

"She's probably known for a long time that I'm the one who published the names in the Sphinx. There are only three names left. She would know that one is hers."

"She said she wasn't afraid."

"Of course she told you that. She's a good liar, isn't she?"

"What are the other two names?" Con asked.

"Mine, for one."

"And?"

"David Call. He's been the hardest to decode, I'm still working on him, but my guess is that she already knows who he is—otherwise she never would have sent you to me. Obviously, she doesn't need me around anymore to reveal his identity, if she already knows it."

Con was shocked to realize what Blume meant. "You think I came here to kill you?"

"I don't know what you thought you were doing, but I know how she thinks. I'm next on the list. Once I'm out of the way, she'll have a clear shot at Call. Maybe he has some special value to her—whoever he is."

Con's mind returned to that surreal late afternoon in Berlin, the purple twilight fading to darkness outside the window, the way all the light was sucked away from Mutti's face until finally she turned on a tepid light.

"When she gave me your name," Con told Blume, "she also gave it to my sister. Emmy. She's a lot like our mother."

Blume's forehead rippled. "Where is she now?"

"I'm not sure."

If the story Blume had told was accurate—that Mutti was the one taking vengeance on old enemies when all Blume had done was reveal them—then he wasn't safe. Suddenly Con's real purpose here shimmered into focus: his job was to find Don Fennell; Emmy's was to follow him and finish Blume off.

Con scanned the apartment: four windows, all high up and sealed. Two doors: the one through which he'd entered, and two others, both closed.

The empty vodka glasses rattled on the coffee table when Con abruptly stood. "Which one's the bathroom?" he asked Blume, crossing toward the pair of doors.

"On the right."

Behind the left door, Con was sure he heard the soft retreat of footsteps and the squealing complaint of an old stair. And then, silence. He flung open the door; hollow and light, it nearly ripped off its hinges. An empty stairway led up, presumably into the main house. At the top, another door hung open.

Con spun around to look at Blume, who calmly replaced his cannula, unfazed. "Lukas, you can't stay here. It isn't safe."

"Let her find me. I'll tell her exactly what I told you. It doesn't matter what happens to me after that."

TWENTY-EIGHT

A Necessary Life

NEW YORK CITY, August 6, 1979

CONRAD CAUGHT up with his toddling son in front of a storefront window on Broadway, just shy of Ninety-first Street. Behind the polished glass, a dozen televisions were tuned to the same channel showing Yankee Stadium. Players were lined up in a moment of silence, their hands clasped behind their backs, in front of an enormous screen showing an image of the team's caption Thurman Munson on the field, dramatically mustachioed, wearing a helmet and a mitt. Munson had died suddenly a few days earlier, at the age of thirty-two, and in some quarters of the baseball-crazed city life had nearly come to a halt. Mesmerized by the repeated image, little Con paused long enough for his father to gather up his hand. Con tried to tug it away, so he could run off again, but this time Conrad had him.

"Not again, my little man," he whispered in broken English.

Laughing uproariously, Con snatched his small hand out of his father's sweaty grasp. August in this city was unbearably humid. Conrad's face dripping, he ran, once again, after his son.

On the corner of Ninety-first Street, a woman appeared out of nowhere just in time to stop the boy from hurdling into traffic. She scooped him up and threw him over his shoulder as if he weighed nothing, though Con was big and sturdy. When Conrad approached, he put out his arms and she handed him over.

"Fast little rascal," she said.

"Thank you."

"I work at a nursery school, so I'm used to it."

Conrad thought immediately of Monika Walz, and his heart sank. Since arriving in the States nine months ago, he'd heard that Ilsa had died. He'd been right: Mutti had tried to plant evidence implicating him in her poisoning, but someone must have been watching over him because the suggestion didn't stick. Someone must have also been watching over Mutti because, as usual, she'd walked scot-free. Whenever his mind drifted to Mutti now, it flew to Emmy, and the guilt of his parental abandonment crusaded through his mind.

"Where are you from?" the woman was asking him now. She was attractive, small with lush brown hair to her shoulders and a round, welcoming face.

Conrad shook himself free from distraction, and answered, "Germany."

"Wow."

Conrad didn't know how to respond; he still wasn't used to Americans and the simplicity of their declarative statements.

"How old is Hans here?"

"Con. He's just one."

"And already he runs like that?" She looked truly impressed.

"He walked at nine months if you can believe that."

"I do if you say so."

"Well, thank you again."

"What's your name?"

"Conrad. And you?"

"I'm Ruth."

Her eyes were luminous hazel marbles. He couldn't think of what to say, but he didn't want to lose her attention. "Do you like baseball?"

"Not me. I guess you do, though. I saw you watching the Munson thing just before."

"Actually, I prefer museums. I wonder if you'd like to join me…I hear the Metropolitan Museum has something interesting at the moment."

"They've always got something interesting, sure, but sorry. I don't go out with married guys."

"Of course." Conrad felt like a fool; he should have explained sooner. "I'm here alone. No wife. It's just me and my boy."

"You left her back in Germany?"

"Yes. For good." He'd heard that, after his defection, Emilie had taken their daughter and fled to the relative safety of the Soviet zone in the east.

"Okay. How about Saturday afternoon? But you've got to bring him along."

Con nuzzled his face into his father's neck, as if lovestruck. "Yes," Conrad answered. "Of course."

TWENTY-NINE

Your Friend Dostoyevsky

NEW YORK CITY, May 27, 2013

JUST OUT OF THE ELEVATOR, Con could hear the hive of the task force buzzing in its conference room partway down the hall. He had a lot to report, not the least of which involved his concern for Lukas Blume's safety. Preoccupied, he didn't notice Artie coming down the hall until he heard his voice.

"Just the man I was hoping to see." Artie smiled. "So—I just got some very interesting news about your friend Dostoyevsky."

Con was surprised to see Artie away from his comfort zone at Hogan; one perk of the investigation being based at OPP had been less interference from his skeptical boss. But Artie got out and about, meetings and lunches and whatnot. Or maybe he'd stopped in just to pry. "I keep telling you, Artie—the guy's not my friend."

"Guess what?" Artie's eyebrows popped high onto his

forehead, sending a flourish of wrinkles over the dome of his scalp. "Guy turned up dead on a beach."

The news was stunning at first, and quickly predictable. "Where?"

"Rockaways. Some lady walking her dog this morning found him. No blood, no struggle. Just dead. Medical examiner's got him now. EMS techs reported froth on his lips. Maybe he drank something."

Dvorshetskii had some mammoth troubles on his plate; poison would have seemed like a viable way out. "How long for the autopsy?"

"Newcombe leaned on them, so it's gonna be later today. Promise." Artie framed the last word in air quotes since the ME wasn't famous for its efficiency.

"Well, so—"

"We've got his buddy Pavel down at Hogan right now, seeing what he can tell us. With his partner gone, the charges are gonna fall heavier on him. We think he might get a little more talkative now, help us crack open the Popov operation. This is very good for us."

"I'd say so."

They had reached the conference room. Loud voices spilled into the hall through the open door.

"How's it going in there?" Artie asked.

"I just got back from New Jersey; had an interesting talk with an old spy who knew my father back in the day. Talk about skeletons in the closet—my parents were hoarders."

"Progress on the alleged murders?"

"You can probably save yourself some breath and drop the 'alleged'."

"Keep me posted, buddy." At the sound of Larry's voice, Artie knocked Con on the shoulder and backtracked in the direction of the elevator.

"Speak of the devil," Vandyke greeted Con. She was standing at one of the dry erase boards, using the heel of her hand to wipe a clean area. "We were just talking about your mommy dearest."

Voices flew, catching Con up. When they were through, he filled them in on his conversation with Lukas Blume. "According to him, Mutti was an experienced assassin who set my father up. Blume admits to publishing the list, but thinks she's been using it to eliminate old rivals."

"Motive?" Larry asked.

Con answered, "He doesn't know."

FBI special agent Suarez leaned forward, arms folded on the table. "And you trust him?"

It was a valid question. "I do. The man's sick, he probably doesn't have long. I honestly don't think he's after anything except to set the record straight."

"Well, according to my contact in the CIA archives," Suarez said, "Blume's the real thing. No red flags. If your gut says he's for real, then I say we can trust him enough to proceed with the line we're on."

"What this guy Blume told Con fits with the mother," Yep said.

Larry told Con, "We were just reviewing what we know about Mutti." He sat beside her at the table. Her notebook was edged with curlicues and badly drawn faces. Inside the chaotic border of Larry-scribbles was a laundry list of information about Con's first family.

"And?" Con asked.

"I'm sorry," Larry smiled at him, softened her voice, "but she's giving off a stink."

"Don't apologize. I barely know her."

"Well, she's your mother."

"Birth mother," Vandyke clarified. "I've got two moms

myself, and trust me, all is not equal in the realm of broken families."

"Let's get back to Emilie Schumann," Suarez said, picking up on where they'd left off before Con walked into the room. "We'll want to find out who she's still in touch with from the old days. Also, if she was maybe around New York or anywhere near the deaths off The Golden Sphinx list. If we can connect her to any of them, we might be able to extradite her for murder or at least wrongful death. I would love to pick her brain."

In front of Yep, on the table, sat the original file documenting the Conrad Mathis, Sr. suicide. It had acquired a couple of new coffee stains over the last twenty-four hours since its renaissance. "We've had cameras on the bridge since 9/11," Yep said. "I'll see what I can dig up."

"What about Emmy, the daughter?" Suarez turned to Con with an expression of tempered concern. "Your sister. Listen, I'm sorry—is this hard for you?"

"No," Con lied. "Not at all." It was hard, but not for the reasons Suarez or the rest of them might have thought. Con refused the temptation of a sentimental attachment to his birth mother and twin sister. Despite everything that had happened between them, or maybe because of it, he did better if he thought of them as stone-cold strangers. They had played with him without mercy. Still, they were a conduit back to his father's past.

"If she's a threat to Blume," Suarez pressed on, "well, we can't afford to lose him just yet. Do you think she'll go after him?"

The answer wasn't obvious. "I have no idea what she's capable of doing. She's probably dangerous, or maybe it's all bluff." Con shivered at the memory of her teeth biting into his dick and then stopping on the verge of breaking skin. "I tried to get Blume to go stay with a friend, but he refused. I couldn't force him."

"Old folks," Yep clucked. "My old man refused to go to the hospital before he passed. Might have had an extra couple of weeks, but you know what? Maybe he had a point."

"Let's put a team outside Blume's house," Suarez said, "just to keep an eye out in case Emmy surfaces there again. I'll make the call."

Con read over the work they'd organized on the dry erase boards, where ribbons of colorful markers overlapping in various handwriting had been replaced by tidy lists and taped-on photos. At the bottom of a section detailing his father's activities, something jumped out at him.

Death 11/5/04

Medical examiner-autopsy review

DNA analysis: Brody Winslow: confirmed

Con asked, "Who is Brody Winslow?"

"Brace yourself." Larry took his hand. Her palm was damp, and she squeezed. "He was homeless, camped out mostly in lower Manhattan. Wasn't seen by anyone after November 5, 2004."

The day Conrad Sr. died.

"And?" Con pulled his hand away. Struck by the sudden coldness of his skin, he rubbed his palm up and down his arm but couldn't seem to warm himself.

Larry shifted to face Con squarely like she did when she needed to have a talk with him. The acids in his stomach curdled and he realized he was hungry. "I didn't want to tell you on the phone. And when you walked in just now, well, I don't think anyone really knew how to say it. Con…Brody Winslow is the person lying in your father's grave. He'd committed a few petty crimes, so he was in the system. But Codis, you know—it's been a work in progress.

This afternoon, it made a match." Her voice could be so soft when she wanted it to. But her words now, these words, were impenetrable.

"They're sure about this?"

"Positive."

"They didn't want me to ID the body when I offered," Con recalled. "Tim Fisher's office told me that someone from Dad's work had already gone down, and I could spare myself the trauma." Con swallowed. He felt queasy. He should have eaten something on his way back from New Jersey. He should have gone down to the morgue; but it was much, much too late.

"What we're thinking," Yep explained, "is that Tim Fisher got paid off by someone. We're trying to find him so we can talk to him. Once we do, we should be able to fly with this."

Con gazed from face to face to face. Every single one of them looked hungry for his reaction. Was this good news? He was too stunned to process it at the moment. He cleared his throat, skimming the lists that now blurred and blended, jumping together in his mind. All his life, the one thing he'd been sure of was his family—his reliably familiar family, up until his father jumped, or was pushed…except apparently, he wasn't the man who fell from the bridge. And now, even a concept as simple and basic as family had lost its discernible meaning for Con. It was like a poem you'd carried in your pocket all your life, taken out and looked at occasionally, for reassurance; and then one day its pliant seams come apart and you're left with individual words, and you realize you'll never reassemble it the way it was. It's gone. Not just the poem itself, but the reason you carried it.

"Where did he go?" Con threw the question out to everyone, anyone. "My father."

They all looked at him. No one answered. They didn't know.

Con turned to Larry, and wanted to ask her: Why? Why did he do it? Leave us like that. The breathtaking cruelty of it: vanishing with such a dramatic flourish. Staging a fake death, leaving behind a real family that had loved him.

THIRTY

Sacrifice

NEW YORK CITY, November 5, 2004

Simon Engemann, *War Hero, Dead at 64*

Conrad didn't recognize the name on the obituary, but the face was unmistakable. Narrow, with the kindest of eyes; once-blond hair that had thinned and silvered; that sharp nose that had helped him blend so well into postwar Berlin when they worked together at RIAS. Conrad could not have mistaken Fred Hicks for anyone else.

"Won't you be late?" Ruth asked upon finding her husband at the breakfast table, reading the morning paper.

Conrad checked his watch. He was already showered and dressed. "No, I'm fine."

Ruth disappeared into the far reaches of their large apartment. From a distance, he could hear her arguing with Sophie, who, at eighteen, was turning her senior year of high school into a harrowing uphill battle. Con Jr. had moved out six years ago, at twenty, and to his father's dismay had taken up working as an undercover investigator for the district attorney's office. Conrad felt a cold blade of regret each time he thought of his son's ill-advised choice. Pretending to be someone else, under any circumstances, was the slipperiest of slopes. But the boy, like the woman who had given birth to him—a viper Con thankfully knew nothing about—could be self-destructively willful. All Con's life, it had been a goal of Conrad's to nurture his son's humanity. They had both made tremendous sacrifices in their break for a life of freedom: a daughter and a sister had been lost to those dark days. And now, after all that, Con was effectively a spy. Sometimes Conrad felt as if he had lost hold. Raising children was nothing like what he'd imagined.

Doors slammed. Footsteps charged the front door. Finally, Sophie departed for school.

Conrad usually left for the office early, before seven, but today he was riveted by news of his old colleague. He had never known Fred Hicks's real name, Simon Engemann. None of them had known each other's true identities back then; working under protection of their covers had been vital to their survival during that politically brutal time. Conrad hated to revisit those years, but now Hicks's obituary brought him back into the very heart of that darkness. Simon Engemann: a name published for all to see. A frisson of dread rattled its way through Conrad. He read on.

In his obituary, Simon Engemann a.k.a. Fred Hicks was described as a member of the elite U.S. Army Counterintelligence Corps, the CIC, that infiltrated the German Democratic Republic by any means possible. Engemann's assignment to Radio in the American Sector allowed him access to the airwaves, whereupon he transmitted coded information to the resistance on the other side of the Wall. He had received a Knowlton Award for his service in Army intelligence. After the Cold War, Engemann returned to civilian life and worked as a software engineer in Oakland, California. He had a wife and three daughters. Tragically, two days ago, Engemann and his family perished together in a house fire while they slept.

The skin shivered on the back of Conrad's neck. He rubbed away the sensation, but it returned immediately when he thought of Jonas Heusler, another former RIAS colleague, who had recently shot himself in the head.

Conrad scanned the paper cover to cover every day; he liked to know what went on. When he'd seen Heusler's obituary, paired with a photograph of a man he'd once known as Leon Jost, Conrad had devoured every word. That was three months ago. Now, Engemann was also dead before his time.

All the way to the office, Conrad was troubled by the coincidence. He settled in at his desk and, before resuming work on the article he'd intended to finish writing today, plugged his old colleagues' names into an internet search. The results were immediate and alarming.

Several weeks before Heusler killed himself, and four months before Engemann perished with his family in the fire, someone had published a list of names in an obscure newsletter for U.S. Army intelligence retirees. Conrad had never heard of The Golden Sphinx; but now, it seemed, it was to determine his fate.

Jonas Heusler
Conrad Mathis, Sr.
Simon Engemann
Valerie Marin

David Volz
Maximillian Haberfelt

Was this the moment he had long feared? Since the release of old Stasi records the previous year, including the Rosenholz files—a breakdown of the GDR's intelligence activity on foreign soil—Conrad had assumed that it was just a matter of time before he was outed. He'd immediately applied to the Birthler commission for records of his own name, only to learn that he wasn't listed anywhere. The news had initially brought relief—he was safe—only to sink in over time that there had to be a reason for his omission from the files.

Now, finding his name publicly sandwiched between those of two recently dead men, along with what were presumably the real names of his fellow former spies, he recognized the essential difference between exposure and concealment after the rationale for secrecy had evaporated with time. Exposed, you were safe in the crowded field of documented history. Concealed, you were a sitting duck for anyone who wished to eliminate you without much of a trace.

Conrad counted six names on the list. Then he thought back to his time at RIAS, and began his own list of the cover names of everyone he remembered:

Julian Wimmers
Lena Froebel
David Call
David Hicks
Don Fennell
Leon Jost
Mia Landry
Tobias Hofer
Fabian Anger

. . .

His list had three more names than the one in The Golden Sphinx. Clearly, someone was out there, decoding covers from a missing part of the files. Now, made public, this minor treasure trove appeared to be a master list from which someone was targeting former adversaries—or colleagues. A hit list, as it were. With an obscure purpose, and lethal results.

With a shudder of foreboding, he understood that Heusler and Engemann had not died by chance.

Someone had wanted them eliminated.

Conrad thought of Emilie. Of course, he thought of her. She was ruthless enough to pull something like this off, though he couldn't imagine why she would want to, after all these years.

As soon as Conrad's thoughts drifted to Simon Engemann's wife and daughters, killed with him, fear erupted. With a shudder he saw Ruth and Sophie, at home with him in their apartment, in the dark of night, flames devouring his beloved family. Or, if not fire, bullets. Or poison. Or blades. There were endless ways in which it could be done. Despair overtook him at the thought that his very existence put his family's lives in danger.

He worked until the end of the day, finished his article, and emailed it to his editor. He called Ruth to say he'd be late coming home and to tell her that he loved her. He called Sophie to ask about her day, which she reported had gone well. He also told her that he loved her. Lastly, he called Con and got his voice mail: "This is your father calling." But then, at a loss for words, he ended the message. Con was a grown man now. The most essential thing that Conrad hoped to impart to his son—another plea to reevaluate his choices—was the one thing that Con had made clear lay beyond their zone of permissible conversation.

The evening was dark when Conrad entered the rush hour fray. Instead of taking the subway uptown, toward home, he boarded a downtown train and alighted at the Brooklyn Bridge. He walked all the way to the Brooklyn side, hardly aware of the dazzling lights of the city against the deepening sky. All he could think of was where he would go, and how much he would miss. How much he loved his family. How what he had to do now was for their protection.

It was over. He loathed leaving them, but he had to free them from danger.

By the time he crossed back to the Manhattan side of the bridge, night had fallen completely. A November chill penetrated his jacket. His stomach grumbled, but it didn't matter. With each passing moment, the physical needs of his body lost their relevance.

No tears, he told himself. No emotion. You just do it. You just go.

The sound of a man weeping caught his attention. Conrad stopped walking. There appeared to be no one there, and for a moment he actually wondered if the man he heard was himself, if perhaps his resolve was not as firm as he'd thought. He touched his face to find out if he had somehow already fled his body in advance of taking any action and succumbed to the pain he worked so hard to repress. His eyes were dry. Folded into a shadow at the foot of the bridge's west tower, he saw what appeared to be a mass of filthy clothes but in fact was a crying man. A vagrant huddled in his own mess.

Conrad approached him. The stench was sickening. "Can I help?" The man didn't answer, and so Conrad tried again. "What do you need?" Finally, when nothing he could think to say brought a response, Conrad removed his gold watch—the Junghans he'd worn all these years as a reminder of the fragility of his choices—and handed it over to the broken man. The man stopped crying long enough to take the watch and thank him in a small, hollow voice.

THIRTY-ONE

Truth Be Told

PRINCETON, May 28, 2013

Lukas Blume sipped oxygen from the pliant tubes of his nasal cannula, plastic prongs chafing the skin inside his nostrils which recently had begun to leak blood. For the scabs to heal, he'd need to keep the plugs out of his nose; but to breath, he'd need to keep them in. Such were the paradoxes of life at its end.

When he'd finished reading the first section of the *Times*, he folded it and placed it on the coffee table beside his laptop, his notebook, and the black index cardholder where he'd accumulated notes relating to his work reconstructing the missing Rosenholz files. Just this morning, he'd completed decoding the list of names of his old truth-hunting lie-wielding colleagues. With a piece of masking tape and blue pen, he'd labeled the box Rosenholz-Complete, knowing it would be looked through. Having met Con Mathis, he sensed that the young man had the will and capacity to interpret the neat fit of past to future.

The resurrected missing piece of the files would be in good hands.

Meanwhile, the world would go on, regardless. One way or another, reality would continue to weave itself from inauthentic scraps.

Beside the box, from the front page of today's newspaper, Senator Kenneth Rapp smiled and waved to a group of supporters. He had officially announced his run for the Republican nomination for president. Even if Blume were to live, he wouldn't vote for that bastard. Politics aside, he simply didn't trust the man.

It occurred to Blume that he ought to cancel his subscription so the papers wouldn't pile up outside his landlord's door. He made the call, explaining (unasked) that he would be leaving on an open-ended vacation.

A passing thought of Julian Wimmers, Conrad Mathis, Sr., brought a smile. For all their differences, he'd liked the man, and had always felt that the regard was mutual. He'd heard from Con that the person in his father's grave was an imposter. It was a nice touch. For a fleeting moment, Blume wondered if his old friend was still alive and if he knew how well he had been loved by his son.

Blume listened to the quiet outside his basement apartment. The lonely song of a bird. The swoosh of a car passing. The unintelligible voice of a young child calling out. From the sound of it, nothing much happening. An average day. And yet he knew that the same unmarked police car from yesterday was still out there, guarding him, waiting for an unfriendly appearance by Con's twin. If she was anything like her mother, unpredictability would be her most reliable characteristic. None of it surprised him. Emilie's daughter's lessons of conceit, greed, passion, rage would have been well taught and well learned.

He considered moving to his bed for a final sleep but

decided that it didn't make a difference. He opened the top of the card box and, from the back corner, pried loose an old piece of tape sealing down the cyanide he'd kept close. He set it on the coffee table, beside the newspaper, and added a Post-it note to the top of the cardholder: You will know what to do with this.

He had saved a box along with its packing materials. After peeling off the old labels, he set the cardholder into a nest of bubble wrap. He sealed the package and addressed it to Con Mathis, c/o the District Attorney's Office at Hogan Place, New York City. Next, he phoned Federal Express and requested a pickup. He removed the cannula, slowly climbed the stairs, and set the box outside his door. Yes, his guards were still there, pretending they weren't seen. Blume saw everything. He waved to the men who wouldn't acknowledge him and went back inside.

Back on the couch, he set aside his cannula and switched off the oxygen's motor. Then he swallowed the capsule with the dregs of his morning coffee, settled his head against the cushion, and waited.

THIRTY-TWO

A Mother's Love

BERLIN, *May 28, 2013*

"WOULD you mind keeping an eye on my stuff while I take a leak?"

Emmy smiles. "Not at all." Waiting in front of her mother's building, she watches the young woman rise from an outdoor table at the neighboring restaurant and vanish inside in search of the bathroom. She's left behind half a beer, a burning cigarette in an ashtray, and her black sweater draped over the chair. No one else is seated outside, perhaps because of the time: the quiet hours between lunch and dinner. Emmy steps away from the door, picks up the beer, and takes a long drink. Smoke curls into her nostrils. She hasn't touched a cigarette in years, ever since her brief love affair with smoking at university. She takes one long drag: a smoldering deep in her lungs.

She presses her mother's doorbell again, this time harder, anger stoked. Finally, when someone comes out wheeling a bicycle, she spirits inside.

Dusty sprays of sunlight crisscross up to the third floor. Emmy knocks on her mother's door, assuming, at this point, that she isn't home; though with Mutti you can never be sure. From her purse, she retrieves a Swiss Army knife she bought duty-free at the airport. She was pretty good at picking locks when she was a teenager, and it comes right back to her. Pick, push, twist, jiggle—pop.

Mutti's scuffed black suitcase sits just inside the door. Beside it, a brown shoe with a thick rubber sole.

A shuffling in the kitchen stops abruptly, leaving a silence broken by Emmy's footsteps.

She smells it right away: the stink of one of her mother's beloved pungent cheeses. All the windows are closed on this warm spring day, trapping the reek of the cheese and wine.

An image of Mutti and Uncle Rolph sitting in the kitchen, drinking wine late at night when she couldn't sleep, returns to Emmy with clarity.

"Join us," her mother offered.

Rolph blew into a dusty wineglass and poured her a glass.

She was ten. Flowers on her nightgown.

Leaving the untouched glass, she returned to her bed and exhaled through her nostrils repeatedly to get rid of the smell of the wine, which had mingled with the memory of Rolph's sordid advances. She couldn't understand it, but Mutti was more than his companion; she was his accomplice…but in what, and why?

Emmy felt it then: This was a mother who couldn't, or wouldn't, love.

And she knows it now: This is a mother who is willing to use the idea of love as bait. A vicious mother, who never loved her and never would.

Mutti sits alone at the square table pushed into a

corner of the kitchen. Her crutches lean against the wall. The cheese leaking out of its rind onto a plate; a ripped slice of brown bread; an open bottle of red wine and an empty glass with lip marks like bites around the rim. She's wearing the pantsuit she likes to travel in.

Standing in the kitchen doorway, Emmy asks, "Where are you going?"

"I didn't expect you."

Emmy sits down, refills her mother's glass, and lifts it to her own lips. The usual cheap table wine. "I found him. Don Fennell."

The lines astride Mutti's eyes multiply under the harsh kitchen overhead. Skin slackens around the clenched jaw. "You have the key?"

"First, you tell me who our Mr. Moneybags is."

"I told you," her mother's voice tight and slippery with aggravation, "that when it's finished, then you'll find out. Not knowing the precise details is a crucial part of the discipline of accomplishing our goal. Now give me the key."

Emmy repeats the lie: "Our goal?"

"You know how to live in the world. I've taught you how it works. You'll know how to handle the rewards when they come to you."

"Controlled by you, Mutti?"

"Nonsense."

"Do you plan to give me a lump sum, or will you dole out my share for the rest of my life?"

The blank look in her mother's eyes tells her that she hasn't yet decided. Mutti holds out the flat of her palm, expecting a key.

Emmy leans in, fingertips tight around the stem of the glass. "Who is he? Show me how well you've trained me.

Test me one more time. Find out if I'm good enough to beat you at your own game."

Closing her hand into a fist, Mutti takes one of the naval-deep breaths meant to demonstrate that she's had enough. She leaves the mess for her daughter, stands, and reaches for her crutches. "I have a plane to catch. The driver should be here any—"

The glass shatters easily on the edge of the table. Wine douses her mother's jacket and blouse, splashing onto her face, seasoning her age-crumped skin with a violet haze.

"You wanted me to kill my own brother." Emmy rises to face Mutti, noticing that they're no longer the same height: she is now an inch taller than her shrinking mother. "You heartless bitch."

"When you failed the first time," Mutti spits, "I knew you'd fail again, even when I gave you an advantage." The pitiless tilt of her head as she surveys the disappointment of her daughter. The way she shoulders her crutches and turns to leave.

"Where are you going?"

The silence when Mutti's bare foot touches the hall carpet.

The crook of Emmy's arm fits around her mother's neck like a nutcracker. The crutches crash to the floor. Yanking the older woman off-balance, forcing her to lean backward, bearing her weight with relative ease, Emmy asks again, "Tell me who he is."

"Not yet."

Soft skin folds over the fractured edge of glass as Emmy touches it to the arch of Mutti's neck. Pressing it deeper, she elicits a gasp. She had never realized that her mother was as fragile as any other human animal. That's what Mutti used to tell her as a child: "People are animals of the human variety. Don't make too much of it." This close, the wine on her clothes smells like a barroom floor.

"Tell me," Emmy whispers into Mutti's ear.

"David Call," Mutti croaks. "Another American."

"I want his real name."

"So do I."

"You're lying. You know who he is—you wouldn't have sent me after Fennell if you still needed him alive to figure it out for you."

"Stop. Please."

"I like hearing you beg."

"Please."

"You're going to him right now, aren't you?"

"David has the address in Schwabing. I'll break in if I have to. We'll be rich."

"What's in Schwabing?" All Emmy knew about the obscure hamlet was that it was in northern Munich.

"I knew you'd fail me."

"Who is he?"

"He owes me. Not you, me."

"You're a killer. And a liar. You drove my father and brother away. I was born in the west—it all could have been different." Emmy digs the edge of glass into her mother's skin, drawing a pinprick trail of blood. "Tell me the truth: Why did you do it?"

Panic jumps in Mutti's brown eyes. Con's eyes, except faded, dead. "He broke me."

"But you were never whole."

"You're wrong—I was whole once. I worked for Wolf because I believed in the GDR. I was his best agent."

"You're a fucking liar."

"Please, stop, you're hurting me."

Emmy holds the broken glass where it is. She likes the sound of her mother begging. "Truth."

"I… I was weak…."

"Go on."

"I… I tried to get rid of Conrad because David thought he was in the way. I passed the Rosenholz files to David, but your father intercepted them." She gags at the pressure of the blade pressing deeper into her neck. "When David left me, he walked away like I was nothing to him. But I know his secrets."

"What secrets?"

"He kept our names out of Rosenholz to protect himself. His people at the CIA—they'll abandon him when it comes out that he did away with his old colleagues…"

"You're rambling, Mutti."

"He's going to pay for what he did to me. You'll have money—it's what you want. And I'll get to watch all the fingers point at him."

"What did he do to you that you didn't also do to him?"

Mutti's voice is faint, barely a whisper: "He made me love him."

Emmy looks into her mother's eyes—they're as cold and as empty as they've always been. "I don't believe you."

"Come closer. I'll tell you who he is."

Her last words are a hoarse whisper: a name Emmy is sure she's heard somewhere before.

The blade of glass slips into Mutti like a knife into butter. Blood now pours from the fat, pulsing jugular. She lowers her mother onto the linoleum, remembering the time spilled milk ran along the slanted floor to the wall just beneath the window, where it pooled white, glistening. Her cheek still burns from the slap that clumsy accident earned her.

Emmy sits back down at the table and finishes the wine directly from the bottle, while her mother's blood collects beneath the window, and her mother writhes and eventually falls silent at her feet.

A phone rings—presumably Mutti's driver has arrived. Emmy ignores it and finally it stops.

Later, wandering the apartment where she was raised by a dead woman, Emmy finds the living room mantle cleared of books. She hunts for a note. Mutti's bed is made, her closet half emptied, not a single toothbrush in the bathroom, a ticket to Washington DC in her purse, and Emmy knows for sure.

Her mother's plan was to leave her nothing.

THIRTY-THREE

Small Packages

NEW YORK CITY, May 29, 2013

THE SMALL BOX recycled from a previous shipment, old labels haphazardly removed, sat innocuously atop a pile of mail on Con's desk at Hogan. He had never seen Blume's handwriting before: it was clear and bold, much like the man himself, with the slightest bend at the end of some letters, suggesting a tremor. Con ached, seeing that. Lukas Blume had struggled. Con didn't blame him for ending his own life, though it saddened him that someone of such apparent integrity had died alone. And frustrated him: he was sure that Blume had more he could have shared with the investigation, had he lived longer.

Con ripped off the tape and the cardboard flaps sprang open.

Under a cover of bubble wrap sat Blume's little black box of file cards with a blue Post-it on top: You will know what to do with this. He'd marked a piece of masking tape across the top of the box: Rosenholz-Complete.

Con felt a rush of blood into his head when he hinged open the cardholder. Just two days ago, Blume had said that he hadn't yet decoded David Call's identity. Clearly, that had changed.

Blume had put Call's card at the front, with a name written in capitals across the top.

Artie was on the phone when Con appeared, with the cardholder, and waved him into his office.

Since Con had last been here, his boss had decorated one wall with a visual map of the Dostoyevsky case, a grainy photograph of Vlad Popov at the very top. Alexei Dvorshetskii's mug shot was crossed out with an energetic X. Pavel Gavrikov's was circled in red. Beneath them, a family tree of co-conspirators spread into complicated branches. Con had helped build this network so that Artie could climb its reaches, and seeing it, he felt a jolt of pride.

Hanging up the phone, Artie grinned. "You like it?"

"Gavrikov still talking?"

"You bet he is."

Con put the small black box on Artie's desk, withdrew the card in front, and handed it over. "Lukas Blume sent this before he killed himself. Looks like he finished the puzzle."

Artie stared at the card. "Shut my door."

Con turned back to find his boss slumped into his chair with his face in his hands.

"I don't believe this," Artie moaned. "Ken Rapp? I'm having trouble swallowing this one."

"I know," Con agreed. "But when you think about… well, the senator talks about his army service all the time. He's proud of it. He was there."

"But he's Newcombe's buddy. And he's running for

president." Artie stared at his Popov wall chart. "This is not good."

"I guess he figured he got away with it. Those guys always do."

"Shit."

"It won't be easy, but we have to go to Newcombe with this."

"Are you fucking kidding me?"

"Artie—"

"Newcombe's been fundraising his ass off for Rapp, and you know as well as I do that if Newcombe comes out for mayor, when he comes out for mayor, Rapp's going to be his best card."

"The man was a double agent during the Cold War."

"So what?"

"He committed treason against the country he wants to lead."

"Close the box, Con."

"We have to look at the bigger picture here," Con argued, "and anyway, it might turn into nothing. What if Blume was wrong? But we have to investigate—you know we do."

"One mention of this leaks to the press," Artie said, "one insinuation against Rapp, and it's over for him. This is a no-fly zone."

"Artie—"

"I mean it: Back off."

Con reached for the card, but Artie pulled his hand back and in two swift motions tore it into quarters.

"It's just a piece of paper, Artie. You can rip it up all you want. It won't make a difference."

"See him?" Artie's finger shook, pointing at the photo of Vlad Popov taped to his wall. "Guess who has the power to pull the plug on my investigation."

"Your investigation? It belongs to this office—it isn't yours."

"I do this to Newcombe?" Artie stalked to the shredder beside his desk, turned it on, and dropped the pieces of Blume's index card into the maw of the whirring blades. Then he moved to his map of Dostoyevsky, stripped-down Popov's picture, and mimed ripping it in half. "He does this to me. And Con? I won't have that."

"Are you telling me you're willing to let one world-class criminal off the hook in favor of another?"

"I'm telling you, drop it."

"Artie, this is wrong. You know that." Con modulated his tone, trying to keep calm. "I understand how you feel—"

"Feel? Who gives a fuck how I feel? I'll tell you what I know."

"You know that we have to add this to our investigation."

Artie ran a palm across his scalp to wipe away a film of perspiration.

"All those people who were killed because—"

"Just hold off a while, that's all I'm saying."

"This can't wait. I'll talk to Newcombe directly."

Coming around his desk, Artie aimed a stiff finger at Con's face. "Do. Not. Even. Think. About. Doing. That."

Con stood there, rage bubbling just under the surface. He said nothing, but he wasn't finished with this.

THIRTY-FOUR

The Candidate

NEW YORK CITY, May 29, 2013

FROM ACROSS THE ROOM, the senator's nose looks like a handle someone pushed, hard, to one side; Emmy wants to take it in her hand and force it back into place. His light brown hair is obviously dyed. His skin is thickened, patchy. And yet, for a man in his seventies, he's fairly attractive; wealth and power have a way of turning old men handsome.

The climax of the fundraiser largely behind them, most of the patrons are either drunk or gone. Classical music has switched to jazz. The once-packed restaurant has thinned to a manageable crowd. Emmy has no intention of leaving just yet; she paid a lot to a scalper for a last-minute ticket to this event and plans on getting her money's worth.

She makes her way toward the bar, where Senator Rapp half-sits on a stool, arms folded across his chest, pretending to be interested while a couple with matching gray haircuts bends his ear. A short line of donors waits their turn for an audience with the Republican candidate. Emmy squeezes past all of them, presses her chest against the edge of the bar, waits for the bartender's attention to land on her. Goatee, pair of small hoop earrings, black vest over purple shirt—some kind of artist probably, making his way. She requests a glass of champagne.

Goatee delivers her drink with an arch smile. Leaning in, he whispers, "I'm off in a few minutes."

"Not interested." He's cute, but she's got bigger, older, richer fish to fry tonight. After that she ignores him. Lingers in her tight red dress and fake diamond earrings. On the bar, her beaded evening clutch contains the essentials: cash, phone, lipstick, gun.

Eventually, no one is left for the senator except Emmy and his minions, an exhausted well-dressed clump at a far table, drinking and doing their postmortem on the event's haul.

Senator Rapp's extended end-of-a-long-night yawn is her cue to face him squarely.

He looks at her and, after a pause, comments, "Those are some bright blue eyes you've got."

"I've heard."

"I don't think we've met. I'm Ken Rapp."

"I know." Her laugh is a calibrated tinkle. "I listened to your speech with great interest."

A smile she recognizes creeps onto his face. "Buy you another glass of champagne?"

"Thank you. Yes."

"Two," he tells the bartender.

She notices that his aids have all filtered out of the restaurant, leaving him to his own devices. He leans close, and whispers, "What's your name?"

"The only way I'm going to tell you that," her lips so

close to his ear she can taste his salty skin, "is if you take me home and…"

Behind her, a cool, dry hand touches her bare arm, igniting a flash of goosebumps. The first thing she notices is the purple cuff. Goatee, bothering her again. "I told you I'm not interested," she says.

But this time, it isn't Goatee.

"He's mine," Con whispers with an urgency that wakes her up to the oddness of this moment. She, this close to snaring Rapp for herself. And Con, dressed in the bartender's uniform, working undercover, no doubt. Birds of a feather. She wonders if he knows about Mutti's death —her murder was in the German papers, but news of the unsolved crime never reached the States—or how much he cares after all the shit they've been through thanks to their dear old mother.

"Excuse me." Senator Rapp shoulders between them. "I believe the lady just asked you to leave her alone."

Emmy almost laughs at what the senator just said, calling her a lady, and the way he jumped to her defense because the horny toad believes he's got her in the bag. She feels a snap of pure frustration. Given the chance, without Con's interference, in a matter of hours, she could have gotten Rapp exactly where she wants him: with his wallet splayed in exchange for protecting his secret past. He has to be good for a sizable lump sum right away; if he wins the nomination, there will be more. And then, if he becomes president, the sky will be the limit. Rapp will understand, when Emmy makes things clear to him, that he's got no real choices left. The way Mutti set things up, he'd look good for the murders of his fellow spies if anyone were to find out who he really is. As for the address in Schwabing that Mutti was after, if Emmy can get that out of Rapp, too, it will be icing on the cake.

"Senator Rapp." Con's voice toned with cool calculation. "I'd like a word."

Rapp grins at Emmy in intimate conspiracy. Without looking at Con, he answers, "I've already asked you to leave us alone."

"David Call," Con whispers. And waits for the reaction.

Close to Rapp, Emmy feels the modulation of his energy as he shifts from predator to prey. The candidate's small eyes slide to Con and lock on.

Rapp slides off his stool and glances furtively around the room, apparently hoping that no one has witnessed him on the verge of being duped by what must appear to be a team of operators of some kind. Emmy can only imagine what he thinks, and she doesn't really care. Her moment with him has evaporated.

"Keep away from me," Rapp hisses, "or I'll have you both arrested." Lifting his chin in a stab at recovering his dignity, he strides away.

Wait, Emmy wants to call out, let me finish this, but doesn't. She turns to Con, and hisses, "You fucked it up."

"What exactly did I fuck up for you, Emmy?"

"He has the address. For the key. When we find it, at least we can—"

Before she can finish, Con rushes out from behind the long, curved bar to follow the senator outside.

No. Rapp doesn't belong to him.

She grabs her handbag and follows.

"Wait!" Con opens his wallet, flashes his ID. "This is official, Senator." Immediately regretting having addressed him by his title.

"You're out of your league," Rapp sneers. A waiting town car emits a snake of exhaust into the warm spring evening. A quick breeze shifts the fumes forward; turning away, Rapp coughs. He makes an odd rotating motion with his hand; a taxi responds by pulling to the curb, but Rapp waves him away. A woman with a shopping bag crosses West Broadway to nab the taxi for herself.

Meantime, Rapp's driver has stepped out of the car—a tall man with a military brush-cut and a gun on his hip—and hustled the senator into the back seat. The door cracks shut. The driver revs the engine and the car lumbers forward and away with the impunity of privilege.

Con watches as the red taillights blur around the corner onto Broome Street and disappear. Only now does he realize that he's broken into a sweat; the polyester shirt doesn't breathe at all. He opens the top buttons and feels the crisp kiss of air on his skin.

He goes back inside to look for Emmy, curious about what she said about an address for the key. Clearly, she knows something that Con doesn't, and he wants to hear more. But the only person left in the elegant bar, sleepy with late-night jazz, is the bartender with the goatee.

"Did you see where she went?" Con asks him. "The woman in the red dress."

Goatee shrugs. "She left right after you did." He turns his back to adjust an already perfect arrangement of bottles, as if to say that, as far as he's concerned, nothing happened here tonight.

THIRTY-FIVE

End of the Afternoon

THAILAND, May 31, 2013

OUTSIDE IN THE COURTYARD, having finished their lunch, the children played and shouted. Shards of sun fell through the thatched roof onto the classwork Conrad was correcting: rudimentary math for the younger students, algebra for the older ones.

A cloud must have shifted overhead because the penciled numbers on Angga's paper suddenly faded. Conrad slid the page under a band of light, and in doing so, noticed that the screen of his satellite phone was flashing. He always kept the ringer off during school hours. Private Caller was trying him for the third time today. He didn't answer.

Only one person knew how to find him, but Blume was dead. Conrad still kept up with the obituaries, his eyes always open for friends and enemies. He had also recently learned of Mutti's murder but had hesitated to believe that the cloud that had chased him all these years could pass that easily.

He finished grading Angga's work and drank the lime juice he'd brought with his lunch. It had taken a long time to get used to the custom of a warm drink on a warm day, but now he enjoyed it.

His thoughts tumbled backward in time, to Berlin. Once, when they were young, Emilie had whispered to him in bed that the whole world was only them. They would chart their course together. No matter what happened, they would never let the other down. But like most heated conspiracies, it was half bullshit. Fifty-two years ago, she had summoned him under false pretenses, and he had flown right into her duplicitous net. He was nineteen. The error had ruined his life.

At the end of the afternoon, the children raced outdoors again. Conrad returned to his bungalow beside the school. He packed only what he needed. At the airport, he would buy his ticket to New York with cash.

As a last thought, he knelt beside his mattress, slipped a hand under, and fished until he felt the tiny pouch. He unknotted the drawstring. Emptied the contents onto his open palm.

Holding the ring up to the light, he read the inscription that matched Ruth's: Joined in love and heart and soul. He'd grown thin over the years, and it slipped easily onto his finger.

THIRTY-SIX

Sunset

NEW YORK CITY, *June 9, 2013*

Con paused to listen to the unreal sound of his parents chatting in the kitchen, stilling his hand as it stirred the keys inside the Betty Boop jar. His father had been back with them for nearly a week, but he still had trouble believing it sometimes. All these years, he had never wished for his father's return. Because he was dead. And Con was no fool. He had been hungry for answers, and wished for understanding; but his hope all along had been to put his father's death to rest in his mind, not to resurrect him.

A decade ago, nothing about this scene would have felt surreal. Dad in the kitchen, talking, the clatter of Mom cooking, the swell of their voices in congress over questions and issues and stories large and small. Nothing would have made Con stop and think about the existence of the conversation. But now he couldn't help listening; he was insatiably hungry for his father to stay and stay and stay, to dispel once and for all the long grief of his absence. It would take time. Con knew that. In the meantime, there were still hard questions to answer.

He peered into the jar and dug until he felt it: the old skeleton key that used to open imaginary dungeons.

Holding the key in his hand, he picked up the postcard that had just arrived in the mail, addressed to him, from Dubai. A camel leaving a trail of footprints in the sand; looming in the distance, on a little island all its own, a sail-shaped skyscraper. The handwritten message read, 60 Ungererstrasse, 5B, Schwabing, Munich. It was unsigned, but Con knew it was from Emmy.

Evidently, she had found her way back to Senator Rapp. Had her way with him. Now it was Con's turn. Given that morning's headlines about Rapp dropping out of the presidential race, to spend more time with his family, Artie's resistance to the task force's interest in the senator's Cold War activities would likely ease up.

Conrad Sr. appeared in the breakfast nook, carrying a tray of four steaming coffee mugs to the table. Sophie's was the black one. The rest were milky. A teaspoon of sugar would have been stirred into one, for Ruth. He was seventy-two years old now. His hair had turned grey in Thailand, his skin leathery from the unrelenting sun. He had been patient with all of their questions from the moment he returned. Stayed up late talking, listening, explaining, apologizing—sometimes even laughing. Spent late mornings behind a closed bedroom door with Ruth. Even managed to coax some food into Sophie. The family was gradually weaving itself back together, but there were still missing threads; Con supposed there always would be.

"Dad, I've been meaning to ask you." Con opened his palm to show his father the old key. "Mutti wanted to get her hands on some key. She thought Lukas Blume had it, but he didn't know anything about it."

"Yes, of course." With impeccable reserve, he looked at the key but didn't move to touch it.

"Last time I saw Emmy, she said something about an address in Schwabing. She planned on getting the address from Senator Rapp. It looks like she did." He showed his father the postcard. "Does it mean anything to you?"

Conrad thought a moment and shook his head. "No." A look of irritation darkened Conrad's eyes. "Rapp had an ungodly amount of plastic surgery, you know. That crooked nose was a stroke of genius. When I knew him, when he was David Call, he was quite a handsome fellow. His cover was as a chaplain—can you imagine that?"

"Any idea what they wanted in Schwabing?"

"Not at all."

"Are you sure?"

"Everything was subterfuge then." Again, Conrad responded without answering the question. "It was almost a joke. We transmitted things in case they came to have value, not necessarily because they already did."

Con wondered if his father was telling the truth. He wanted to believe that he was. But the decisive feel of his father's hand closing Con's fingers around the key, the refusal to look deeper, troubled him.

"I never passed along the key," Conrad said. "I kept it. Whatever they wanted it for, it would be too late by now."

"Mutti didn't think so, and neither did Emmy."

Conrad smiled, his eyes brimming with love and forbearance and regret. "Munich's easy enough to get to, if you still feel it's important to dig into the past."

"Will you come with me?"

THIRTY-SEVEN

Dusty Pictures

MUNICH, June 11, 2013

THEY STOOD side by side in front of a yellow building on Ungererstrasse, on the quiet street in Schwabing that had lit Mutti's and Emmy's imaginations on fire. Maybe his father was right: maybe this was a fool's errand. But maybe it wasn't.

Cars drove past on the street behind them, but not many; it was still too early for rush hour. Bicycles leaned against number sixty-one. An elixir of coffee and bread and motor oil perfumed the air.

The building's front door was unlocked. Inside, the modest lobby smelled of bacon. There appeared to be no elevator and so Con led his father up the five flights. In the harshly lit hallway, they passed varnished wooden doors until they found it: 5B/Leopold Sommer.

Conrad ran a finger along the letters embossed on the nameplate, his brow rippling with thought. "I don't understand this. It doesn't make sense."

Con stared at his father, as the older man appeared to struggle with a memory.

"Leopold Sommer died in the war."

"You knew him?"

"I knew of him."

"Who was he?"

Conrad drew a breath as it came back to him: David Hicks entering the broadcast booth at RIAS, handing him a slip of paper with an announcement to read on the air. On the back was the cipher that would lead him to the safe deposit box at Steglitz. VB10961. He could still see it clearly.

"Sommer was an art dealer who worked for the Nazis," Conrad explained. "He collected so-called degenerate art to get it out of the mainstream, so it wouldn't pollute the masses."

"Collected?"

"Stole. From the Jews. He also assisted in trafficking looted art out of Germany—paintings taken from people's homes, masterpieces taken right off the walls of museums, whatever they could get their hands on."

"That's disgusting."

"Yes. And it was ironic because Sommer himself was Jewish, but he was a well-known art dealer—maybe the Nazis didn't give him a choice."

"What happened to the art?"

"Sommer's widow released a statement saying that it was destroyed in the firebombing of Dresden in forty-five. I remember thinking it was strange to report news that was so old." Conrad, suddenly eager to open the door, said to his son, "Let's have that key."

Con reached into his jeans pocket and pulled out the old key. It turned crankily in the lock as if it hadn't been tried in a long time.

The dark living room reeked of sour abandonment. Heavy curtains were drawn across the windows. Their steps kicked dust into frantic motion, captured in competing blades of sunlight. Con tripped on something and steadied himself against the frame of a painting that leaned against the arm of a sofa. Conrad stood back and took it in, as Con made his way through what appeared to be a minefield of art, found the nearest window, and pulled open the curtains.

Con had to cover his eyes until they adjusted to the sudden brightness. And then he saw.

Sculptures and paintings, portraits and landscapes, napping animals, naked women, boys in stone. Facing out from a stack of paintings, a portrait of a seated woman caught Con's eye: simple lines, blues and yellows, her eyes averted and pearls around her neck. He wasn't an expert, but he'd taken an art history class in college and the painting reminded him of something Matisse might have done. Maybe it was a good forgery—or maybe it was the real thing.

"Did you—" Con started to ask, and then stopped himself. He had been about to ask if his father had known about this.

Conrad stood there, jaw dropped, eyes flicking around the room.

No, it wasn't possible. His father couldn't have tossed the key into a kitchen jar and gone about his life as if it was nothing, especially when the price of his silence had been so high.

Had they all known? Emilie certainly had, and Call, and possibly Hicks. Wolf, definitely. But Fennell? Maybe. There had been numerous operatives at RIAS who might have been aware of the illicit stockpile. The voracious sons of bitches. Conrad was glad, at least, that in their greed they had inadvertently preserved something true and good that had grown out of Germany in its worst possible moments. Incredible. It was incredible. All that idealism and the GDR had been run by common thieves!

"Well," Conrad stepped through the garden of paintings and patted his son's back, "you were right. It's a good thing we came."

"They never needed the key," Con said. "It would've been easy to break in."

"Exactly. But your mother liked to play her games to perfection."

"She wasn't my mother."

Conrad smiled, with tears in his eyes. "No, she wasn't. Not really."

The two men looked into each other's eyes. Conrad felt his growing damp and turned away. "That old newspaper there." He pointed to the broken leg of a small table that had been propped up with folded sheaves of time-yellowed newspapers. "Let's take a look." Better to divert themselves than to give in to emotion.

Con tilted the table and lifted the topmost paper, its dry edges flaking at his touch. Half the front page turned to powder when he unfolded it: Unser Heer.

"Our Army," his father translated. "I remember this newspaper, though my parents didn't exactly subscribe."

The German print was tiny and, to Con, indecipherable. The paper was dated 17 August 1942. On the first page, a grainy photograph showed a young man smiling into the face of an older, seated man. Both wore brownish uniforms with armbands emblazoned with a swastika. From the neck of the man who sat smiling into the face of his protégé hung the thick black iron cross of Hitler's Third Reich.

The image gave Con a stiff chill. He looked at his

father, whose face showed no reaction, just the familiar placid expression of a willingness to accept anything, and a refusal to betray an inner life that had to be impossibly complex. The chaotic look on the young guard's face, leaping from east to west over a coil of barbed wire, was beginning to make sense to Con. His father had been raised on a shifting ground of radical ideologies, one crazier than the next. Jumping that border in 1961 had been impetuous. Escaping the Stasi in 1979 had been a feat of bravery. Staging his suicide in 2004 had been an act of love.

Con locked up and they returned to the street in search of a cell signal. It was a relief to be out of the tomb of stolen paintings. He'd report in to Larry; she'd get the ball rolling on the other side. Listening to the faraway sound of her phone ringing and ringing, he asked his father, "How did the key to that place end up in the hands of the Stasi? I thought the Communists hated the Nazis."

"They did." Conrad's smile sent waves of intricate lines across his face. "But as far as I can tell, there's nothing more human than greed."

THIRTY-EIGHT

Orange Carnations

AN AFTERNOON CONCERT was in session when they arrived at the nursing home. Brahms. Through a pair of windowed French doors off the main lobby, Conrad saw a cluster of elderly residents in various states of listening.

He and Con introduced themselves at the front desk, presented their identification, and waited for an attendant.

"Are you nervous?" Con asked him.

Was he? He hadn't seen his mother in 52 years. He had been a boy when he left his parents without warning, and now he was an old man. "Yes. I suppose I am a little nervous."

"I'm Monika," the attendant introduced herself. Conrad's heart jumped, but of course, it wasn't his Monika. This one was relatively young, younger than Con. She wore the kind of cheerful, decorated nursing scrubs you might expect to see at a pediatric hospital. "I'll go fetch

Bettina. Why don't you two wait in there?" She directed them to a family visiting room behind the reception desk.

A vase of orange carnations signaled an effort to override the blandness of the room. Polished linoleum. Beige walls. Blonde furniture. Plastic seats. Oatmeal-hued curtains framing a busy road. But it was clean. Conrad was glad to see that. And the nurse had been kind.

A swell of music through the open door and then the rattle of wheels. "Here she is," Monika said brightly as she pushed Bettina's wheelchair into the room.

His mother was ancient. Withered and white. Bending, Conrad held one of her gnarled, speckled hands between both of his. She was as warm as ever and softer than he remembered.

"It's me," he spoke quietly, "I'm here. I'm back."

She blinked. "Hello, old man."

Didn't she recognize him? "Can she see?" he asked Monika.

"A little."

"What about her hearing?"

"It's pretty good. But with Alzheimer's, the words kind of tangle up in her mind. Some days she's clearer. Just do your best."

"I'm Conrad," he tried again, "your son. And this is Con, my son."

Con stepped forward to meet his grandmother.

"Conrad." She pulled her hand out of her son's and reached for her grandson. "I knew you'd come back." There were tears in her voice. She smiled, her old loving smile, even if it was somewhat misdirected. Conrad didn't mind; in one way or another, she was receiving him back. "I have something for you." Her voice hoarse as a whisper, but louder, as if she worried it wouldn't be heard. "Pfeffernusse, just out of the oven. Wait. I'll sugar them now." Her eyes drifted closed as in her mind she retreated to a long-gone kitchen to powder the spice cookies her son had always favored. "Can you smell them?"

Conrad nodded at his son, urging him to indulge her, to put words to memory on behalf of his father. "They smell great."

"Taste. Careful of your shirt. The sugar gets everywhere."

Obligingly, Con hummed, "Delicious."

Conrad smiled in gratitude for his son's kindness.

And then her hand drifted back to Conrad's as if drawn by something inchoately familiar. The pressure of her fingers moved in his hand, recognizing him in some small way. In the silence that fell between them he listened as, outside the window, a horn honked. Someone shouted. A siren wailing in the distance moved rapidly closer.

About the Author

Katia Lief is the author of bestselling crime novels, most recently *Last Night* and *A Map of the Dark* published under the pseudonym Karen Ellis. She teaches fiction writing at The New School and lives with her family in Brooklyn. Learn more at katialief.com

CRIME NOVELS

Last Night (as Karen Ellis)

A Map of the Dark (as Karen Ellis)

The Money Kill

Vanishing Girls

Next Time You See Me

You Are Next

Here She Lies

One Cold Night

Seven Minutes to Noon

Five Days in Summer

Names of the Dead

Waterbury

FICTION

The Beautiful Years (novella)

The Rise & Fall of Rocky Love

Love, Sex & the Wrong Bride

Soul Catcher (young adult)